COULD HE ASK A WILDFLOWER TO BECOME A HOTHOUSE ORCHID?

Colin stepped to the bed and stared down at the dress Maggie had left behind. Her old hat was gone, the one he'd resisted burning just because it seemed to define her. He glanced toward the window. She must have slipped away while he was at drill.

He sat on the bed and smoothed a hand over the dress, imagining her inside the fabric that slid softly against his palm. Where would the cold, dark night find her? Was she alone in the wilderness? His first instinct was to find her and bring her back and then to protect her, to mold her into someone she was not. But he knew better. He had no reason to keep her here. She was a free woman, free to choose her own destiny.

Only he'd hoped she'd choose to share that destiny with him.

Just thinking the idea, it sounded foolish. He and Maggie Hayes had no more in common than the wild prairie flowers and the tame geraniums his mother had grown in brown wooden window boxes. She'd never have learned to live his life, never been able to give up her independence, her uniqueness to conform to polite society.

Colin rose and walked to the window that looked out across the wide parade ground and to the gates beyond. Rare sunlight broke through the clouds, dappling the trampled and stirred ground.

"Guard and keep her," he said to the peek of prairie visible through the open gates.

Dear Romance Reader,

In July, we launched the Ballad line with four new series, and each month we'll present both new and continuing stories set everywhere from medieval England to the American West—the kind of passionate, romantic stories you love best, written by the most gifted authors. At the back of each book, we'll tell you when you can find subsequent books in the series that has captured your heart.

This month beloved author Jo Ann Ferguson completes her riveting *Shadow of the Bastille* series with **A Sister's Quest,** as a French schoolteacher embarks on a perilous—and passionate—adventure with a Russian count. Next, talented newcomer Elizabeth Keys offers the second book in her *Irish Blessings* series, **Reilly's Gold.** What happens when a man determined to find his fortune in America meets a spirited woman instead?

Beginning this month is a series from rising star Kathryn Fox. In 1874, three men—loyal, brave, and true—ride into the Canadian wilderness to fight for justice as *The Mounties.* In the first installment, a recruit trained as a physician will capture a bootlegger—yet *she* will claim his heart for **The First Time.** Finally, new favorite Shelley Bradley presents the second book in her breathtaking *Brothers in Arms* series, as a Scottish knight bent on revenge finds the power of true love with **His Stolen Bride.** Enjoy!

Kate Duffy
Editorial Director

The Mounties

THE FIRST TIME

Kathryn Fox

ZEBRA BOOKS
KENSINGTON PUBLISHING CORP.

http://www.zebrabooks.com

With deepest respect, I dedicate this book to those who also served—the Red Serge Wives.

Prologue

Lonely specters of damp fog wrapped themselves around Colin Fraser's face as the ancient smell of decay and forgotten herbs rose up from beneath his horse's churning hooves. Despite an air of mystery and loneliness, the moor was beautiful, and he loved the feeling of desolation it presented. But after four years of medical school, four years of the cloying odor of chloroform and dark, cavernous halls, the Scottish moor seemed almost a sunlit escape.

He pulled his horse down to a walk, content to turn his attention from the landscape to the woman who rode at his side. Dark curls framed her face, wisps of errant hair allowed their escape only when she was riding. At other times, they were swept up in perfect symmetry, as befit the daughter of a professor at the University of Edinburgh. But here, with him, she was simply Elena, relaxed and contented to ride a huge beast that masqueraded as a horse.

Seventeen hands high with feet like dinner plates and a chest twice the width of most horses, Goliath plodded along, surprisingly agile for a beast that made the soggy ground tremble with each step. Foul-tempered, stubborn, loyal, he responded only to her, hanging his great head in comical fashion when admonished by the woman he respected above all other humans. Not a single horse aficionado in all of Edinburgh could put a breed name to Goliath, and none dared ride him—except the beautiful Elena.

His Elena.

They would marry on Saturday in a quiet, secret ceremony, then enjoy each other on the return trip to Canada, where they would put on innocent faces and marry again for the benefit of happily tearful parents. Even the thought of their clandestine plan was arousing, exciting, making him instantly want her, right here and now, with the soft moss as their bed and the mist as their concealment.

"I'll race you," Elena challenged, shaking him out of his reverie.

"I think the ground's too soft, Elena. After the rain last night—"

Goliath's thundering change from walk to gallop drowned out the last of his words, and she charged away, cloak flying out behind her. Alarm edged into his thoughts. Rain had deluged the moor for the last three days, softening the already soggy ground and hiding holes with debris. But Elena cared little for danger when she was astride her beast, completely absorbed in the rush that accompanied plunging headlong unchecked.

"Elena!" Colin called again, but she only glanced over her shoulder long enough to smile a challenge at him.

Against the voices that cautioned in his ear, Colin urged his own mount into a lope, but Elena was yards ahead and rapidly drawing away.

Colin's own horse stumbled then, and he instinctually slowed his pace, but Elena raced away from him. He called to her once more, not expecting her to hear his words, but she turned and looked back over her shoulder. Then the world slowed.

She pitched forward over Goliath's head as he crumpled to the ground with the groan of a mighty tree, the bones in his leg snapping with an audible crack. Elena flew on, her cloak fanning around her like wings of a black bird. Then she, too, pitched to the ground, her head bent beneath her.

When Colin reached her side, she lay still, her body limp and crumpled like a shell already discarded by the soul that soared above it. A cold lethargy settled onto him. The emotions that ruled his body slithered back to their secret place, and the physician in him took over. Falling to his knees, Colin felt for a pulse and found none, only the loud quiet of the moor filling his ears—and Goliath's labored breathing.

"Elena. Oh, dear God. Elena." He lifted her hair and probed her neck, finding the place where the spine was cleanly snapped.

She'd died instantly, perhaps before she even felt the pain of her vertebrae snapping in two. Despite his years of study and hours of dissecting cadavers, there was nothing any mortal being could do to bring her back to him. And the magic that had buoyed him these last few weeks dissipated, his hard-won knowledge paling in the presence of death's callousness. He'd convinced himself he could hold life in his hands, meet death on its level, and defeat it with his skills. But Fate had reached out a cold hand and, with the flick of a finger, put him back into his place.

Rolling Elena over, Colin gazed down into her fixed violet eyes that bore an expression of mild surprise. He pulled her onto his lap and bent over her, willing her to blink and smile at him, praying that by some miracle God would return her to him.

Time lost its value, and only when his legs grew stiff did Colin gently place Elena onto the spongy ground and rise. By his side, Goliath's massive chest heaved up and down, and his eyes rolled in fright and pain. Numb, Colin stood over the horse, hearing the pain and anguish Elena would never voice coming from the horse she loved. His leg was broken horribly, bits of bone and sinew protruding from his slick black hide. There was no saving the animal, especially this far from Edinburgh and help. The best he could do was send him to his beloved Elena with a quick prayer to watch after her.

On trembling legs, Colin walked back to his nervous mount and retrieved the pistol he always carried when riding on the moor. The gun was a small caliber, hardly large enough to penetrate the skull of so massive a horse, but Colin prayed for a miracle as he cocked the gun and looked into the horse's large eyes. Fear seemed to leave the horse, replaced by quiet acceptance. Colin tightened his grip on the trigger, and the part of his brain that still worked wondered if Goliath knew what was about to take place. Colin had never killed anything in his life, let alone a magnificent horse like this. He looked down one last time, allowing his gaze to meet the horse's and saw a deeper intelligence than he could have ever imagined, a silent message passing between man and animal.

Protect her.

Then Colin closed his eyes and pulled the trigger.

Chapter One

Only the haunting warble of the meadowlark rivaled the sweet voice of the wind as it caressed the tall golden grasses into a sensuous dance. Maggie Hayes rethreaded the reins through her fingers and waited, her eyes fixed on the far-off ridge in an endless landscape of rolling hills. She squinted one eye, looked up at the sun, and was rewarded with a sneeze. Wiping her nose on the old, ragged shirtsleeve, she shifted on the hard board seat and returned her gaze to the hills beyond.

Pa had said the men would come this morning. And if she was any judge of time, the sun said it was long past morning. Maybe they'd gotten cold feet. Maybe one of the U.S. Cavalry patrols had caught them and taken away that lovely load of whiskey Pa had talked about for weeks. Pa'd be mad if he didn't get his load of whiskey. Maggie shrugged to herself and smiled to the prairie that stretched to the horizon. She couldn't care less about the whiskey, but she secretly hoped there would be a patrol of cavalry that would burst over that ridge, resplendent in their blue-and-gold uniforms. How she did love a good chase.

She'd been hauling rotgut for her Pa ever since she was old enough to handle a team, and she could handle a two-horse hitch better than any of her Pa's men. Pa said so, but he didn't have to tell her; she knew she had *the touch*. Pa said some folks had a way with horses and some didn't but that she had something special.

A soft clang of metal on metal and the groan of wood drew her attention to a rise nearby. She stood up, still holding the reins in her fingers, ready to flip them against the horses' shiny backsides and gallop back across the Canadian border and out of reach of the boys in blue. But when a wagon much like hers came lumbering up out of a draw, one man hunched on the seat, her spirits plunged.

Another boring transfer of goods.

She waited until the other wagon drew alongside. Arnie Stevenson squinted at her before spitting a long brown stream into the dirt at her horse's feet.

"Where's yer menfolk?" he asked, squinting against the bright sun.

"They's helpin' Pa at the still."

"Well, I ain't unloadin' this stuff by myself."

Maggie looped the reins around the brake and

swung down. "I ain't askin' you to. I reckon I can load and unload a wagon by myself. I been doin' it fer years."

Arnie swung around in the seat and watched her lift the first box from the tail of his wagon and carry it to hers. "Ain't fittin' fer no gal to be a-doin' this sort of work. Yer Pa oughta be whupped fer not already marryin' you off."

"I ain't a-wantin' no husband. Just gittin' underfoot's all they's good fer."

Arnie grinned, showing stained and gapped teeth. "Now, missy, that ain't *all* a man's good fer."

"You applyin' fer the position, Arnie?" Maggie stopped in her tracks, settled her hands on her hips, and stared at him until he shifted his gaze first.

"Naw, girlie, you know I was just joshin'."

"I don't josh about things like that. I got enough men to have to pick up after and such. Don't need no husband to add to the workload."

Smiling to herself, she shuffled around behind the wagon and soon had the entire contents reloaded. Swinging up onto the wagon seat, she picked up the reins and opened her mouth to send Arnie on his way when the unmistakable jingle of tack and harness rose above the voice of the wind.

"Cavalry," Arnie breathed, and flipped his reins, sending his horses and wagon back down into the coulee and quickly out of sight.

Maggie waited, enjoying the way her heart surged with excitement. The border was less than a half mile away, and if she had judged right, the cavalry patrol would top that rise right over there, about a mile away. As soon as she saw the first glint off their polished brass, she'd set the horses into a gallop and scoot across the border just ahead of them.

True to her judgment, the patrol topped the rise just where she'd estimated. She cracked the reins, and the horses bolted into a gallop. Clenching her teeth, Maggie drove them across the flat top of the rolling ridge, glancing back over her shoulder once to be sure they were following and found them at full gallop, mere spots on the drab grassland.

In the wagon's bed the large glass bottles clanked and lurched. If just one bottle broke, Pa'd whip her for sure, but not even the threat of a whipping was enough to dissuade her from indulging in a rollicking race.

A small line of low trees came into view and with them the Canadian border. Once across the line, the patrols rarely followed, content just to have her out of their territory. They'd flirted like this for months, she and this dandily dressed patrol, and they never followed her once she reached the tree line. But now the closer she came to the border, the more they gained on her. True panic began to replace her arrogance. If they got this entire load, Pa would be furious and might stop her from driving delivery. That would be worse than the whipping.

She barely noticed the trees and the cooling of the surrounding air as she rattled across the border and never stopped to look back until she ceased to hear the thud of horses' hooves behind her. Only then did she slow the team and turn to look over her shoulder. The men in blue sat on heaving horses, their hats pushed back on their heads. She could have sworn she saw them smile.

Ceaseless, pelting rain drenched Colin's clothes, ran down his neck, and pooled at the small of his back. Hands shoved in his pockets, he hunched his shoulders against the onslaught and hid beneath the hat pulled low over his eyes. Leaning against a handy wall, he watched the rest of Toronto hurry past him, eager to return to warm, dry homes.

The gray sky hovered ominously above him, as if reminding him of his sorrow. For all the years he'd spent studying that breadth of time between this life and the next, for all the techniques and schemes he'd learned to cheat death, death had triumphed, snatching her away in a heartbeat, a breath, giving him no time to call into use his hard-won knowledge. And now, after staring into the face of death, his godlike knowledge seemed puny, useless, pointless. And so his life. For if he could not save the woman he loved, what good could he do the rest of mankind?

A small knot of men had gathered at the end of the puddle-filled street, drawing Colin's attention away from the mud forming around his feet and to the men and horses waiting there. He shoved away from the wall and shuffled in that direction, promising himself that whatever had given rise to the gathering would not interest him above a moment's distraction.

In the center of the covered sidewalk sat a rickety table. Rain streamed off the overhang and plopped loudly on the gouged boards. A young man, resplendent in a scarlet jacket cut in military fashion, guarded the damp table that was covered with neat stacks of papers. Sure that the British Imperial Army was staging some recruiting program, Colin turned around, intent on heading back to his alleyway, when a finely saddled horse stole his attention.

The blood bay was sleek, dark from the rain, saddled with tack recently oiled to a golden sheen. Colin touched the horse's back, felt the warm, damp hair, and smelled the pungent horse scent that was so tightly woven into his childhood memories. Then, as in his nightmares, he momentarily saw again Elena's still body, her hair spread around her like a silken fan and Goliath's heaving body at her side.

He jerked his hand away just as a man brushed roughly past him, staggered a moment, then lunged toward the horse. He scrambled into the saddle, gathered the reins, and sawed cruelly at the horse's mouth. The horse rolled its eyes and sidestepped daintily as if puzzled at this rough treatment.

Anger, long banked, began to uncoil in Colin, slowly and deadly. "You don't have to pull on the bit so hard," Colin said, placing a hand on the horse's neck. "He'll come around with a gentle tug."

"If I'd a-wanted yer damn opinion, I'd a-asked fer it," the drunk drawled, and yanked the reins. The horse shied and grunted, nearly unseating his rider.

"You stubborn bastard." The rider balled up a fist

and landed a blow directly between the horse's ears. The horse half-reared and stumbled backward.

With muffled oaths, the drunk drew a rifle from a leather scabbard, dropped the reins, and took aim at the horse's head.

Full-blown fury burst free inside Colin. He lunged toward the man and knocked the barrel of the rifle upward as it discharged with a roar that sent the skittish horse one way and his rider the other.

The horse danced away a few feet, then stopped and stood quivering, ears pricked forward, intelligent eyes alert. Colin approached with soft words and extended hand, then caught the reins and looped them over the hitching rail.

A crowd had gathered, huddled under the dripping roof. Scrambling out of the mud, the drunk lunged toward Colin, clutching and gesturing with a short, stubby knife. "I'll split you from asshole to appetite," he growled, seemingly cold sober as he began to circle Colin.

The man's reactions were sluggish and irregular, and his breathing was shallow and rapid, indicating he was still very drunk despite the appearance otherwise. Turning on his heels, always keeping his face toward his attacker, Colin waited. Then the drunk stopped, took a deep breath, and dropped his arms for a second. Colin seized his chance. He lunged forward, striking the man midchest with the heel of his hand. The drunk looked surprised for a moment, then dropped his knife and clutched his chest before dropping to his knees, gasping.

Colin kicked the knife out of reach, then squatted down in front of the drunk.

"You'll be all right in a minute, I just knocked the breath out of you." Colin placed two fingers on the man's neck and felt a steady, strong pulse.

"Ye . . . ye didn't even use . . . yer fist," the man stammered.

Colin smiled and pushed to his feet. "No, I didn't have to."

The observing crowd murmured for a moment, then straggled away to other interests.

"How did you know just where to hit him?"

Colin turned at the smooth voice. The young man dressed in scarlet stood behind him, offering his hand. "Subinspector James Walsh of the Northwest Mounted Police."

"Colin Fraser and a dubious skill, I assure you." Colin shook the man's hand. Mounted Police? Someplace in his sluggish brain Colin remembered hearing of the new police force that was touted as the army of men that would tame western Canada.

"You're a physician, aren't you?"

Surprise robbed Colin of his words of denial. "Yes. How did you know?"

Walsh smiled and gestured to the man who had climbed out of the mud and now sat on the sidewalk, one hand pressed to his chest. "I've seen that done before. Ends a disagreement quickly and without a lewd display, doesn't it?"

Colin nodded, then pulled the last of his money from his pocket. He stepped over to the drunk, threw the currency onto the man's lap, and took the horse's reins. "That's more than a fair price for the horse and the saddle. Get yourself a mule."

The drunk squinted up at him but made neither comment nor argument.

"We could use someone like you in the Mounted Police." Walsh said, handing Colin a recruitment brochure. As he read it, he tried to push away the slight trill of adventure that sang through him as visions of wide-open land and expansive blue skies raced across his mind's eye.

"We're looking for one hundred fifty enlistees to make up the initial force."

Colin glanced back down at the paper in his hand. Men of "sound constitution, able to ride, active and able-bodied" were being sought. Knights mounted on horseback, wearers of scarlet, the color that had commanded respect for the British army for decades, defenders of Canada's laws, abolishers of the hated illegal whiskey that was destroying the lives of the Blackfoot, Peigan, and Blood Indians. He remembered now the fine and elegant words that had been used to romanticize the proposed force of men, intended to sway public opinion to the side of those that believed the Territories needed policing and civilizing.

"We need physicians," Walsh gently prodded. Again, Colin thought of open sky and endless wilderness, enough space for a man to lose both himself and his soul. Why not? He had to work someplace, sometime. Why not in the west, as far from anything that resembled Scotland and a foggy moor as he could get? But not as a physician.

"I wouldn't have to serve as a doctor, would I?"

Walsh looked at him curiously. "No, not if you insist. We need good men. In fact, we already have a physician signed up."

"I'd just like to be an enlistee, if that's possible."

Walsh looked him up and down, obviously taking in his rumpled clothes, and the vivid images of freedom and hope dimmed.

"You'll need an examination by the physicians just through that door and a character reference."

Colin stared down at the paper again. He knew no one in Toronto. His parents were in Ottawa, with no idea where he was. They only knew that Elena had died, Colin had disappeared, and they had been left to deal with both their sorrow and his. *What a selfish bastard you are,* he thought for the first time since he'd dropped out of sight.

"I don't know anyone here." He handed Walsh back the leaflet, his fledgling hopes dashed.

Walsh stared at him for a moment, then quickly penned something on a form and handed it back. "The doctor is waiting for you through those doors," he said, gesturing over his shoulder.

Colin took the form and looked down at the writing. "Mr. Fraser is of fine character and sound constitution. It is my pleasure to recommend him to the Northwest Mounted Police," followed by Walsh's flowing signature.

"Why are you doing this?" Colin asked, warring

with the temptation to accept the kindness or to slink back to his hiding place and sink again into oblivion.

Walsh turned the quill pen over in his hands and stared down at it. "I've always been a good judge of men, Mr. Fraser, and I've seen the look that's in your eyes before. Some men never shake the devil off their back, and some do." He raised his eyes to Colin's face. "I think you will."

Colin stared at Walsh's fine, looping writing again, fighting the sudden wave of emotion that threatened to overtake him. In his self-imposed state of misery and anger, he'd forgotten that kindness and trust still existed in the world.

"Through those doors lies your destiny, Mr. Fraser."

Colin tightened his grip on the papers and met Walsh's steady gaze. "Watch my horse, will you?"

Chapter Two

A stranger stared back at Maggie Hayes from the shiny surface of the stagnant green water. She gazed at her reflection, tugged at an errant strand of blond hair, and chewed one side of her mouth. Then she folded the sides of her old felt hat down over her cheeks, mimicking the stylish straw bonnets she'd seen in the store windows in Benton. On Pa's last trip down, she begged to go along, eager for new sights and sounds. And there in the store windows, she'd seen the hats. They were woven of delicate straw and trimmed with bright blue ribbons. Dainty and fragile, they would hardly survive a windblown rain or offer much shade from the unrelenting prairie sun. But she'd wanted one all the same.

Slowly, she released the hat and let the felt brim drift back up to its natural floppy position. She was what she was, and so was her hat. Neither was soft and frilly; both were substantial in build and demeanor. She'd bet not one of those city women could handle a four-horse team as well as she. And yet, since the last time she accompanied her father into Benton, there had been within her a yearning, a growing dissatisfaction with something she could not name or correct. She'd tried once or twice to broach the subject with her father, but he'd quickly turned the conversation to something less personal. And in those moments, she'd have given anything she owned to talk to her mother.

Amanda Hayes was only a wispy memory, a jumble of soft touches and soothing words without face or form. Maggie could vaguely remember a home once filled with small creature comforts, but some days she wondered if she remembered those things at all or if she'd made them up to satisfy this growing void that gnawed at her insides.

The wavering reflection dissolved as her father spat a stream of tobacco juice out into the pond. "Wagon's loaded," he said without preamble.

Maggie turned toward her father. Bags and shadows rimmed eyes as blue as hers. Years in the prairie sun had turned his skin the color and texture of leather and traced tiny lines at the corners of his eyes. Would she one day look this way, old and dried, worn down by the sun and wind?

"Earl'll meet ye at the usual place across the border. Watch out fer them boys in blue." George Hayes was not a man of words, and what few he spoke were usually gruff and sharp. But standing there, staring into her father's aging face, Maggie knew without reassurance he loved her despite the fact he expected her to make a ten-mile ride alone and at night to meet his whiskey distributor. Thus was the nature of their life; it had been so for as long as she could remember.

But sometimes when the prairie night was silent and no insect songs kept her company on her lonely rides, she wondered about this way of life and the strength of her father's love. But in those times a small voice inside her was always quick to point out that he'd done the best he could, raising her alone in a harsh and unforgiving country where men were just as coarse and merciless. Whiskey making was his only talent, and he'd used that knowledge to provide for her the only way he knew how. And through this life, she'd learned valuable lessons about men.

"Is Earl gonna have money for me tonight?" she asked.

"Yep, this week and last's. You know where to hide it."

"I'll be back by dawn."

He nodded. "Me and the boys'll have us all packed."

Maggie turned her head, puzzled. "Are we a-goin' someplace?"

"I'm movin' us up along the Bow River. I hear tell it's a trader's heaven, with plenty of Injuns fer customers."

"You mean we ain't comin' back here?"

"That's what I mean. Now go on and get on the trail 'fore Earl thinks you ain't comin'."

She expected him to turn away, but he remained for a moment, his fingers lingering on her arm, his expression softening in a way that was detectable only to her. His eyes crinkled around the corners, and a slight smile played over his lips. "You be careful, Maggie girl."

"I will, Pa."

"I hear tell the government is sending a police force to wipe out the likes of us. Mounted Police, they're callin' 'em. Dandies on horseback."

Maggie felt her eyes widen. "Are they here now?" All she needed was more soldiers to watch out for.

"No, but we'll have to be on our toes once we get into Canada proper and away from the border. Gonna wipe out the whiskey trade, they say. Keep us from ruinin' the Injuns."

Then, as quickly as his face had softened, it hardened again, and he turned away, shuffling off toward the group of men clumped around the still.

An odd assortment of pipes and tanks, the still gave off a sweet-sour smell Maggie had hated as a child but now ignored. For the last five or six years her father had dragged himself out of bed, rain or shine, cold or heat, and tended the still. And because of the still and the product it produced, there'd been a constant stream of men in and out of their home. Old, young, evil, and those who had simply strayed from the path had all crossed their threshold at one time or another.

Safe under her father's ever-vigilant protection, she'd listened to them talk, watched them earn money, then lose it all on a single poker hand. Yep, she'd learned a lot about men.

And as the years passed and she grew into womanhood, she sometimes dreamed of a home of her own, a husband, children. But as quickly as such a treacherous thought surfaced, a man would come along with a particularly odd assortment of personal vices and send that romantic notion scurrying back into the depths of her mind. There was no room for such in her life. Her father needed her, and besides, who'd marry the likes of her?

"Don't look like much of a going concern, does it, now?" Braden Flynn cocked an eyebrow toward Colin, the words rolling off his tongue in a sassy Irish brogue.

Colin shifted in the saddle, the tight collar of his scarlet uniform jacket chafing his neck. Tension rippled through the air like the waves of heat they'd left behind on the plains only a few weeks ago. In front of them, thick cottonwood trunks formed a formidable palisade wall around Fort Whoop-Up, infamous stronghold of the illegal whiskey trade in the Northwest Territories and the end destination of the Mounted Police.

As they watched, a dog ambled across the hard-packed ground, threw them a curious glance, then poked aimlessly at piles of debris.

No whiskey traders crowded the enclosure.

No wagons loaded with illegal rotgut rumbled past.

No encampments of Blackfeet filled the grassy flats to either side of the fort where now ponies grazed peacefully between telltale rings of stones and trampled circles in the grass.

The fort was recently deserted.

Or so it seemed.

Tack squeaked as men shifted nervously in their saddles. A bastion of squared timbers guarded the northwest corner, its hollow windows possibly hiding guns trained on the slim column of men. And above it all fluttered, inappropriately, the American flag. Exclamations of surprise rose despite the order of silence.

Expecting armed resistance, Assistant Commissioner James McLeod had ordered the column to load arms and approach the fortification with caution. Two field guns—nine-pounders—and two mortars had been strategically repositioned in case they were needed.

Somewhere to Colin's right, a warbling field lark broke the tense silence, trilling a sweet song that lifted and grew until it abruptly ended. A chill wind ruffled the guidons, reminding them it was October and winter was not far away.

James McLeod rode forward and sat studying the structure ahead, scout Jerry Potts at his side. Then, amid gasps of amazement, McLeod dismounted and strode toward the open main gate alone. He paused briefly, glanced up at the towering walls, then walked inside.

Colin slid his Springfield rifle from its leather scabbard, his heart pounding and all his senses alert. A robust vegetable garden rambled alongside the walls, and nearby were several corrals and a rickety hay shed. To the south was a pile of charred timbers, reminders that Fort Whoop-Up had not been the first stronghold to be built here where the stream St. Mary's swept gracefully into the Belly River.

Time crawled by. Horses shuffled tired feet, shifting their weight from side to side. Men whispered ominous predictions. They'd been instructed to expect crowds of whiskey traders, their wagons packed for transport northward into Cree country, and camps of drunken Indians, already victims of the traders' business.

McLeod reappeared, a little gray, bent man at his side.

"Gentlemen, this is Dave Akers, the only inhabitant of Fort Whoop-Up." His voice was edged with sarcasm. "He asks that we dismount and take supper with him."

"And what do ye make of that?" Braden removed his white helmet, balancing it on his knee and raking at his red hair. While the helmet was an integral part of their uniform, it was also the bane of their existence. Hot, unwieldy, and downright uncomfortable, it was nonetheless striking from a distance, reflecting the sun with a clean brilliance the organizers back in Ottawa hoped would intimidate all who dared challenge the Mounted Police.

"Looks like they were warned," Colin said, searching the walls for signs of resistance, his heart hammering beneath his coat. He glanced at Braden, who sat slumped comfortably in his saddle, none of the nervousness Colin was feeling apparent. But then Braden rarely lost his good humor no matter how tense or dangerous the situation.

"Ye don't suppose they saw this proud display of finery marchin' across the plains, now, do ye?" Braden grinned as he set the helmet back on his head and drew the chin strap tight.

Braden was the closest thing Colin had to a friend. Maddeningly cheerful, Braden saw the world through an irreverent Irish humor and applied his gift liberally on all who would listen. Especially Steven Gravel, a fellow humorist, perched on a small bay horse on the other side of Colin. He, in fact, had left behind a career as a professional clown to follow the call of adventure. Between the two of them, Colin had learned to laugh again.

"I don't think we could be missed. I guess that was the point, though," Colin said.

"What do ye think the old man'll do now?" Braden nodded toward where McLeod stood, head bent, talking to Akers and the two Indian women at his side.

"I expect he'll take him up on his offer, and by the end of the meal, McLeod will have charmed the truth out of one of them."

"Aye," Braden said with a smile as he urged his

horse forward. "The men of Scotland and Ireland have a common gift . . . tongues of silver."

A cold, bitter wind keened across grass already bent beneath the hand of winter. Colin hunched his shoulders against the cold and glanced at the group surrounding the newly dug grave.

"We commit his body to the earth, oh, God," McLeod was saying. Colin shut his ears against the painful words and gazed across the open area to the half-finished stables made of cottonwood logs. Constable Godfrey Parks was the first casualty of the Mounted Police. The young man with laughing eyes and tousled hair had contracted typhoid when the troop passed through the Sweet Grass Hills and died despite the efforts of the surgeon.

Colin glanced at James Kittson, the surgeon, who stood with hands clasped in front of him, his eyes also on the grave. Kittson had struggled to save Parks to no avail, discovering as Colin had, that man's struggle against death was futile.

And Colin had offered no assistance.

He'd have done nothing different, Colin told himself. Kittson was obviously a very capable physician. So there was no reason to break his vow to himself and reveal his background. And yet, during Parks's illness, he found himself listening to the surgeons' conversations, measuring their opinions with his own. And while the first shovelful of dirt thumped onto the wooden coffin lid, he renewed his promise to leave behind the practice of healing.

"McLeod wants to see ye in his office." Braden fell into step beside him as the group trudged across the area now morbidly designated as a cemetery.

"What does he want?" Colin asked, a prick of irritation digging at him. An audience in front of McLeod always meant a battle of wits. Dignified and intuitive, McLeod had a way of working his way through any and all excuses to get at the information he wanted. And anytime Colin was called in front of McLeod, his legs turned to jelly, certain McLeod knew all his failings.

McLeod's door was cracked open, and with a quick rap, Colin received a mumbled "Come in" from the other side. The door skimmed open, brushing lightly against the plank floor. James McLeod hunched over the desk, scratching wandering loops of script onto a page of paper. He paused and looked up.

"Constable Fraser. Have a seat." With a nod he indicated an empty chair across the desk.

Colin slid into the seat, balancing his helmet on his knee. McLeod continued to write what was obviously a letter. He signed with a flourish, then carefully placed the page to one side. "My wife worries if she doesn't hear from me," he said with a small smile.

Colin nodded. James and Mary McLeod lived the love affair most people only wished for. Although the width of a continent separated them most of the time, each was deeply devoted to the other. And yet despite the distance between them, they sent their love back and forth across the wilderness, tender words penned on fragile paper.

"Are you up for a little adventure, Constable Fraser?"

"Yes, sir," Colin replied, surprised by the question.

McLeod rose and walked to the window. Hands behind his back, he stared out across the common ground defined by the hastily erected buildings that surrounded it. "How do you feel about lying, Constable?"

Jarred, Colin frantically searched for an answer as the guilt of his own lie of omission haunted him.

McLeod turned and leveled his honest, piercing stare on him.

When no glib answer would come, Colin raised his eyes and met McLeod's gaze. "Lying is dishonest but remains a human fault, Commissioner."

McLeod watched him, assessing, measuring. "I'm about to ask you to lie, Constable. One of Jerry Potts's relations, a minor Blackfoot chief, has brought me information that there's a whiskey camp about fifty miles north of here in Pine Coulee. George Hayes is the bootlegger's name. He's a brazen sort, operating out in the open, challenging us to catch him. I'm willing to wager that his arrogance will be his undoing."

"What would you like me to do?" Colin asked, a measure of relief working through him. McLeod had not found him out.

McLeod sat down and leaned across the table. "I want you to pose as a trader, infiltrate their camp, get to know their weaknesses and their strengths, then report back to me."

"But why me, sir?"

McLeod leaned back in his chair and toyed with the edges of the blank pages of papers neatly stacked in the center of his desk. "I like to think that I'm a good judge of character, Constable, and I sense that appearing to be a little less than you truly are is a special talent of yours."

Colin felt as if he'd been punched in the stomach. McLeod's words were gracious and cloaked, but the meaning was unmistakable. He knew.

Should he confess all? Admit that he possessed valuable medical knowledge that could be of service to his companions? And in doing so, admit that he had lied on his application?

He ceased his perusal of the room and met McLeod's eyes, reading in them no disapproval or censure . . . only expectation.

Colin opened his mouth to confess, to give voice to the words that could result in the loss of his position and discharge from the Northwest Mounted Police.

"Someday when you are ready," McLeod said in a deep, soft voice, "I will expect a complete explanation."

He paused, and Colin remained silent, waiting.

"Until then, all I require is your answer to my question."

"I will be happy to do as you ask, Commissioner."

McLeod smiled slowly, showing white teeth beneath his carefully trimmed mustache. "This is our chance to strike the first victory here, to let those who wish to challenge our justice know that the Mounted Police will suffer no disobedience. Welcome to the world of intrigue, Constable."

Colin drew his horse to a stop in a thicket of twisted and entwined branches. Summer's leaves had long since turned and dropped to the ground. He hunched his shoulders against a cold wind and shifted as the horse's spine dug into his backside. He'd ridden bareback as a child, but on a fat mare whose top speed was a bored shuffle and whose back was a soft pillow.

Together he and James McLeod had invented this new persona he would use to gather information on George Hayes's whiskey operation. He would pose as another wanderer, seeking his fortune in whatever manner he chose, legal or not, in the fast-diminishing lawlessness of western Canada. He'd wander into Hayes's camp with intimate knowledge of the bootleg trade, gleaned from various stints among whiskey traders. Once there, he'd participate in the business and find out when and where their shipments were being dispersed, then report back to McLeod. When the time was right, the men of Fort McLeod would sweep in and achieve their first victory against the whiskey trade.

The camp was laid out like a village. A cluster of rough log huts squatted in a grove of aspen and birch. A long log building stood in the center of the cluster, a metal stovepipe poking out of the center of the roof. The sky was leaden and gray. Smoke clung to the ground and along with it the unmistakable scent of souring mash.

To the right was the Bow River, a ready source of water—disposal for the used mash and a perfect means to bring customers to them. All in all an ingenious plan, Colin thought, scratching the two-week-old beard that itched mightily.

He prolonged the scratching when a movement to his left caught his eye. Someone watched from a neighboring thicket. A sentry, probably, instructed to watch from cover, then circle around behind him once he moved on. The leather scabbard beneath his leg held his Springfield rifle. He shifted on the horse's sharp backbone, moving his leg for better access to the weapon.

"I don't mean ye no harm," Colin called, slurring his words slightly. "Heard ye was making liquor. Made some liquor myself in my day."

Colin waited, his hearing trained on the bushes to his left, even though he kept his eyes on the camp in front of him.

Nothing. Not a sound in reply.

"I know yer in them bushes. I heered ye thrashin' around."

A small stir rustled the leaves, then a gaunt man stepped out, rifle drawn. Worn and greasy buckskins hung from the man's frame. Dark circles surrounded eyes sunk in a colorless, pasty face.

All the signs of a heavy drinker.

"Speak yer business or I'll drill a hole in yer gut."

"Stopped down at the Whoop-Up. They said some of ye'd moved up here. Said business was good. Thought I'd come up and hire on." Colin met the man's gaze steadily, praying his eyes were selling his story, but the man didn't lower his rifle.

"Whoop-Up's done cleared out."

"I know. I talked to Dave Akers. Said buffalo hunters told him there was some fancy police force coming from the east." Colin managed a cocky smile. "Dandies on horseback," he said.

The man lifted his face from the gun sight. "Who you been workin' with?"

"Benny Parsons, outside Benton. Jess Hartley in the Sweet Grass Hills."

The gun lowered another inch or two, but the shadowed eyes continued to drill a hole in Colin's gut. The names and places of whiskey traders rioted through his thoughts, and Colin prayed he'd gotten the information right.

"What did Ollie Swift call that rotgut he made and sold down along the border?"

Colin's mind went blank. Panic inched through him. A bullet could do a lot of damage when fired into the lower abdomen. The lower intestine would be perforated. Bowel contents would spill into the body cavity. Death would be slow and painful.

"Ollie's Hooch." The answer came to him as if placed there by a divine force. Somewhere, somehow, he'd heard the name, and it had stuck. He offered a silent prayer and braced for the next test.

"That was good stuff, won't it?" The man lowered the rifle to his side and grinned. "It had a bite to it, that's fer sure, goin' in and comin' out. Ollie was heavy-handed on the red pepper, but the Injuns couldn't get enough of it." The man laughed and stepped forward. "Abner Smith."

He held out a grubby hand, and Colin grasped it with relief. "Colin Fraser."

Abner dropped his hand and started toward the camp, the gun cradled in his arms. "George can always use another hand. Business's been good up here. The woods is usually full of Injuns sittin' around waitin' fer the next batch to work off. Just sit out there in the trees, squattin' and waitin'."

Abner shook his head and looked up at Colin as his horse shuffled around behind. "Gives me the willies sometimes seein' how they love the stuff. Some buck tried to trade George his little girl once."

The desperation evident in that act shook Colin to his center. He'd heard it before, stories of emaciated men dragging starving families behind them, their one purpose to obtain another bottle of liquor. And then another. Trading or selling anything they could to feed the beast within.

He passed the first row of cabins, and men filtered outside like silent ghosts. They stood staring with their sunken, blood-shot eyes, silent disapproval in their piercing stares. He was invading the inner sanctum, walking among those who could snuff out his life with one word, one action. He teetered on the edge of death, danced on that fine edge where Elena had danced for a brief moment before she plunged into the void beyond.

Surprisingly, he felt no fear, no anxiousness for his situation. Not even as the shadow men wandered down off rickety porches and moved in his direction, surrounding him. He didn't care whether he lived or died. And for a brief moment, he knew what it was like to be immortal.

Chapter Three

"State yer business," said a tall man with a scraggly black beard as he leveled an ancient rifle directly at Colin's chest.

"I heard ye were lookin' fer men to deliver liquor," Colin said, careful not to overdo the slur of his words.

"Could be," the man said, and spat at Colin's feet. "Brazen, ain't you, strollin' in here like this? Abner, what the hell's the matter with you?"

Abner hesitated, and without turning around, Colin knew he was fumbling for an answer. "He knows Benny and Ollie. Said he worked for 'em."

"Any damned fool can say that, you idiot."

Abner moved around in front, his expression sheepish. "I don't think he's lyin', Tom."

Tom leered darkly, studying Colin. "Let's see about that. What did old Benny put in his liquor?"

Again, Colin searched his memory. One hot summer's evening James McLeod had explained the eccentricities of the whiskey trade and the Indian's fascination with it.

"Benny liked a combination of alcohol, molasses, tabasco, and tobacco juice. He called it Hell Hot Jump Up."

Tom's face remained impassive, his alcohol-soaked brain sorting through the information.

"Any fool could know that, too. Where'd he get the tabasco?"

"He grew 'em himself."

Again, Tom stared expressionless, then he smiled. "Ol' Benny'd be mad ifen he knew somebody else had his recipe. He always said the Blackfeet'd sell their women for one cup of the stuff."

Colin let out his held breath. Tom lowered his gun, stepped forward, and held out his hand. "Welcome to the Bow River traders. . . . Buccaneers of the Plains, we like to call ourselves."

His flowery announcement brought shouts of approval from the assembled crowd, who obviously also fancied themselves a special breed.

And then, from behind the crowd, emerged a small man who sauntered forward with a confidence reserved for men of greater stature and girth. And as he approached, an incongruity began to nag at Colin's thoughts.

Something about this fellow seemed out of place. His body swayed slightly as he walked. A fluid gracefulness propelled him forward instead of the jerky, lumbering gait of most men.

And then it hit him.

He was a she.

Colin flickered a glance at the surrounding crowd. Did they know? He watched their faces as she neared and saw that they moved aside slightly to let her through.

She wore the same nondescript clothes as the men. Torn and ragged pants, too-large shirt tucked into a rope belt. Floppy hat pulled low over her eyes. Aside from her feminine walk, no one would suspect.

Or were they supposed to be fooled?

She stopped by the side of Colin's horse and raised the bluest eyes he'd ever seen. Not even the October sky on a clear day could rival the depth and hue of the color that now stared at him.

She said nothing, staring up at him silently, her gaze neither threatening nor angry, simply inquisitive.

"Are you one of Benny's runners?" she asked. Her sweet-rough voice ran up his spine and teased something in his brain to life.

"Was."

She studied him for a long breath. "How's Earl?"

The question caught him off guard, and he had no ready answer. Was this an interrogation designed to catch him in the threads of his own lie when direct questions could not?

"What?"

Still, she gazed up innocently. "I said how's Earl? Did he use that potion I sent him when he was sick?"

"Yes." Colin nodded. "He's better." He prayed that was the right answer and that Earl had not seen fit to die and make him out a liar.

"Good." She nodded as she spoke, a relieved expression softening her eyes. "I was worried 'bout him."

The intuition Colin had once relied on heavily during his medical training and practice sprang again to life. The realization was so jarring, Colin felt a shiver run up his spine. Not since Elena's death had he allowed himself to utilize that instinct. In fact, he'd not allowed himself close enough to anyone to sense anything in a very long time. But now that intuitiveness was running at full tilt.

He thought of the Scottish thistle, a tough, thorny plant with delicate pink blooms that struggled to show their colors past the gray-green thorns. She was a bloom among thorns, he decided, watching as the men moved aside to allow her to pass. As she pushed her way through them, not a single man turned to ogle her well-fitted, if ragged, pants. She commanded respect, well-earned respect, he sensed. These men would not be easily impressed or tamed, and she seemed to have done both.

Maggie willed herself not to turn around and stare. She walked through the men and straight toward the house, feeling his eyes on her back as she climbed the steps, opened the door, and went inside. Once the door was shut behind her, she hurried to the window and peeped outside.

He sat unconcerned, smiling down, answering questions. Now he was swinging one leg over the horse's back. Was he dismounting? No, no, he was just relaxing. How on earth could he relax on a horse's backbone that thin and sharp?

A hat shaded his blue eyes, but she could see his mouth as he laughed. She imagined his face as he'd gazed down at her. No mustache drooped over lips that were thin and soft. His face was clean shaven, a rarity here. Every man she'd ever known had worn a beard of some description. As she watched him shift his position, she wondered how his cheek would feel against the palm of her hand, his skin slipping beneath her fingers, soft and smooth. Perhaps he would smell of lotion, the warm, enticing scent she'd smelled outside the open doors of the barbershop in Benton.

He smiled then and laughed at something someone said. She could imagine he had a deep, throaty laugh, that jiggled his shoulders and bubbled up from deep within him. Something in Maggie's belly stirred, an odd sensation that made her grip her abdomen. Was he some spirit sent to punish her for her disloyal thoughts of late? She remembered bits and pieces of a Blackfoot tale that warned of such punishment for those who wished for more than they had. And she had certainly been longing lately, but for what she did not know.

No, that's silly, Maggie. He's just a man, another one

come to work for Papa. He'll be gone in a few weeks, like most of the rest.

His name was Colin, she'd heard. She said the name again, letting the syllables roll off her tongue. It sounded exotic and rich.

He slipped off the horse's back and began to walk away, followed by the pack of men, their rifles lowered, clasped in their hands. Although his clothes were ragged and stained and torn, he wore them with a pride unrivaled among her father's other followers. Dim recollection stirred, and she saw in her mind the cavalry officers that strode the streets of Benton, handsome in their blue uniforms. Shaking her head, she dispelled the ridiculous notion and resumed her peeking.

The last of the men followed him into the still building and closed the door behind them. Maggie dropped the curtain and turned away from the window. As she began to gather the breakfast dishes together, Colin Fraser stayed in her mind. Of all the men who'd ever crossed her path, why did he haunt her thoughts?

Many a man had tried to corner her in the still house, and many more had attempted touches in the dark, but she'd dealt with them swiftly and convincingly, just as her father'd taught her. And they'd not tried a second time. But something told her there was more to business between a man and a woman than fumbled clutches and lustful groping. No, there was more. Something that would bind two people together through adversity and joy—as it had her parents.

Maggie lifted a pan of dishes and stepped out onto the porch; a washtub filled with hot water awaited. Bubbles rose into the morning air and popped with a tiny spray as the dishes settled to the bottom of the tub. She poked a finger at a large one that rose, quivering in rainbow shades. She smiled as the shower of soapy water hit her face. Yes, Colin Fraser would be the kind of man that would stay.

Colin watched a rat crawl along the beam over his head. The rodent paused for a moment, looked down, then scurried to the other end and disappeared into a hole in the wall. Colin had been here a month and already had enough information to put George Hayes out of business for good. But he delayed returning to Fort McLeod. And although he told himself many reasons, he knew the real reason was Maggie.

Once he returned, McLeod would quickly organize a group of men who would swoop in, take everyone into custody, and destroy as much of the product and equipment as possible. And where would that leave Maggie? In jail? On her own? Adrift in a country where women were rarely wives and more often little better than slaves?

Colin turned over. Orange embers winked at him from the fireplace. Various versions of the same snore echoed around the room. He shared this cabin with eight other men, all in the end stages of cleanliness.

The warm fire soon produced an odor guaranteed to make the strongest eyes water.

He was due to make a delivery today to the small Blackfoot village about ten miles north. Maybe he'd ask if Maggie could go along. The thought brightened his thoughts. Despite the fact that her face was constantly smudged with soot and her clothes were likely castoffs from the men in camp, something about her awakened thoughts within him he'd considered long since dead.

There was no reasoning with this place within him that first fluttered, then burned, whenever she came around, with her clear blue eyes and sharp mind. There was no reminding this place that he still mourned Elena, that he had given up all that he was to keep the memory of his pain alive. No, this mysterious place within him refused to mourn or cling to old sorrow. Instead, it throbbed and glowed within him, awakening first his body and then his mind to Maggie Hayes.

Even the thought of her set his blood to rushing, and he closed his eyes against the realization that this was the same desire, the same consuming need, he'd once felt for Elena.

No. He could not—would not—feel that way for another woman. But his body ignored him and grew warm and ready.

Colin sat up and placed his feet on the cold, rough board floor. He'd make this one last delivery for George, then he'd make his excuses and leave . . . before he did something foolish.

* * *

"I want you to go with Colin today."

Maggie looked up from the dishpan and wondered if she'd heard her father correctly.

"What, Pa?"

"I want you to go with Colin. He's going to the Blackfoot village, and he don't speak no Blackfoot."

Maggie shook the suds off her hands, dried them on a towel, then drew her coat tighter around her. A cold November wind whined around the corner of the house, skittering long-dead leaves across the uneven boards of the porch.

Her first instinct was to jump at the chance. Ever since the move to the Bow River, her life had been far less interesting than when she drove most of the wagons of liquor over the border. She longed for adventure, for the thrill of escaping by the nape of her neck. But her father's eyes wore an odd expression.

"Is somethin' the matter?" She stepped toward him, and he shook his head.

He turned away and again stared down at the piece of copper tubing in his hand. "I promised yer Ma I'd take you down to Benton and raise you there."

The unexpected comment caught Maggie by surprise, and the regret in his voice rippled across her. "You done fine, Pa." She watched sorrow play across his face and wondered what had brought about this conversation. Pa wasn't one to talk about personal things.

"She didn't want you raised in no bootlegger's

camp. She made me promise. She wanted you raised in town with decent folk, but there just weren't no other way by then." His eyes were so filled with pain and remorse that Maggie slid her arms around his waist and laid her head on his chest. His hands full, he awkwardly hugged her with only his elbows and gently laid a cheek against her hair.

"She wanted you to marry a good man, one who'd love you and take care of you. She knowed you wouldn't find that here."

Maggie drew back and stared into his face again. "I ain't set on marryin' nobody, Pa. I've cleaned up after folks all my life. I ain't anxious to do that fer the rest of it. I want to see things and do things."

He stared down at her, that curious expression still on his face. "I only want you happy, girlie."

"I am happy, Pa, here with you."

George stared down at the top of the floppy hat that she wore like a suit of armor. She didn't know it yet, but his little girl was in love. Her heart was in her eyes every time she looked at young Fraser, and he gazed back at her the same way. And if Fraser was more than he seemed, as George suspected, then maybe one day he'd take her away and fulfill her mother's wish.

"You go on with young Fraser," he said, stepping out of her embrace. "Make us a good deal. Don't let them Injuns put one over on you, now."

"I won't, Pa." Maggie stepped back, and her father, obviously embarrassed, hurried off toward the still house to finish the repairs he'd started earlier that morning.

Maggie looked out across the yard, where snow had begun to fall as tiny, stinging bits of ice, and wondered at her father's odd words. A hastily erected lean-to squatted at an odd angle and provided shelter for the two teams of horses that pulled the delivery wagons. Colin was leading a matched set of bays outside, a set of reins in each hand.

Maggie stepped down off the porch and slogged across the muddy, churned yard, pausing beside the outhouse to watch him. He tied the horses to a hitching post and walked between them, smoothing their necks and talking to them in words lost in the patter of the snow. Maggie watched his hands and wondered how it would feel to be caressed so, to have someone's hands glide over her skin, warm and comforting.

As he bent over, picked up the tangle of harness, and gently laid it across the bay gelding's broad back, Maggie moved closer.

"Bo don't like the belly band so far back," she said, stepping into his line of vision.

He raised his head, surprised. "Really? Thank you." He stepped to the side of the bay gelding and moved the cinch forward before tightening it. "Does Bo have any other preferences?"

He was making fun of her. Maggie bristled, more angry at the flush of embarrassment heating her cheeks than at his words. Her thoughts had been wanton, shameful . . . and thrilling. "No, he just don't like the band rubbing against his—"

"I get the idea," Colin interrupted, glancing at her with a crooked smile. He'd lived among them for weeks now, and Maggie could count on one hand the number of words they'd exchanged. Truth be known, Colin Fraser frightened her. A simple glance from him made her stomach do flip-flops and her insides do things not nearly as playful. The sensation was frightening and addictive. She'd often made excuses just to walk past him and have him nod in that polite way of his and wish her a good day.

"Pa says I'm to go with you."

Colin paused in the task of threading two leather straps through their buckles. "Don't you think that's dangerous?"

Maggie's temper flared again at the implied incapability. "I was running liquor over the border when I was barely big enough to hold the reins."

"Where was your mother?" His voice softened, plunging into that velvety range that reminded her of new corduroy and how rubbing her hand across the grain of it sent chills up her spine.

Months had passed since either she or her father had mentioned her mother. And now her name had come up twice in a day—from two different men. Had Colin and her father had some conversation she didn't know about? "She died when I was little."

Compassion filled his eyes, and he took one step toward her. "I'm so sorry."

"It's all right. Happened a long time ago." Maggie crossed her arms over her chest, suddenly very uncomfortable with his nearness.

"That must have been hard for you . . . and your father." He had moved still closer and touched her shoulder with one hand. Despite the layers of fabric between them, she could feel the heat of his touch as intimately as if they touched skin to skin.

"Pa raised me by himself." Intimate thoughts lined up in her brain like little tin soldiers. Things she'd never told anyone jockeyed for position to be the first out of her mouth. What on earth was wrong with her? She clamped her teeth shut so hard on the next thought that the sound was audible.

Colin glanced at her curiously, then turned his attention back to the horses.

"You'll need to bring some blankets," he said, abruptly changing the subject. "We're in for snow this afternoon." He glanced up at a threatening sky teasing them now with an occasional snowflake.

Maggie turned away, grateful for the chance to leave his company and regain her sanity. And as she trudged back to the cabin, she vowed to keep her mouth shut the whole way there and back.

"Three." Maggie held up three fingers and shivered.

Painted Ax squinted his good eye and seemed unconcerned that snow coated his hair. "Two."

Maggie shook her head, then drew the bearskin closer around her shoulders and held it tight with one hand. "Three."

The old Blackfoot relaxed his lined face and smiled,

obviously enjoying the bargaining. He and Maggie had haggled over the last box of whiskey for the better part of an hour. He'd offered two wolverine pelts, and Maggie had refused and countered with three. He'd refused, offered two again, and Maggie had still refused. And on and on they'd continued.

Colin looked from Maggie to Painted Ax. Each glared at the other, neither willing to give, both considering the final agreement a matter of honor. Colin looked down at his feet and wondered if they would ever be warm again. "Maggie, take his offer and let's go," he said when the chattering of Maggie's teeth grew louder than the patter of snow.

"No," she said, never taking her eyes off the old man.

"It's only one box of whiskey."

"No."

"Maybe he doesn't understand—"

"He understands perfectly, don't you, Painted Ax?" The old man quirked the corner of his mouth.

"He understands English just fine when it suits him," she said, continuing to stare. "I speak in Blackfoot to honor him, but he's being just plain mule stubborn now."

A quick breeze shook the bare aspens that filled the grove surrounding them, and a shower of fine snow sifted down. Painted Ax shifted his weight and glanced toward his tepee, where smoke curled out of the smoke hole and a new case of whiskey waited.

"Two pelts and that." Maggie pointed at his wrap,

an elegant white deer hide adorned with tiny blue trade beads.

Painted Ax's chiseled face melted for the first time, and he stared at her with open amazement. Apparently, Maggie had just upped the offer. He stared at her a moment longer, then lowered the wrap from his shoulders. He stepped forward, draped the hide over Maggie's shoulders, and pulled it snugly across her arms, pausing to smile at her.

"Maggie woman is good trader."

Then he stepped back, picked up the wooden crate of bottles, and trudged toward home, the snow melting as it fell on his bare back.

Maggie watched him go, amazement on her face. "I didn't think he'd take me up on the offer," she murmured. "Everybody knows this is one of his most valued possessions."

"Well, apparently his frozen feet won out over his pride. Now get in the wagon and let's go before it gets dark."

Maggie threw him a glare but shuffled toward the wagon without further comment. The sun was a dim orange disk through the gray clouds, and night would be upon them before they could make it home, a prospect Colin did not relish . . . for more than one reason.

The snowfall increased until the backs of the horses were white and the prairie was bathed in blue reflected light.

"We'll have to stop and go back in the morning."

Colin drew the wagon to a stop and pulled the team around to head back toward the village.

"Wait. No." Maggie grabbed his sleeve and pulled. "We can't go back. They'll all be drunk."

Colin stared at her, realizing for the first time the incongruity of how she and her father earned their living. He'd heard the evils of the illegal whiskey trade extolled across Canada for more than six months while a saddle rubbed his backside raw, but he had yet to witness the evidence firsthand. But apparently Maggie knew well what happened when the Blackfeet drank the liquor.

The question of how she could participate in the manufacture of something that produced such a terrifying response in those that consumed it begged to be asked, but one look at her face changed his mind.

"All right, we'll go on." He turned back to look across the horses' snow-encrusted backsides. If the snowfall stayed light, they could make their way home in a few hours. But if the storm intensified, they would be in real trouble. Either way, Colin thought, noticing the way a strand of Maggie's hair had captured a large, perfect snowflake, *he* was in real trouble.

Chapter Four

The snowfall quickly robbed the plains of their soft browns and golds, replacing them with hard white that dulled to a faint blue as the sun set and night descended. Large, heavy flakes fell in clumps, lingering only a second before they melted on the horses' rumps and the sharp crunch of the wagon wheels became a soft *swoosh*.

By the side of the trail, the voice of the Bow River gurgled to keep them company, its path Colin's only landmark beneath a starless sky. Colin questioned their decision to travel home tonight.

Maggie hadn't said a word since they left the Blackfoot village, seemingly absorbed in watching the road in front of them. Colin longed to ask her questions, to entice her into conversation, to hear the slight drawl of her words and watch the quirk of her lips as she never quite smiled.

But she sat there, bundled up to her chin in her ill-gotten beaded wrap, teasing his imagination into naughtiness. What would it be like to peel away the layers of clothes she now drew around herself? To touch her soft skin and revel in the warmth of her body. To feel her respond to his touch, the ultimate acknowledgment of one's being. He pulled his gaze away from her and wondered if he desired Maggie or simply longed for the touch of a woman's hand.

"How long you think it'll take us to get home?" she asked abruptly, her words muffled by the furs in which she buried her face.

"We should be back before dawn." *Wishful thinking,* he mused, *and only if the snow doesn't intensify.*

"It's purty, ain't it?" She raised her face and nodded toward the sparse stand of trees surrounding them. Branches hung heavy and frosted with snow, and a foggy haze hugged the ground.

"Pretty and dangerous."

"You don't take much pleasure in anythin', do you?"

Her words jarred him, for he'd been thinking the same thing about her. "Of course I do. Why do you say that?"

"You don't never smile," she said with a shrug.

"Of course I do."

"Nope," she shook her head. "I ain't never seen you smile once."

"Well, here, I'll remedy that." He grinned widely.

"I seen dogs do that. Folks' smiles creep all the way up to their eyes and then down to their toes so's you can feel it all over your body." The corners of her mouth turned up. "I like those kind of smiles."

He'd never thought of it that way before, but he'd have to concede she was right. How long had it been since he'd smiled? More accurate, how long since he'd felt a smile down to his toes? "I was just thinking the same thing about you."

She looked as surprised as he'd felt, and he was immediately sorry for his words. "Ifen you smile too much, you look like you're up to somethin'. That's what Pa always says."

"Is Pa always right?"

She shot him a quick look of disapproval before glancing away. "Most of the time."

Fearing he was trodding on sensitive ground, Colin turned his attention back to the rapidly disappearing road. Was it possible Maggie was not as loyal to the whiskey business as it appeared? Did she disapprove of her father's practices?

And could he use her disapproval to aid in wiping out the Bow River Traders?

He was instantly appalled at the cunning ruthlessness of his thoughts. He had apparently been trained well by the Mounted Police. The success of the mission above all else.

Ribbons of pastel streaked the sky as the sun struggled to peep above the last of the clouds. The snow had stopped hours ago. Along the river's edge, trees groaned under the added weight, and here and there snow toppled from a branch with a soft plop.

Maggie slept with her head on his shoulder. Soft, warm breaths teased his neck, tempting him to wake her with a kiss. But he resisted and was glad that night had finally released its seductive hold. With the light of day, his thoughts might not turn so often to that which was forbidden.

The traders' camp came into sight suddenly, hidden as it was within a thick copse of trees. And with their return, Colin was sorry he no longer had Maggie to himself. He drove the wagon straight into the lean-to and halted the exhausted team. The camp was still asleep. Only faint smoke curls from the chimney of a cabin or two gave evidence that it was occupied.

Colin paused before climbing down, relishing the last few seconds of Maggie's head on his shoulder, her body close to his, her fate completely in his hands. Gently, he shook her, and she roused with sleepy eyes.

"We're home."

She looked at him and blinked slowly, still lost between sleep and wakefulness. And in that moment, Colin knew he'd never again have the courage. Slowly, he lowered his face to hers and touched her lips. She smelled of smoke and the outdoors and herself.

He'd only expected to get away with a peck, a small something to assure himself he was still alive, still a man. But, to his surprise, she responded.

Eagerly.

An edge of guilt pricked Colin as he wondered if she realized what she was doing or if she was responding to some unfinished dream. But the cut of guilt was not enough to make him break away.

She kissed him with honest desire, unfettered by contrived mores or accepted traditions. Her breathing increased, and a small sound of pleasure bubbled up from within her. The realization was shatteringly arousing, and a rush of desire swept through Colin such as he'd never before experienced.

He gathered her to him and pushed aside the double layer of furs that brushed her chin, exposing the delicate white skin of her neck. His lips played along the hollow of her shoulder, his teeth nipping at her collarbone, marveling that she allowed him this intimacy. A few inches lower was the round of her breast. He stopped, leaned his forehead against her shoulder, and sighed.

Her fingers slipped inside the blanket that covered his back, seeking that same small hollow on his own shoulder, her lips seeking the same satisfaction as his. As her skin slid across his, gooseflesh rose on his arms, and he leaned toward her, willing her never to stop touching him, demanding time to stand still until he'd been touched all he could endure.

Her fingers slid around his shoulder and buried themselves in his hair, stroking his scalp with butterfly touches, raising the hair on his neck with pinpoints of pain. How exquisite was her torture. He pulled back and looked into her face. She stared back wide-eyed, a hint of fire in her eyes as the woman within her awoke and stretched.

Was she a consummate seductress? Did she know what she was doing, or were her actions innocent? These considerations passed briefly through Colin's thoughts as he fought to regain control. Then she leaned forward and pressed her mouth to his. No polite pecks for her. She closed her eyes and drew him closer, moving her mouth beneath his, begging him to come closer with a silent language between them.

Colin's heart began to thud in double time. Heat poured into his veins, and he longed to throw off the buffalo hide that draped his shoulders. She moaned softly against his mouth, put her arms around his neck, and with one hand pulled his mouth hard against hers.

Never had he been so quickly seduced, so aroused as to reach the point of no return with a woman.

When she broke the embrace, he leaned his face against her shoulder.

"Maggie . . ." He breathed against her neck.

She raised her head to look directly into his eyes, her breaths coming quick and shallow.

"You're cold." Colin touched her cheek.

"My insides feel funny. Do yours?" The innocence in her question brought him out of the fog of desire consuming him. She was practically a child and very likely a virgin. She wouldn't understand that her honest, fervent kisses would drive a man over the edge, give him approval she did not intend. And he had been only too eager to accept it.

He climbed down off the wagon, then held up his arms for her. Frowning in confusion, she leaned down and allowed him to help her to the straw-strewn floor of the lean-to.

"Did I do something wrong?" she asked as he stepped away from her and began to unharness the team.

"No, you didn't do anything wrong." He turned his back to her, shame rapidly overtaking him.

She stood behind him, waiting for his next words, some explanation for his abrupt dismissal of her. But he had none. He'd contemplated an action of which he'd never considered himself capable—callous, unemotional seduction. How could he have slipped so low? Was his withdrawal from even the possibility of loving again so apt to create such a monster?

Or could he be falling in love with Maggie Hayes?

No, he berated himself. He was incapable of love. He'd buried his heart in cold, damp Scottish ground.

"You should get inside," he said without turning.

He heard her sniffle, then turn and start for the door. She was crying, and he'd left her without explanation or apology. Would she judge all men from this point forward by his sorry example? But not even these thoughts that speared his heart could bring him to call her back. If he opened his heart to seek an apology, she might slip inside.

* * *

The melting snow was haunting the grove in the form of a low, creeping mist that snaked and coiled itself around the trees. Stars winked overhead in a clear night sky, but not even their beauty appealed to Maggie. The camp was long since asleep, but slumber was no longer her refuge.

Kissing him had changed her forever.

Wrapping her arms around herself, she wandered listlessly through the grove of trees and wondered at how his lips could have set her insides on fire and made her want him to touch her in ways that were forbidden. What magic thing had happened to make her forget her father's dire warnings about men and love? Perhaps Colin had bewitched her, worked some evil magic that bent her to his will. No, she told herself, she'd gladly kissed him back and felt a thrill of satisfaction when he whispered her name.

She wandered down to the river's edge, hoping its happy chuckle would lift her spirits. In a few weeks its babbling laughter would be silenced by winter's hard grasp.

Through the increasing mist, Maggie saw a figure moving toward the riverbank. Her curiosity piqued, she followed and hid in the brush by the side of a well-used trail. As the figure neared, she recognized Colin.

He moved down the trail to where a horse was tied to a bending willow tree. He untied the horse, swung into the saddle, and rode into the water. A faint splashing told his location long after the mist had swallowed him.

And then he was gone.

A steel hand closed around Maggie's heart, extinguishing the warmth his touch had ignited. She closed her eyes and summoned the memory of his kiss, his touch. And then she tucked them away deep within her where her disappointment could not reach. She turned and trudged up the trail toward camp. Morning would come soon, and there would be hungry men to feed.

Colin fastened the neck of his scarlet uniform jacket and then ran a finger around the inside of the collar. Funny, he couldn't remember it being so tight. But then, many things had changed in the month he'd been gone. The stables, which had been merely skeletons of upright, twelve-foot cottonwoods when he'd left, were now chinked with mud and topped with sod roofs. The hospital was finished, the construction of the men's quarters well under way.

He stepped back from the cracked oval mirror dangling on the center post of the canvas tent and surveyed the shine on his knee-length, fitted boots. Inspection was in ten minutes on the parade ground, and McLeod would want to see him immediately afterward.

He would ask him what he had learned from the whiskey traders—their weaknesses, their frailties. How best could a mounted force flank them, take them into custody, destroy all they had, and strike the first victory for the Northwest Mounted Police?

He'd gotten personally involved, broken the first rule in espionage. And now his heart would pay the price.

Colin picked up his white helmet off his narrow cot and seated it carefully on his head. Then, with a final tug to his white gloves, he turned and walked out the door.

James McLeod strolled down the rows of scarlet coats, hands clasped behind his back. Nodding and speaking softly to an occasional constable, he stopped when he came to Colin.

"Constable Fraser. Glad to see you back in one piece." His words held a slight scolding note. Colin had not checked in with his commander upon his arrival. Somehow, immediately divulging George Hayes's weaknesses seemed like a betrayal, a dangerous attitude. He'd decided to sleep on it first, if only for an hour or two.

"Yes, sir."

McLeod squinted. "When did you arrive?"

Colin swallowed. "At first light this morning, sir."

McLeod stared at him a moment, as if pondering his choice of times of arrival. "I'd like a few moments of your time later."

"Yes, sir."

With a final assessing look, McLeod moved away, and Colin released his held breath.

"What was it like, sleepin' in the den of thieves?" Braden Flynn whispered at his side.

Exquisite. Arousing. Unforgettable. "Dirty and cold."

"And are ye leavin' somethin' out of yer account?"

Colin slanted a glance at Braden, whose eyes twinkled with mischief. "What do you mean?"

"I heard ye thrashing in yer cot early this mornin'."

"I was tired."

"Dismissed!" McLeod's voice carried across the troops, and the men moved away in scattered groups.

"Ye talked in yer sleep, lad." Braden fell in step beside Colin. "Ye called her name. 'Maggie,' ye said."

Colin's heart began to pound, but he shrugged casually. "She was a woman I knew . . . before."

"She must have been a wondrous girl." Braden shook his head and moved off toward the stables without further comment. Colin didn't dare ask what else he'd said.

McLeod was standing at the window, staring out across the parade ground, when Colin rapped once and pushed open the office door.

"Come in, please," he said without turning around.

Colin entered, removed his helmet, and sat down on a chair across from the desk.

"Dreadful, cumbersome things, aren't they?" McLeod pointed to the helmet resting on Colin's knee.

"Yes, sir, they are."

"Perhaps one day we will replace them with something a little more suited to our surroundings."

"That would be an improvement, sir."

McLeod sat down at his desk and looped his fingers together. "Tell me what you've learned."

Without emotion, Colin related all the military facts about the Bow River Traders—their location, their weaknesses, their strengths. And with every word,

Colin wondered if he was neatly sewing up Maggie's destiny.

McLeod listened patiently, scratched an occasional note on a piece of paper, and drummed his fingers. When Colin had finished, an odd sense of guilt settled on his shoulders, and he knew it would perch there for a long time.

"I plan to send a patrol there as soon as possible, before the river freezes over. Travel will be limited, and their guard will be down. Now is the time to strike." McLeod offered Colin his hand. "You've done a fine job, Constable."

"Thank you, sir." Colin stood to leave, a thousand questions he dared not ask drumming in his head. What would happen to the men captured? What would happen to Maggie?

"I have another matter I'd like to discuss with you, Constable."

Colin eased back into his chair, dread creeping over him. McLeod slid a letter from beneath some papers on his desk. Colin immediately recognized his mother's delicately looped script.

"One of Baker's wagons was kind enough to also bring our mail packet up from Benton. Your mother sends her regards. It seems she found out you were a member of the Northwest Mounted Police when she read your name in the Ottawa paper."

Although McLeod's face held no reproach, Colin still felt like a child forced to stand in the corner.

"This matter is between you and your parents, Constable. However, her letter did impart an important piece of information."

"And that is?" Colin already knew the answer.

"Your mother wonders if you are a good doctor."

Colin swallowed. Lurking in the back of his mind had always been the fear that one day he would have to face his lie by omission.

"She says that you graduated from the University of Edinburgh last year." McLeod smiled slightly, barely moving the ends of his carefully trimmed mustache. "She sounds as if she's very proud of you."

"Yes, sir, she is."

"And for some reason you chose not to disclose that on your application."

"I chose not to practice, sir."

McLeod stared over the edge of the letter, his quick mind judging. "I suspected you were hiding something. You are under no obligation to use your medical knowledge in the service of the Mounted Police, of course, but I would appreciate it if you would reconsider that decision."

"You'd like me to reconsider?" The request was so sudden, so unexpected, Colin searched for a response that did not make him sound like a parrot. "My reasons were personal."

"I guessed as much. However, as you know, Dr. Richard Nevitt, our assistant surgeon, remained behind at Dufferin. As the winter closes in on us, I would like for you to assist Dr. Kittson whenever he sees fit."

How crooked a path fate takes to have its way, Colin

thought as he felt his life snatched from his hands. He had taken an oath, one sworn in reverence and compassion, long before he swore a second oath out of bitterness and grief. And now he was being forced to live up to the ideals of Hippocrates. How could he say no and leave the burden of winter ailments to Dr. Kittson, now that he had been found out? And yet the thought of again holding another's life in his hands, of playing God with someone's soul, was repulsive and not the nurturing impulse it should be.

"I'd be glad to fill in for Dr. Nevitt, sir," he heard himself say, his heart deciding before his mind had time to argue.

"Good." McLeod carefully folded the letter and slid it back into a delicately flowered envelope.

"May I read my mother's letter?" Colin held out his hand.

"No."

Colin stared, wondering if he'd heard right.

McLeod opened a drawer and slipped the letter inside. "She was very specific that her letter was to remain private between herself and me. However," his hand reemerged, clutching an identical envelope, which he passed over the desktop to Colin. "She wanted you to have this."

One look at the delicate writing and the reality of the lie to his parents crawled out of its dark hiding place and filled his thoughts.

Surely they'd worried about him, wondered where he was and how he was. Mother always was a worrier, and for an instant an image of her filled his mind.

She was standing by the gate, her hands entangled in an apron sprinkled with blue flowers, waiting for him as he rounded the corner on their street. He'd tarried to play marbles in Tom Gaelen's yard, and twilight was turning to night. As he'd approached her, dreading explaining his tardiness to his father, he'd seen her, her face lined with worry and the last rays of sunset highlighting her hair. She'd spotted him then, and the worry eased smoothly into a smile filled with pure love. As fleeting as it was, that image of his mother had become how he saw her whenever he thought of her. Had her face been lined with worry when he'd dropped from sight? Had she waited by that same gate, hoping to see him swing around the corner?

Tears filled his throat and threatened to choke off his voice. "Thank you, sir," he managed to say.

He rose, put on his helmet, and left the office without another word or an official dismissal. He strode toward the stables, where he knew he'd find understanding ears and privacy to search his soul for wisdom.

Chapter Five

Thunder crashed overhead, rattling the stoppered glass bottles that lined the shelves in the adjoining examination room. Colin turned over on his narrow bed and squinted against lightning that splintered the dark and momentarily illuminated his bedroom. Thunderstorms in November were a rarity, and the presence of the monster that now raged over their heads foretold trouble. Colin felt it, saw it in every blue flash of anger the storm unleashed.

He pulled the coarse, Force-issued blanket up to his chin and glanced between his feet to the stove where fire flirted from behind holes punched in the door. Another bolt of heaven's anger split the sky with a ripping sound, and Colin wondered about Maggie. Was she on some long, dark trail peddling her father's illegal brew, hunched against the rain?

Or was she curled up beneath quilts, her skin warm and soft.

Either possibility was disturbing.

Colin rolled to his feet, walked over to the stove, and threw in another piece of wood. Then, since sleep had abandoned him, he put the kettle on the top of the stove and sat down on the foot of his bed to wait for the tea water to warm.

Beyond, in the outer room, he now practiced medicine. Dr. Kittson, well ensconced in the newly finished hospital, occupied the only space designed for sleeping there, so halfway between the hospital and the stables, a hastily erected cabin had been built with the understanding that Colin's skills might be needed in either place if John Poett, veterinary surgeon, also found himself needing an assistant.

Colin's first case had been a broken leg. Traders from the Montana Territory brought their trade goods and families to Fort McLeod. A child had fallen from his father's supply wagon and had been brought here. As if months of nonuse and sorrow had not passed, Colin's fingers had begun their spider-walk examination of the boy's leg, relaying information to his brain about the broken tibia that was snapped cleanly in two. A cast, a few weeks, and the lad would soon forget he'd ever had a broken leg. And with that victory, Colin had known he was lost to his own destiny.

The kettle began to sing, and its lid rattled, demanding immediate attention. Colin poured steamy water into his cup, then shook in some tea from a tin. He stirred the darkening water, staring down at the tea leaves that swirled within a tiny whirlpool and wondered again about Maggie.

Her presence had been unsettling, but her absence was more so. He'd tried to shake off his growing awareness of her since his return to Fort McLeod, but more and more often, his thoughts turned to her. She was bits and pieces of memories in his head. A glance. A touch. A laugh. She'd crawled inside him and refused to leave, coiling dangerously close to his heart.

Colin took a sip of the hot, bitter tea and walked to the window that looked out onto a sodden parade ground. Raindrops pounded dimples onto the shiny surfaces of huge puddles that winked and flirted with the stormy sky.

Dark figures rode through the uprights of the front gate, then split into two groups, one riding to the right and the other straight toward Colin.

He set down his cup and pulled on his uniform pants, snapping the suspenders onto his shoulders. The door flew open with only a hint of a knock.

"Need your help, Colin," Braden's voice said from beneath a soggy felt hat. He held one end of a squirming, thrashing bundle, and Steven Gravel held the other. Arms emerged from the blanket shroud, flailing and swinging wildly.

"We raided the Pine Coulee operation tonight. Took the whole bunch into custody except the old man. Poured out gallons of whiskey, broke up the still. But somehow George himself got away."

Why had he not been included on the raid? Did McLeod not trust him, since he'd lived as one of them? Or did he hesitate to endanger one of his physicians? Colin nodded, tucking away the questions until later.

"Get him up on the table," he said, stepping forward to help.

"I'm thinkin' ye'd best let us wrestle the lad to the table while we've got a hold on 'im," Braden said as wrapped his arms around the bundle and hoisted it off its feet. " 'E put up a splendid fight. On three, Steven, lad. One. Two. Three." They swung the blanket to the table, and the body inside landed with a plop, lurched up to a sitting position, then fell back, still.

"Why didn't you take him to Kittson?" Colin asked, pulling aside the layers of wet, clinging blankets.

"Kittson's delivering twins."

Colin glanced at the dripping men. "Twins?"

"For one of Baker's men."

Shaking his head, Colin pulled aside the last layer of muddy blanket and stared into Maggie's pale face.

"Where did you find her?" Bolts of lightning to rival those stabbing the night rioted through Colin's chest. He laid the back of his hand across her forehead, and it warmed his skin with a dangerous heat.

"Her?" Braden and Steven exchanged looks.

"This is Maggie, Hayes's daughter." She lay so still, her chest barely moving, her skin a chalky white.

"She was fightin' alongside the men. Better than

most, I'm thinkin'. Ask Steven there. She belted him with a frying pan across the midsection.''

Steven absently rubbed a hand across his stomach. ''We couldn't tell who was who when the scuffling started.''

Colin pulled the blanket back further. She was soaked to the skin and muddy, yet beneath the dirt, something was different, odd. Colin stepped into the bedroom and picked up a lamp from his bedside table. He lit it with a sliver of wood from the stove, then moved back to her side and held the light over her.

A strand of muddy blond hair was plastered across her face. Gently, he moved it to the side with one finger, but she never flinched as his skin grazed hers. She was thin, her face gaunt and pale. Terror began as a kernel of doubt. He tested her forehead again, then slid his hand down to cup her cheek and touch the tender skin of her neck.

She was on fire.

''Hold this.'' He shoved the lamp at Steven, then grasped the front of her shirt and ripped it open. Beneath the creamy swell of her breasts an angry red rash fanned out across her ribs and continued down to disappear into her pants.

Typhoid.

The same vicious disease that had taken young Godfrey Parks only weeks before.

Colin took the lamp back from Steven, his thoughts whirling. If Maggie was infected, then so might be the others. There could be an epidemic at the fort that would surely spread to the traders' villages outside the gates. He and Dr. Kittson had only limited medical resources, dependent on I. G. Baker's unpredictable delivery of supplies.

"There's some hot water on the stove. Pour it into the bowl over there and wash your hands, both of you. Use the soap in the washstand. It's strong; I use it for surgery."

With the medical detachment he'd mastered after years of practice, he bent over her again. Her ribs poked up in ridges beneath her skin. "Lather up to your elbows; then get out of here."

"What is it?" Steven asked as he rinsed off his hands and shook them dry.

"Typhoid. She has typhoid."

The silence behind him was more telling than anything they could say. Typhoid struck suddenly and fatally, killing its victims slowly, eating them from within until they were mere ghosts of their former selves. He had seen many cases of it while in Scotland. It preferred the poor, stalking those who made their homes in hovels or in the streets. Colin had long suspected the disease was caused by tiny organisms that somehow found their way from victim to victim through touch or breath, but he had never been able to prove his suspicions.

"Is there anything we can do a'tall?" Braden asked.

Colin shook his head. "Go tell McLeod we have a case of typhoid. Have him quarantine the prisoners."

The door opened, and a fresh onslaught of rain swept in.

"Wait."

The two men turned, their felt hats and long coats stern silhouettes when lightning next flashed.

"Tell McLeod to keep the prisoners as clean as possible. Give them clean clothes. Have them bathe. Spread them out; don't put them all together. Give them chamber pots—and make them empty them often."

At their quizzical looks, Colin said, "I'm hoping I can prevent this from spreading."

Then the door closed, and he was left in the stormy dark with Maggie—or what was left of her.

By dawn, the rain had slowed to a thin drizzle that hung from the eaves in lazy icicles. The temperature had dropped, and puffs of wind blew down the fireplace, scattering ashes across the plank floor.

He'd bathed Maggie, dressed her in one of his nightshirts, and tucked her into his bed. With the darkening dawn sky, he'd lit another lamp and placed one on each side of the bed. And yet, despite his hopes, she lay listless, as she had through all his ministrations. Behind her eyelids, her eyes did not move, as in peaceful sleep, and her breaths were labored and uneven.

Colin ran a hand over his face and propped his elbows on the rough fabric of his pants. How long had she been sick? And how had she summoned the strength to fight?

He leaned forward, took the damp cloth off her forehead, then replaced it with one dipped in cold water. If he could keep her temperature down, perhaps she could fight off the disease. Many had survived bouts of typhoid but were left weak and never fully recovered.

Someone knocked on the door. Reluctantly, he left her side and opened the door. Commissioner McLeod stood on the porch, a large buffalo skin, thrown across his shoulders, whitened with snow. Colin looked beyond McLeod's shoulder. A light snowfall was dusting objects and trees and gradually covering the wet ground.

"Constable Flynn tells me he brought you a prisoner last night."

Funny, he hadn't thought of her as his prisoner until now. He resisted the urge to glance over his shoulder.

"Yes, he did."

"What's the matter with him?

For a moment, he entertained the idea of not telling McLeod who she was and by that omission allowing her an avenue of escape, but he quickly dismissed the idea.

"It's not a him, sir. It's Hayes's daughter."

"Daughter?" McLeod dropped his usual serene demeanor and looked shocked, if just for a moment.

"She was in the camp with her father."

Recovering quickly, McLeod took off his helmet and scratched his head. "How is she?"

Colin stepped outside into the biting cold and closed the door behind him, preserving the precious heat. "She has typhoid. I don't know how long she's been this way."

McLeod threw a glance out across the fort that bore his name, taking mental account of the souls under his care. "Are we looking at the possibility of an epidemic?"

Colin followed his stare, seeing the fine snow and the muted and softened shapes of everyday things, and thought of Maggie laughing in autumn sunshine. "It's a possibility."

McLeod sighed, and his shoulders moved up and down in exasperation, allowing the burden of command to show for just a moment. "I've done what you asked. The prisoners were ordered to bathe, and we gave them clean clothes. We're using the old traders' camp down near the river. They've been detained two to a room and have been given chamber pots." McLeod smiled. "Some of them have never seen one before. They were amazed, to put it mildly."

"Make sure all their waste is buried, away from the river."

McLeod swung his blue gaze away from the snow and looked Colin directly in the face. "Was she your informant?" He nodded toward the closed door.

"Yes."

McLeod studied his face. "Take care of her."

Colin nodded. "I will."

Then McLeod moved away, a dark figure against the white snow.

Colin returned to Maggie's side and found her the same as before. He went outside, scooped snow into a bowl, and used the cold water it produced to dab her forehead. Morning skimmed away beneath gray clouds, and afternoon moved toward night. When the fire burned low, Colin would resupply it, then return to Maggie's side. And so they'd passed the afternoon together.

Night came swiftly, accompanied by a howling wind that buffeted the corners of the house and rattled the windows. The fire cast shadows, tall, thin, dark demons that seemed to draw their energy from the mischievousness of the fire, dancing frantically whenever the wind puffed down the chimney. Colin watched the shadows move over Maggie's face as he sat in a rocking chair, nodding with exhaustion. With a mind numbed by lack of sleep, he wondered fuzzily which of the shadows was Death himself.

Maggie's skin was hot and dry, the fever showing no signs of breaking. He dozed off once and dreamed, seeing Maggie in the spring, twirling happily on the prairies while nodding wildflowers kept time to her humming. When he awoke, she stared straight at him, her eyes blue and feverish.

"I'm dreamin' you, ain't I?"

Colin moved his chair closer, unsure if he should call her out of her delirium. She would surely struggle if she awoke fully and realized she was his prisoner.

"Yes, you're dreaming me."

She smiled slowly, as if the stretching of her facial muscles were an effort. "I thought so," she said slowly. "I missed you."

"Missed me?"

"Yeah, since you left. I'm glad you're back." She lolled her head to the side, and he thought for a moment she'd drifted back off to sleep. "I liked kissin' you. Liked the way it made me feel inside. Kind of mushy and softlike. Pa says that's sinful and I'll sure burn in the fires of hell fer feelin' like that 'bout a man. But you know what?" She rolled her head back to stare at him. "I don't care. Ain't that awful?"

He leaned back in the chair and set it to swaying as she drifted off again. Warmth from the fireplace effused him, lulling both his body and his thoughts, and then it hit him. He'd fallen in love with Maggie Hayes. Against all good sense, his own vows of an empty heart, and every rule of law enforcement, he had fallen in love with a whiskey trader's daughter.

No, that couldn't be. He hadn't given his grief permission to leave or his broken heart to heal. And yet both had apparently happened without his notice. A burden lifted from his shoulders, and he breathed deeply. Elena had passed on to that realm into which no mortal could follow, taking with her a piece of his heart. They were no longer of the same world. And yet, mysteriously, his heart seemed to have replaced that severed piece and reserved it for Maggie—a feat unattainable by medical science, a skill reserved only for God.

Colin glanced over at her. Gaunt, dirty, reeking of sickness, still he longed to gather her to him, to cradle her in his lap and rock her as if she were a baby, long before whiskey trading had robbed her of her smile.

If God would but grant him one wish, he longed to have the chance to return that smile.

* * *

The snowstorm plowed on for days, blurring day and night with dark, ominous clouds that dangled from the heavens. Maggie thrashed and clawed at the air, delirium from the fever and the disease taking a firm hold on her. Colin's world narrowed to the aura of light given off by the fireplace and Maggie's pale face.

The ravages of the disease were ugly, and bouts of diarrhea gnawed at her. Help came from an unlikely source. Tall, genteel Steven Gravel quietly offered his aid without request. Together he and Colin tried to keep enough fluid in Maggie to survive these spells, and they took turns watching over her at night while the other fell into an exhausted sleep on the hard examining table.

Outside, the business of the fort continued. The new quarters for the officers turned from gaunt skeletons into snug dwellings. Blackfeet became routine visitors, appearing at the front gate without warning, just for a look at the red-clad men who were rumored to have exacted a fair white man's justice—an event rare enough to warrant several days' ride just to witness.

McLeod checked on the prisoners and gave Colin daily updates through the closed door. So far no one else had fallen ill.

A week passed, and Maggie failed to improve. Her color worsened, and her cheeks sank further into her face. She drifted between confused consciousness and sleep and never seemed to realize where she was or who was with her.

Perforated bowels was one of many devices typhoid used to kill. Deep in the night, when he was alone with her except for Steven's gentle snoring, Colin often stood over her, willing himself to see through her flesh, to her insides, and determine if all their efforts would be to no avail and she would die in awful pain and agony.

After two weeks passed and she failed to improve, Colin examined her again. He stripped back her nightshirt, exposing her chest and stomach. The red rash had crawled its way up her chest, covering her breasts and down her sides, claiming her ribs. Gentleman that he was, Steven moved a discreet distance away. Caught up in his own worry, it wasn't until he noticed Steven's absence that Colin realized how unaware he was of anything else around him.

Colin gently probed her stomach, watching her face for some sign of discomfort—a wince, a groan, some sound to give him a clue. But she remained limp and unresponsive. He felt for bulges, lumps, anything to tell him she was still intact. She'd been unconscious for more than two days this time without opening her eyes once. Colin closed the nightshirt, pulled the blanket back over her, and sat down at her side. He picked up her hand, still calloused and rough, but thinner. So frail. So unlike her.

Again, he was helpless, at the mercy of God and Nature, for both hid their secrets well. He knew every bone in the body, every muscle, and yet he could do no more than hold her hand. A sorry attempt. The only effort he had been able to make for Elena. And now the only one he could make for Maggie.

Chapter Six

Maggie fought her way through the confusion that seemed to hold her like phantom arms. So many images swam in her head. Some she suspected were memories called forth for an encore by the sickness that had gripped her. Some were more recent, but whether reality or dream, she was unsure.

Gentle hands had cared for her, soft skin smoothing her brow, her arms, fingers raking back her hair. These touches she knew were real, and she'd learned to look forward to them, lost as she was in her world of whirling pictures.

She struggled to open an eye. Her lids were heavy, so heavy. The world was a pleasant blur, coming into focus only slightly as she blinked and focused on the light at the end of her bed.

A figure was silhouetted there against the golden

glow of the fire. A man, slim and tall, braced both hands on the mantel and hung his head to stare into the flames below. He was sad, beaten. That part of him reached out and touched her.

Broad shoulders were arched as if in pain, and a wide *X* cut across his back. Maggie blinked again. He wore dark pants that settled on slim hips, and a white undershirt provided the background for the *X* formed by dark suspenders.

He squatted, fed a log to the flames, and resumed staring into the fire. One slim hand combed through his hair, then rubbed the back of his head and around his neck. He leaned his head back, and the same hand slid across his chin, rasping the dark shadow of a beard.

She was in a room whose log walls were hung with bunches of dried herbs and sparkling glass bottles. The bedding on which she lay was clean and smelled of the outdoors, not grease and smoke.

Was she dead?

She opened the other eye and turned her head slightly, careful to make no sound, an instinctive caution warning her to take care.

A room beyond this one held a solitary, bare table, and more bottles sat on shelves against log walls. Her head ached, but she closed her eyes and spun back in time to the last thing she could remember as being real.

There were men, lots of them, in brilliant scarlet jackets. They rode into the camp with guns drawn. The camp had been asleep, and men emerged from their cabins in saggy underwear and without their weapons. The men in scarlet had dismounted and calmly herded the men into a circle. Maggie had watched it all from her window, fear paralyzing her and a persistent headache blurring her vision. These were the dreaded police from the east, the scarlet-uniformed men who had been sent to wipe out the whiskey trade. Then she saw her father being led outside by an arm. He wore only his suit of red underwear, and there was a look of terror on his face. So vulnerable. So frightened. Maggie couldn't bear it.

She had dragged on her ragged pants and shirt, then shoved up a back window and slipped outside. Edging around the corner of the cabin, she'd run straight into a broad chest. Arms like steel bands clamped her arms to her sides. She struggled and heard a soft chuckle that infuriated her. She stilled, hoping he would release his grip and her head would stop spinning so she could think. Then she saw the frying pan leaning against the side of the cabin where she'd left it after scouring it with sand yesterday. She doubled over in his arms, and he released her. She closed her hand around the iron handle and swung, catching him across the midsection. She heard him *oof* in pain as she raced away toward the lean-to where the horses were kept.

Twisting cramps gripped her stomach, and her steps faltered. She hadn't eaten in three days, every taste of food bringing on wrenching pain. She stumbled and dropped to her knees. If she could just make it to the barn . . . And then there was nothing.

Maggie peeped open her eyes. He had moved from the fire and stood in the open doorway. One hand was braced against the door frame, his hips swung to the side in a casual stance. Another man faced him. A man in a scarlet jacket. Full consciousness returned.

She was a prisoner.

Summoning all her strength, she bolted from the bed and made for the door, struggling to keep her wobbly legs under her. She ducked under his arm and barreled straight into the tall man's chest when he stepped neatly into her path. He caught her easily and hoisted her over his shoulder.

"I believe this belongs to you, Colin," the tall man said, carrying her back into the room.

He set her on her feet, and she summoned the last of her strength to charge past him. The tall man caught her slim wrists in one hand as the last of her strength dissipated. "Lady, I know all about you and frying pans. You won't get a second chance."

The man in the doorway turned her around and caught her under her arms and behind her knees, lifting her into his arms. She kicked and flailed, arching her body to spring out of his arms, but succeeded only in twisting against his chest. The hands that held her were gentle, not hard or restraining. He laid her gently on the bed and held her down with one hand in the middle of her chest, the other on her stomach. Devoid of strength, she resorted to words, cursing him with a string of oaths.

"Dear God, she's got a foul mouth," the tall man

said from the doorway. "Now that she's awake, I don't envy your job, Colin."

Maggie stared up into Colin's face, the same face, the same lips, that had deeply stirred her in a barn on a snowy dawn.

Traitor.

He looked down at her, grinning like an idiot. Well, if he thought he had the best of her, she'd show him. Docilely, she returned his gaze, waiting.

"Is anyone sick today, Steven?" Colin asked, turning his attention away from her for a moment.

Steven shook his head. "No one."

Colin grinned some more. "If anybody else was going to come down with typhoid, they would have by now. How's Braden's cold?"

"Sneezing and miserable but able to ride today."

Colin returned his gaze to her face. "Good."

Typhoid. The word made Maggie's blood run cold. Talk had come from traders in the Sweet Grass Hills that typhoid had wiped out an entire camp. A group of Blackfeet had found them when they came for their whiskey. Was that what had happened to her? And what about her father?

But she didn't dare ask. She'd wait, then slip away and find her father. The rest of the men must be here somewhere. Wherever here was.

His hands moved over her again, touching her forehead, smoothing back her hair. Familiar hands. Had he been the one to care for her these days she could not remember? His fingers slid down her arm and rested lightly on the inside of her wrist. He stared down at her arm, then raised his head and smiled.

"Colin?" The tall man motioned toward the door with a nod.

Colin tugged the blanket over her. "You stay put." Then he patted her leg, rose, and stepped outside.

Maggie could hear voices coming through the door, muted words that rose and fell in normal tones. She strained to hear but could make out none of the words. What kind of game was this man playing? To pass himself off as a whiskey trader, to live among her people, then disappear without a word of explanation? Pa simply shrugged it off, saying that men come and men go, but something about him had remained, buried beneath her skin like a briar.

She looked around the room. Hanging on a nail on the wall was a red jacket, neatly tailored, a gun belt draped over it. On a chair beneath the jacket was a gleaming white helmet.

She looked toward the closed door, fury clearing away the last of her fogginess. So he'd set a trap and neatly caught her. Well, she'd teach him the lesson of the spider who caught the wasp.

"This came in by rider." Steven handed Colin a folded piece of paper once the door was closed. "It's from her pa."

Colin opened the paper, a ragged, faded label from a can of beans. The note said in a shaky handwriting:

*My girl is all I got. I promised her Ma I'd do better
for her than I have, and it pains me to know I didn't
keep my end of the bargain. I know who you are, and
I'm askin' a favor of you, man to man. I'm a-hopin'
that you feel for her like she feels for you. Make her a
decent woman. Don't never tell her you heard from me
or she'll want to come and find me. I don't want her
to ever come back to the whiskey trade. It's all I know,
so there ain't no help for me. I ain't offering nothing
in return for this, 'cause I ain't got nothing to offer.
I'm just hoping that you're the man I think you are
and that you'll do what's best for Maggie.*

It was signed "George."

Colin looked up at Steven. "When did this come
in?"

"A rider brought it just before dawn. William Bagley
was on guard duty. The fellow handed it to him, said
it was for you, and rode off."

"Thank you for bringing it to me." Colin turned
to go back inside, but Steven caught his arm.

"I'm not one to give advice," he began, then
paused and dropped his hand. "And I don't meddle
in others' business." He stopped as if searching for
words. "But I'm a good listener," he finally finished.

Colin nodded, a thousand thoughts of fractured
loyalties sprinting through his head. How could he
love the daughter of the man the entire division was
trying to take into custody and still honor his oath
to the Force? Especially now that her father knew his
heart?

He glanced back at Steven, seeing understanding in his eyes. They were friends, but neither had spoken of personal things. Colin suspected that Steven, too, had brought pain with him to the Territories, but an unspoken code kept either from asking.

"Thank you"—Colin held up the note—"for this."

Steven stopped, one foot in the yard and the other on the bottom step. "Who knows? I might make a fool out of myself one day." The comment was delivered with a good-natured smile. Then Steven stepped down into the snow and strode away.

When Colin returned to Maggie, she had turned to her side, eyes wide open, watching him. He pulled up a three-legged stool and sat down at eye level by her side.

"You've been very sick," he began, "and you were brought here to Fort McLeod."

"You're a damned liar." She didn't flinch as she said the words, even though hate dripped off her tongue. So much for wondering if she recognized him.

Colin looked at the packed dirt floor and hoped words would come. He opted for the truth despite its harshness. "I'm a constable in the Northwest Mounted Police. We were sent to close down the whiskey trade here in the Territories. I came to your camp to gain information for that purpose." His words sounded distant and stiff, and his thoughts drifted again to the softness of her lips and the passion in her soul. How easily he'd become another man, a victim of his own scheme.

"When ye ain't lyin', ye come right to the point, don't ye? Where's my pa?"

"We don't know. We didn't capture him."

She smiled then, bitterly. "And you won't, neither. He'll come and get me. You'll see."

Colin felt the weight of the note in his pocket. "The rest of the prisoners are being held here at the fort."

"What about me?"

"I don't know yet."

Fear flitted through her eyes. "I don't want no special treatment. Whatever you got planned fer the boys, I can take, too."

"You and I have to come to an agreement."

She slitted her eyes. "What kind of agreement am I supposed to have with a liar like you?"

Colin flinched inwardly. Lying, it seemed, was becoming a way of life for him. "You're not completely well, and I'd like to keep you here until you are. But I can't watch you all the time, so I want your word you'll behave."

She studied him with blue eyes, now bright and alert, and even as her gaze cut through him with its coldness, he rejoiced that a dullness no longer robbed them of their color. "What'll you do ifen I don't?"

"Then I'll lock you in the jail with the rest of the men."

She blinked, the only sign his words had given her pause. And behind her eyes, he knew she considered and measured, part of her wanting to defy him and march off to the makeshift cells just to annoy him. But the logical part of her was winning, telling her that was not wise. "I reckon you got me over a barrel . . . for now."

Colin propped his elbows on his knees, threaded his fingers together, and leaned forward until her breath brushed his face. And for a moment, he was seized with the urge to kiss her. Jarred, he looked into her eyes, wondering if she'd seen that momentary weakness. "You'll keep your word?"

"I always keep my word."

The rest of her thought went unsaid, and Colin knew that he, indeed, had joined the ranks of fools.

"You sent for me, sir?" Colin stepped into Mc-Leod's office, which was crowded with men. Braden Flynn stood by McLeod's side, a handkerchief held up to a red nose. McLeod was intent on a paper on his desk, which he signed with a flourish, folded, and handed to Braden.

"Yes." McLeod put his quill back into the inkwell. "The prisoners have all paid their fines, and I'm releasing them."

Had he heard correctly? "Beg your pardon, sir?"

McLeod looked up. "I said I'm releasing them. They've all paid their fines."

"But, sir, aren't you afraid they'll go right back into the whiskey trade?"

McLeod sprinkled sand onto the paper, tilted it to roll the sand around, then dumped the remainder onto the packed dirt floor. "Word comes from the Blackfoot Confederacy that the whiskey trade is waning. Word has passed, partially thanks to your efforts, Constable, that the Mounted Police will no longer tolerate the manufacture and trading of whiskey. Demand has diminished, and therefore so has the supply."

He carefully laid the paper to the side. "How is your patient?"

"She's recovering very well." Colin felt the eyes of the entire room on his back. Or did he imagine it?

"Her name is Maggie Hayes?"

"Yes, sir, George Hayes's daughter."

"Constable Flynn has explained that she was captured along with the men but that her father escaped."

"I believe that is also what Constable Flynn told me, sir." Colin failed in keeping the edge of resentment out of his voice. Still, the fact that he'd been excluded from the raid, for reasons he'd been left to imagine, grated against him.

"Dismissed," McLeod said quietly to the men surrounding his desk. They filed out without further comment.

McLeod stared at him a moment, long enough to let Colin know he had not missed the insinuation. "Do you feel that Miss Hayes is capable of living on her own if she is released?"

Immediately, their intimate conversation in the lean-to came to mind, and visions of someone taking advantage of her innocence gave rise to anger.

"I think it would be better if she were returned to

her father, if possible, rather than set free to her own devices." He could well imagine Maggie's reaction to such a comment, if she'd heard it, which hinted she was incapable of looking after herself.

"And therein lies the problem."

"Sir?"

"Certain of the Blackfoot chiefs rejoiced at our arrival, having already decided that the white man's firewater was dangerous to their people, but they were at a loss as to how to separate their people from their addiction. Once we stepped in and struck this first blow, many traders have closed up shop and moved on. However, George Hayes is one who has voiced, loudly, that he has no intention of doing such and that he intends to reestablish his trade farther north as soon as possible. In short, finding George Hayes maybe somewhat of a problem. Approaching him unarmed would be suicide."

"What do you suggest, sir?" The words of Hayes's note ran again through Colin's head, the news casting a different light on the meaning. Was Hayes leaving Maggie in his care?

McLeod leaned back in his chair. "You became acquainted with Miss Hayes while you were in her father's camp?"

"I knew her, yes, sir."

McLeod picked up his quill and twirled it in his fingers, studying it. "You came to us, Constable Fraser, under tragic conditions."

The abrupt change of subject was sudden and

jarring, setting Colin's defenses on edge. "My fiancée had recently been killed, yes, sir."

"And that's why you decided not to practice medicine. Because you could not save her. Am I right?" He squinted up from the long feather, and Colin nodded, speechless.

For another long minute McLeod ran the fluffy edges of the feather between his fingers. "As men, we don't often speak what is in our hearts. It seems too"—he shrugged his wide shoulders—"intimate." Another long minute passed, and Colin shifted his weight from one foot to the other.

"If something were to befall my Mary—" He bit off his words and swallowed, then leaned forward and drew toward him a piece of notepaper. "She has loved me for many years, even though I am seldom with her." He fingered the paper gently. "This is our only link, this and my scribbling, which somehow she can understand." He smiled softly, then cleared his throat and leaned back in the chair. "I have found that the ways of the heart are as painful and mysterious for a man as they are for a woman, but we seldom admit it. You are not without friends here, Constable. You are a fine physician and a fine officer. Don't let a wounded heart cost you those things."

"No." Confused, Colin could not discern if McLeod was speaking of Elena or Maggie. How much did McLeod know of his relationship with Maggie? Was he so transparent that the entire fort knew of the loss of his heart?

His words cloaked and difficult, McLeod might

have been addressing either situation, and Colin felt the color creep up his neck. He must look a sotted fool to the assistant commissioner—first pining after a dead fiancée and now suffering from the bite of a rough, foul-mouthed brat, the daughter of a whiskey trader.

"Is that all, sir?"

"No." McLeod stood and moved around the desk to stand at Colin's side. "I haven't done a very good job of this," he muttered half to himself. "I would like for you, your duties permitting, to see if you can incorporate this young woman into our midst. She seems to have a certain . . . attachment for you. More businesses arrive each day to build stores at our gates. In time, Fort McLeod will become a small town, and there will be a place for a young woman like Miss Hayes. It would be good if she were prepared for such an opportunity."

"Me, sir? I'm sure there are ladies about that would surely know more about . . . things young women should know than myself, sir." Grasping for straws, he tried to think of one lady who would gladly accept such a responsibility.

"Most of the ladies present in the settlement outside our gates here would be shocked right down to their petticoats after one conversation with Miss Hayes. No, you are her only link to salvation."

Astounded, Colin stared at his commander. McLeod returned to his chair, took up his quill again, and pulled a stack of papers toward him. "Dismissed, Constable Fraser."

* * *

Having exacted a promise from Maggie that she would stay in bed, Colin prowled the traders' wagons and shops that constituted a small town perched right outside the gates of Fort McLeod. I. G. Baker and Co. had been contracted to provide the first supplies needed by the Mounted Police. Quick on their heels was T. C. Power and Bros., bringing wagons heavy with expensive items. Almost every man at Fort McLeod was already in debt, as pay had been slow in arriving from Ottawa.

Eyes turned toward him as he wandered the muddy alleys in his scarlet uniform and gleaming helmet, and he wondered how many eyebrows would shoot up when they learned he was looking for a bright blue calico dress.

Chuckling to himself at the commotion his purchase was sure to cause, he wove between the wagons, resisting hawked offers for pots and pans, bolts of cloth, and new harness. Then, far at the back, he saw a tiny, brightly painted wagon. The top was yellow and the body the same shade of scarlet as his jacket— a color scheme obviously intended to strike a chord of recognition in the men who wore scarlet jackets.

Ready-made dresses twisted in the chill wind on hooks fashioned into the overhanging top of the wagon. One caught his attention, a bright blue affair sprinkled with tiny red and white flowers, reminiscent of his dream of Maggie in the springtime. Delicate lace edged the sleeves and neckline.

It was perfect.

As he approached the cart, a little dark-haired man parted curtains and stepped out of the back of the cart. His skin was the color of well-oiled saddle leather, and he walked with a limp that spoke of more years than his face showed.

"How much for the dress?" Colin said, pointing to the desired garment.

The old man held up two fingers. "Fifty cents," he said in a thick accent Colin could not place.

Colin fished in his pocket and brought out the amount that equaled more than half a month's pay.

The old man accepted the money, took down the dress, wrapped it carefully in brown paper, and presented it to Colin with a smile and a slight bow.

"Thank you," Colin said, and the man nodded.

When he turned, a small crowd scattered. He was sure his purchase would be the talk of the fort before the sun set.

He stopped once more for a small amount of horehound candy, then strode toward the fort and remembered for the first time in months that Christmas was only a few weeks away.

Chapter Seven

Colin teetered on a chair, nails in his mouth, stringing a piece of rope across the doorway that separated his two rooms. Then he hung a blanket across it and stepped down. "What do you think?"

"It's a blanket on a rope. What do you expect me to think?"

She crossed her arms and frowned at him. Guilt tweaked her when he looked crestfallen for a moment.

"It'll have to do." He climbed down, his expression veiled, and neatly placed the chair under his desk.

He was a neat one, she'd have to give him that. Even the corners of the sheets on her bed were folded and tucked with lines straight and tight. But his kiss had convinced her that beneath that calm, neat exterior ran a river of passion, one that threatened to draw her down and hold her in its grasp.

With a conscious shake, she banished those thoughts to the depths of her mind. She couldn't let herself think like that, not if her plan was to succeed.

"Are you cold?" he asked from across the room. He'd shed his uniform jacket, revealing the top half of a suit of underwear crossed by suspenders. The neckline of the garment teased the ridge of his collarbone, drawing her gaze to that tiny hollow where her lips had found the skin soft and warm.

"No, I ain't cold. How can I be cold bundled to my neck in this damned bed."

He moved to her side and pulled one of the blankets down to the foot, then folded it. "We've got to do something about your language."

"What's the matter with my language?"

He glanced back at her with a crooked grin. "There's too much of it, and it's far too colorful."

"Whatcha gonna do with me, anyway?" She rumpled the covers just to annoy him.

She was at once sorry for her words, for he came and sat down beside her, far too close for comfort. "I was hoping you would decide to stay here at the fort once you're well. Maybe find a job with a seamstress or in one of the stores being built."

For a moment her hope soared as she envisioned life in neat, clean clothes and time for picnics and walks.

"I can't sew a stitch, and Pa didn't teach me no ciphering." There was no place for her here, prattling on to fat matrons, playing Yes, ma'am, No ma'am, with some eastern prisspot. Her place was with her father, where it had always been. No matter the temptations dangling before her to stay.

"You're welcome to stay until you decide what you want to do."

"Well"—she picked at little balls of fuzz on the coarse blanket—"I don't know what I want to do. Don't know how to do but one thing."

"You can't do that here."

She flopped her hands down on the blankets in frustration. "I know that. I ain't stupid. I was just sayin' that that's all I know how to do."

He left her, squatted by the fireplace, and swung the iron arm out that held that night's supper in a black kettle. Maggie leaned to the side to watch him, then blushed and straightened when he glanced back at her.

"You like buffalo soup?" he asked, lifting the lid and waving away a cloud of steam.

"I guess if that's all you got." Her stomach rumbled in anticipation.

"That's the menu for tonight."

"What's a menu?"

He laughed and stood, his eyes dancing. "A menu is a list of things available to eat that a restaurant hands out to it customers."

"What's a rest-a-rant?"

"It's a store that sells food already cooked."

She remembered tiny stores with bright curtains

and delicious smells, but Pa'd always said there was no money for such foolishness.

"What do you need a list for? Don't they just bring you whatever's fer supper?"

He moved toward her again and sat down on the bed, the mattress dipping under his weight. His thigh rested against her arm, sharing the warmth of his body through the blanket that covered her. He leaned forward and covered her forehead with his hand, the softness of his palm against her skin.

"No, they give you a choice of what you want to eat. Have you ever been to a restaurant? Maybe on one of your trips to Benton?"

She shook her head. "I been to a saloon with Pa and the boys."

"Did they serve food there?"

"Yeah. Steaks."

"Well, the saloon probably also has a menu, a list of food men can pick from to order."

"I didn't see no list of food, but there was a list of women. Right up above the bar. There was Sarah and Maybelle and Mary, and right after their names was a price."

His ears turned an endearing shade of pink, and he swallowed. "That's sort of the same thing."

The two ideas swarmed around in her head but made no sense. "Why on earth would somebody order them women off a list?"

"Well . . ." He stood and moved to the fireplace. Picking up a stick, he stirred the embers until they collapsed into a glowing orange pile. "Well, the men ask those women to eat dinner with them, and they pay them for their time.''

"Hogwash. All them men want is to get those women in the bed for a poke.''

Colin turned an amused face. "Do they, now? And how do you know that?''

"I heared men talk. They talk a lot about that.''

Colin rearranged the fire some more.

"You're gonna put that fire out ifen you don't quit.''

He dropped the stick into the coals and returned to his spot on the bed, grown cold since he'd left.

"Lesson number one. Pokin' is something you don't talk about in polite company.'' His voice was serious and scolding, and Maggie's anger lashed back.

"You ain't polite company. Besides, Pa and the boys talked about it all the time. At breakfast, at supper, and especially when new men came to camp. Then they'd talk all night about pokin' women in the bushes and in the barn, and once this fellow swore he'd done it in a tree.'' She threw her hands up and then noticed that he stared at her wide-eyed. "What?''

"What exactly is poking, Maggie?'' he asked, his eyes narrowing.

Maggie squirmed. "Well, it's rollin' around and around with a man and . . . havin' fun.'' She wasn't exactly sure about the details, but she wasn't about to tell him that. Pa'd always shooed her away from the conversation before she found out the whole story. The little bit she'd just told him she'd gleaned from straining her ears to hear campfire talk long after Pa'd sent her to bed.

"Humph," he grunted.

"And then once this bunch of traders come through, and they had this woman with 'em. Well, late after supper she and one of my Pa's men went down to the river, and I heared the bushes breakin' and they was a-groanin'. I thought they mighta been in a patch of briars that was down there, so's I went down to see ifen I could help, and there they was, naked and all up on top of each other. Rollin' around, like I said. Old Jerry, he was a-layin' on top of her, a-goin' up and down, and she was a-layin' there with her—"

Colin stood abruptly and walked back to the fireplace again.

Taming Maggie Hayes was going to be a formidable task. What other subjects would she feel compelled to comment on?

"Did I say somethin' wrong?" Her innocence was both alarming and arousing. But if she was to remain here, he'd have to somehow unwind this tale she'd put together for herself before he could teach her what *not* to say. He could just imagine this subject coming up in conversation unexpectedly.

He leaned down and dipped a bowl of soup from the black kettle, replaced the lid, and swung the pot back over the embers. When he approached the bed with a tray, she glared at him from beneath lowered brows.

"You didn't say anything wrong, Maggie. You've just got things a little mixed up."

He put an arm behind her back and helped her sit up in the bed, noticing how her skin slid beneath the cotton fabric of his nightshirt and how her warmth had permeated his pillow.

Placing the tray on her lap, he sat down at her side and dipped up some soup. She was perfectly capable of feeding herself and had done so for several days, but tonight he guiltily allowed himself the pleasure, knowing his motives were not exactly pure.

"How have I got things mixed up?" she asked, her eyes fixed on his face.

Colin struggled to formulate some explanation that was not too straightforward and yet accurate.

"Well, first, pokin' is the same thing as relations."

"The same thing as what?"

"Making love."

She frowned and accepted another spoonful.

"Making babies."

Her eyes widened to beautiful blue ovals. "Is that what they was doin'?"

"Yes."

"Damn." She reached for another spoonful before he got it to her mouth.

"And it's something very private between a man and woman who are married."

She shook her head vigorously. "It couldn't be that, then, 'cause Old Jerry and this whore weren't married."

"You shouldn't use the word 'whore' in polite company, either."

"Well, just what kind of company can I talk in?" she asked, slapping her hands on the blanket.

"We'll talk about that later. One thing at a time."

"Yeah. This is more interesting."

Colin's hand tightened on the spoon, and he felt the waters of frustration rising around him. "A man and a woman don't have to be married to have relations, but . . . they should be."

"Says who?"

"Says everybody." Yep, he was in deep here and with no sign of salvation.

"Like who?"

"Like the Bible."

She took another spoonful and was silent for a few moments. Colin could almost see the thoughts spinning in her mind, and he braced himself for the next question.

"The Bible tells who oughta have a poke?"

"Sort of."

"Pa made me read the Bible every night. Is this where all that begettin' came into things?"

Colin nodded, feeling firm ground again under his feet.

"But if a man and a woman who ain't married have . . . relations, what does God do?"

"Well . . ." She had him there. "Let's leave God out of this for right now."

"So, that whore—that woman coulda had a baby 'cause of Old Jerry's a-goin up and down on her?"

The bottom of the bowl was beginning to show, and he wished her questions would run out as quickly. "Yes."

"They looked like they was havin' fun. Is it?"

Again, she turned those wide, innocent eyes on him and stabbed him in the heart. The wagon had just plunged off the cliff. "Do you want some more soup?"

She nodded, and he rose and walked to the fireplace, a hundred explanations coming to mind. How on earth was he going to explain his way out of this one?

"Is it, Colin?" She'd never used his name before, and the sound of it rolling off her tongue made his stomach tighten.

"I don't know. I'm not married." He answered her with his back turned and hoped she'd let the subject lie. No such luck.

"You ain't never done it?" she asked when he sat back down.

"No." He lifted the spoon to her mouth, struggling to keep his hand from shaking.

"I done it once."

Colin nearly dropped the bowl but saved it from a slide to the floor in time. "You have?"

She eyed him suspiciously for a moment. "Yeah. One time this here boy come to camp. He said he'd show me a real good fishin' place he'd found, and when he was down there a-sittin' on the bank, he pushed me backwards and got on top of me and started a-goin' up and down." She opened her mouth, but Colin spilled the soup on a napkin he'd tucked into the neck of her nightshirt.

"Did you take your clothes off?" he asked as calmly as he could muster.

"Of course not," she answered incredulously. "It was cold. I'd a-froze to death."

"So he didn't touch your skin with his?"

"No. He just did that some, then he rolled off and huffed off back toward camp. But I caught a fish after he left."

Colin shook his head, relief flowing through him. A multitude of explanations came to mind, but misguided youth on both sides was the most likely one. The thought of anyone else touching her in that way fired an anger in him that was sudden and searing and dangerous.

Forcing himself to keep calm, he scraped the bowl and lifted the last spoonful to her lips.

She stared straight into his heart. "Did you ever want to?"

Colin emptied the spoon into her mouth, his gaze fixed on her lips as the silver of the spoon reappeared.

"Yes, I have."

She studied him for a moment. "Was she somebody you loved?"

"She was to be my wife."

Maggie's eyes drooped as the warm liquid and limited strength took their toll. "Oh. Why didn't you?"

Colin wiped her mouth with the napkin and pulled it out of her collar, allowing the tips of his fingers to brush her neck.

"Because I wanted to wait until we were married."

"That's nice," she said groggily. "Do you think I'll ever want to?" Her eyes drifted shut and stayed closed.

He rose and stood over her, looking down into her angelic face. "I hope so, Maggie," he said, "I hope so."

The night air was cold and crisp, almost bitter. Just what he needed, Colin decided, throwing a buffalo robe over his shoulders and stepping out into the slushy snow that stubbornly clung to the ground. The sky overhead was inky black, and stars by the millions winked and glistened, silent sentinels in their slowly revolving world.

Leaning against the fence that bordered the corral, Colin inhaled and breathed deeply to clear his head. He felt as if he'd just defended the fort against a three-day attack.

"So, she's run ye out of yer home, has she?" Braden Flynn's soft brogue rolled out of the dark.

"Just wanted to get out for a bit and get some fresh air," Colin answered, wondering if Braden would buy that.

"Fer sure ye did, lad. Fer sure."

Maybe not.

"Yer in up to yer eyebrows, I'm thinkin'."

Colin sighed. "How'd you know?" He leaned his chin on his crossed arms and stared into the night for wisdom. Or amnesia. Whichever God saw fit to dole out.

"Do ye think I'm blind, Colin, lad? Yer wearin' yer heart in yer eyes."

"Is it that obvious?" he asked with a rush of panic.

He was sure his feelings were in violation of his oath . . . somehow.

"No one else suspects; put yer mind at rest. Steven and me and no one else. She's a fine lass, fer sure. Needs a firm hand, though."

Colin raised his head and looked at Braden. "This is a ridiculous situation I've gotten myself into, and I'll just have to think of a way out."

"Why would ye want to get out of it? I'd give me right leg to have a woman look at me like that." He threw a nod toward the yellow light spilling from the windows. "Even if she could out cuss me."

"I must be out of my mind."

"Sorrow'll do that fer ye."

Colin shot Braden a glance, wondering how he knew of his past, but Braden stared off, wearing an expression of detachment Colin had come to know well. Colin waited for him to continue.

"She was a beauty. Eyes the color of May grass, lips like roses." Braden smiled softly. "She loved the wind along the beach. Barefooted in the surf she'd run, her hair fanned out behind her."

"What happened to her?" Colin ventured.

Braden roused himself from his memories. "She died. Starved to death with most of the rest of Ireland."

"The potato famine?"

Braden nodded. "I watched her waste away, a little

thinner each time I held her. Her dad was a fisherman and brought in food that way, but when the whole countryside was fishin' "—he shrugged—"there weren't enough fish to go around." Braden turned abruptly and walked away into the dark. "Don't turn down love when it's offered, lad. Ye never know when God'll go back on his word."

"I ain't wearin' that thing." Maggie crossed her arms and tilted her chin.

Colin sighed. They'd been at this for the better part of an hour. He'd tried reason, cajoling, and threatening, and nothing had worked. She absolutely, flatly, refused to wear anything other than pants despite his best efforts to explain that ladies simply did not wear trousers. And she'd answered with her now-standard reply, "Who says?"

He'd had her clothes burned when she arrived, and now she padded around in his nightshirt. And nothing else. A distraction, to say the least.

So he was now reduced to blackmail. "I'll get you some candy if you'll put it on."

She cocked her head and looked at him with one eye, reminding him of a robin planning the demise of an unsuspecting earthworm. He being the earthworm.

"All right. I'll try it on. Just once."

Colin held it out, and Maggie slid carefully off the bed, her legs still weak. He closed the blanket that separated the bedroom from the examination room, where he'd spent many restless nights trying to sleep on the examination table.

He heard her rustling her clothes, heard the stiff, new calico slide down her body, and willed himself to listen no more. How many cold walks around the fort could one man stand?

"Can you button these damn—I mean, darn buttons for me." She swept aside the curtain and presented her bare back to him. He'd seen as much of her as a husband in the last weeks, but now, with her standing in front of him, vibrant and alive, his hands trembled.

"What's the matter with you?" she asked, craning her neck to study his fumbling efforts.

"Buttoning a lady's dress is not something I do every day."

"Bet you'd like to."

Colin stopped and leaned around her. "Beg your pardon?"

"I said I'd bet you'd like to. Pa and the boys used to say that if a man went for long without—"

"Stop right there." Colin held up a hand. "Not another conversation today about what Pa and the boys said."

She dropped her hair and turned around. Colin caught his breath. She was beautiful. The dress clung to her in all the right places, then drifted down to her feet in delicate folds of fabric. She looked innocent and sedate.

He wondered how many people would be taken in by her ruse. "It's very pretty."

She looked down. "I ain't never had nothin' this purty." When she raised her face, her eyes glistened, and Colin felt his heart turn over.

"Why'd you buy this for me?"

"Because young ladies don't wear pants, especially dirty, ragged ones." She started to protest, and he held up a hand to still her. "And . . . because I wanted you to have it."

"Thank you," she said in a thick voice, and Colin knew he'd never received such sincere thanks.

Eyes glowing with warmth, she advanced on him. He stepped backward, the vein of their recent conversations flashing to mind. When she had backed him all the way to the other side of the room and his back was firmly melded with a table, she raised up on tiptoe and kissed him on the cheek. "Did I do it right?" she asked, her breath sweet and soft on his cheek.

He swallowed. "You did it exactly right."

She sashayed away, looking down, seemingly fascinated with the way the dress swayed and swished around her ankles. *Are women born seducers, knowing from the womb how to excite and deflate a man repeatedly until he is but malleable clay in their hands?* Colin closed his eyes, battling to quiet his thumping heart and at the same time appear unaffected.

"Drill is in ten minutes. Do you want to come and watch?" he asked as he pushed away from the wall and snatched his coat off the back of a chair.

She turned around and let her gaze rake over him. He felt every second of her assessment in the pit of his stomach. "No, I'm tired. I think I'll stay here." And with that she skimmed closed the curtain.

"You'll stay here. Right?" he asked, gritting his teeth at sounding like an idiot. After all, *she* was the prisoner.

"Of course I will. You promised me candy, remember?" sang her sweet voice from behind the curtain.

Before his thoughts could focus on the sounds behind their thin barricade, Colin escaped to the safety of the parade ground.

Chapter Eight

Maggie folded the dress and laid it gently on the bed. She adjusted the lace around the sleeves and smoothed out a crease. The material felt cool and slick beneath her palm. She jerked her hand away. She couldn't let the temptation to stay overcome her. Pa needed her, and her place was with him.

She glanced toward the door, suddenly feeling self-conscious of the fact that she stood in the center of the room naked. She glanced around. In the corner was a chest, battered and scratched, its brass corner pieces glowing in the firelight.

Garments lay on top of each other, folded and carefully stacked. A pair of blue pants with a white stripe down each leg lay on top, just like the ones Colin wore every day. Maggie held them up to her and found that they stretched nicely from hip to hip.

They should fit her, and besides, he had another pair. Quickly, she slid into them.

She dug through to the bottom where a fine white shirt lay beneath books and papers. The material was cool and smooth like the dress. And although she sensed that the garment was somehow special, she couldn't resist the tiny bit of luxury it represented. Dredging up the last bit of anger toward him she could muster, she slipped her arms into the shirt and pulled it over her head. The shoulder seams hung nearly to her elbows, and the tail stopped around her knees. She crammed the excess material into the pants band. Now all she needed was shoes.

She searched the room but found nothing. Glancing out the window, she saw that snow still fell as a light, glistening haze. She couldn't leave barefooted. Then she saw the buffalo robe. Using a knife she found in a drawer, she sliced out large squares of the hide and tied them around her feet with some long, narrow strips of leather.

Again, she glanced toward the door, indecision gripping her. If she stayed, she might never see her father again. If she left, she'd never see Colin again—at least not on the same side of the law.

Ignoring the squeezing of her heart, she crammed her hair up underneath her old felt hat, the only article of her clothing Colin had not burned.

Although he'd closed the door, she could hear voices soar and drop in the singsong cadence she'd heard over and over again. If she didn't make her escape now, there might not be another chance. She had to find Pa and know he was well. As part of her mind debated her flight, the other half sifted through bits and pieces of overheard conversations. Where would Pa go? Surely not back to Pine Coulee. That would be the first place the police would look. Farther north? The Cree reservation was farther north. That's where she'd go, she reasoned.

With a last look around the room, she eased open the small window set into the back wall. She climbed out and closed the window behind her. Ahead loomed the palisades of the back fort wall. To her right, the cadence of drill and the *clop, clop* of horses' hooves drew louder. Darting from building to building, she finally worked her way to the front gate. Now, how was she going to get through unseen?

She glanced up at the guard post. A lone sentinel stared off across the river. She'd heard Colin say that the Blackfeet and the police were on good terms and vigilance at the fort had been relaxed. Gambling on the guard's distraction, Maggie pulled her hat low, stepped into his view, and shuffled out of the gate unnoticed.

When she reached the first line of stores in town, she darted behind the structures. Here and there, horses were tied to crates and wagons, awaiting their riders' return. Maggie spotted a fat bay mare and moved toward her at the casual shuffle she'd perfected.

The mare nickered and poked her nose out as Maggie approached. No one was in sight, so Maggie quickly untied the reins, swung up into the saddle, and rode away at a trot, expecting any moment to hear shouts and curses behind her. But she heard nothing as she rounded the corner of the stores and rode toward the open prairie. When she passed the last trader's wagon, she broke into a gallop, eager to put as much distance between herself and Fort McLeod as possible.

Colin waded through ankle-high dirty snow, weaving and dodging to avoid newly arrived traders' wagons. The hard November weather should have deterred them from venturing north, he thought as he stepped into a frigid puddle hidden beneath a thin skim of ice. But the opposite had occurred. More and more businessmen had set up shop around the fort, an island of civilization in an ocean of wilderness. Numerous restaurants, dubbed "eating places," had sprung to life, and a log billiard room enticed off-duty men into its dark, smoke-filled interior.

Colin found Mr. Bailey's cart with ease, only now a partly finished storefront loomed behind the rickety two-wheeled conveyance. Marveling at the speed at which building was progressing, Colin stepped up to the cart and smiled at Mr. Bailey.

"A nickel's worth of horehound candy, please," Colin said, depositing the money onto the shelf of the cart.

Mr. Bailey smiled, skimming a hand through his thinning hair. "Good afternoon, Constable Fraser. That's some sweet tooth you have. I haven't sold this

much horehound in a year." He ducked his head to
fish underneath the counter and glanced up, a twinkle in his eye. "Is there a lady involved in this?"

Colin felt a thousand eyes on his back and heard
the wheel of the gossip mill begin to turn.

"No. Horehound was always my favorite." There,
he thought, he'd lied again. A small lie, yes, but a lie
nonetheless.

Mr. Bailey wrapped the candy in brown paper and
handed it across the cart.

Distant raised voices caught Colin's attention. He
hurried back through the fort gates and saw an arriving patrol dragging a draped body off the back of a
packhorse.

"It's Wilton Svenson," Steven Gravel said as he
eased the body to the ground. Long, bloody scratches
etched across Steven's face, and his clothes were torn
and muddy. "We were ambushed down along the
river."

Colin slipped his package in his pocket, fell to his
knees, and yanked open the blanket. A neatly bored
hole marred Wilton's scarlet jacket. Colin felt for a
pulse, tossed aside his helmet, and leaned down to
place an ear near the man's lips.

"He's still alive. Get him inside."

Steven led the exhausted, muddy horses toward the
stables while the rest of the battered patrol struggled
to get Wilton's limp body inside and up on the examination table. Doffing his coat, Colin rolled up his
sleeves and searched the counters for his surgical
instruments.

"Get his jacket off him," he instructed the startled men looking on. Obediently, they stripped away Wilton's coat and cut off the top of his suit of winter underwear, baring his broad chest. Of Swedish descent, Wilton was a huge man with rippling muscles. Seeing him lying there, blood oozing from an ugly, puckered wound, reminded Colin of his own mortality, a thought he could do without. Taking a deep breath, he summoned his surgical experience to mind. Calmed, he carefully selected the instruments he would need.

A scalpel, forceps to remove the bullet, a pan, and rags to pack the wound.

"Maggie? Is the water hot?" he called over his shoulder.

There was no answer.

"Maggie?" He turned and looked into the other room. The bed was neatly made, and in the center was the carefully folded blue dress.

She was gone.

There was no time now to think about where she'd gone or what she'd done. "Get the kettle and pour some water over these instruments," he said to one of the constables behind him.

Whitening to his hair line, the young man mumbled something and moved back a step.

"I need that water now, Constable."

The harshness in his voice stirred the young man out of his fear. He hurried to the stove, lifted the kettle that huffed little puffs of steam, and poured water into the pan.

"Well done," he said with a nod to the young man, who looked up at him with huge, frightened eyes. Colin couldn't blame him. He felt a little woozy himself. He'd hadn't done surgery since medical school. "What's your name?"

"John, sir."

"John, come over here and hand me the instruments I need."

Obediently, John took the forceps Colin dipped into the hot water and fished out the other instruments as Colin pointed to them.

He probed the wound and found that the bullet was shallow, probably having struck a rib that stopped its flight.

"Can I help?" Steven Gravel asked from across Wilton's body.

Colin glanced up. Steven's expression was as serene and unruffled as ever. "Stay here and help me hold him down if he wakes up."

Steven took off his coat and rolled up his sleeves. Colin went to the washbowl and scrubbed his hands with the soap and water he kept there. Then he returned to the table, and John moved to his side.

"Hand me the forceps, those things." He pointed to the maze of instruments in the pan.

John fumbled with the instrument for a moment, then picked up the forceps neatly and held them out with a slight smile. Colin inserted the end of the tool into Wilton's flesh and felt the big man groan as the metal ends dragged across the bullet. Just as he'd thought. The bullet had hit a rib.

Changing the angle of his attack, Colin forced the gaping flesh to one side and poked around. Wilton groaned again and moved one hand.

"Be ready to hold him," Colin said to Steven, who nodded and swallowed.

Then the lead slipped into the grip of the forceps. Tugging, he pulled the bullet free and dropped it into the pan of water with a clunk. A red haze spread over the water's surface.

"Hand me that thread and a needle," he said to John, pointing to the table with his elbow.

John set the pan down with trembling hands, threaded the needle, and handed it to him. Colin glanced at John's pale face. All he needed was for John to crumple into a pile at his feet.

Colin inserted the needle into Wilton's flesh and slowly drew the wound closed while Wilton mumbled and wiggled. They all stepped away from the table as he sat up, blinked, and swung his great head around. "Vhy are all of ya lookin' at me?" he asked in his deep Swedish accent.

"You were shot, Wilton."

"Shot? Vho vould shoot Vilton?

"You and your patrol were ambushed. How do you feel?" Colin asked, stopping the man when he made a move to climb down off the table.

"I feel fine. I vant to get down." He inched his large body to the edge of the table, then stood. He wavered a second, then looked down at the wound on his chest. "You sew guud, Doc," he said with a crooked smile; then he lumbered for the door, bare-chested.

"Wait, I need to bandage that," Colin called, start-ing forward.

Wilton waved over his shoulder without turning around. "Vilton will bandage it himself." Then, with a slight stagger, he stepped down off the porch and sauntered across the parade ground as if he'd been stung by a bee instead of a fifty-caliber.

Steven followed him to see that he made it across the parade ground to his barracks. Colin stepped back and sighed.

"Can I put this down now?" John asked in a weak voice, holding out the basin as if it were a sacrificial bowl.

Colin nodded, and John set the bowl down with a thud and hurried out the door. Colin closed the door and turned to the silence that now filled the room.

Passing the bloody table and instruments, Colin stepped to the bed and stared down at the dress. Her old hat was gone, the one he'd resisted burning just because it seemed to define her. His buffalo robe had two large, square holes in it. He glanced toward the window. She must have slipped away while he was at drill.

He sat down on the bed and smoothed a hand over the dress, imagining her inside the fabric that slid softly against his palm. Where would the cold, dark night find her? Was she alone in the wilderness? His first instinct was to find her and bring her back, then to protect her, to mold her into someone she was not. But he knew better. He had no reason to keep her here. She was a free woman, able to choose her own destiny.

Only he'd hoped she'd want to share that destiny with him.

Such a thought sounded foolish. He and Maggie Hayes had no more in common than the wild prairie flowers and the tame geraniums his mother had grown in brown wooden window boxes. She'd never learn to live his life, never be able to give up her independence, her uniqueness, and conform to polite society.

Colin rose and walked to the window that looked out across the wide parade ground and to the gates beyond. Rare sunlight broke through the clouds, dappling the trampled and stirred ground.

"Guard and keep her," he said to the peek of prairie visible through the open gates.

The grove of aspen and birch was silent except for the occasional rasp of two naked branches rubbing together in a gentle breeze. The cabins sat silent and cold. The still house seemed deserted.

No smoke coiled out of the stovepipe.

No odor of sour mash wafted through the trees.

No voices boasted or argued.

Maggie drew the little mare to a stop and sat listening. Broken bottles and smashed kegs littered the ground that had long since thirstily soaked up the spilled liquor. Disappointment swelled up within her. Apparently, no one had returned after being released.

She heeled the mare forward. For two days she'd ridden in anticipation of being greeted by familiar faces and sounds.

Cabin doors hung open like gaping mouths; dry leaves had been scattered across the stoop by autumn's wind. A few belongings were scattered across the common ground, probably by curious otters. She drew the horse to a stop in front of what had been her cabin and waited, listening again. But she heard only the sigh of the wind.

She dismounted and climbed the steps, starting when the boards creaked and protested, the sound loud in the quiet. Inside, things were much as she'd left them. A quick glance around told her that her father had not been back to retrieve his things. A spare pair of pants hung on a nail. A half-empty bottle of liquor stood on the table, miraculously upright and unspilled. His cup sat on the table, just as he'd left it the morning the police came.

Nothing to tell her where he'd gone.

She snatched the blanket off her cot and spread it across the table. Then she piled supplies and utensils into the center of it. She ran outside and found the frying pan where she'd dropped it after Steven Gravel grabbed her. Then she lifted the grass-filled mattress of her cot and pulled out a piece of folded hide. Inside, the tintype was as she remembered—her father in a suit, looking uncomfortable, with a wide banner in the background proclaiming a horse race in Benton, Montana Territory. She smiled back at the picture and wished, as she had a thousand times, that she had such a picture of her mother.

She wandered around the cabin again, but it was practically bare. They'd had few belongings, only their presence making it a home. Still, there was no clue as to her father's whereabouts. She hoped for some sign, something missing, maybe a note in the event she could escape and return, but there was nothing, only the eeriness of the camp, seemingly waiting for . . . something.

Grasping the corners of the blanket, Maggie made a bundle and threw it over her shoulder. She tied the blanket behind the saddle, then headed for the still house. Inside, the air stank of stale mash and mustiness. Light spilled through the open door, and the dried remains of the dumped mash arched up from the soil in yellow sheets. Maggie stepped inside and moved to the opposite wall. She squatted down and dug at the loose board. It gave way, revealing a hidden cache of six bottles of liquor.

Pa'd always said to put something away. Smiling, she retrieved all the bottles, walked outside, and added them to her saddle roll. Then she stood and looked over the camp once more.

If not here, then where? Where was her father? She had no idea in which direction to ride. Colin had said they didn't capture him. Could he be camped someplace near, waiting for her to return? Could he be sick? Dead?

She shook away the momentary panic. No, she

wouldn't think that. Maybe she should make camp someplace and wait. She glanced at the cabins again but rejected the idea. No, the still camp was just too eerie, almost like graves in a cemetery, peacefully waiting. No, she'd travel downriver a bit and make camp in some thicket. She'd take some more blankets with her, and maybe there was even a tent among the abandoned belongings. He'd find her. She had to believe that, she told herself.

An hour later, she rode away from the camp. She'd found the tent she'd used when they operated on the other side of the border. It was rodent-gnawed a bit, but aside from that, it was sturdy. She took all the blankets she could find and anything else she could use, for she wasn't coming back.

She found the perfect thicket about ten miles downriver. Brambles formed a natural barrier from the north wind, and the river gurgled nearby for company and water. She pitched the tent with little trouble, having to cut new stakes with an ax. When the tent was up and her meager possessions were stored away, she sat on a felled log, gazed at the river, and for the first time let the hopelessness begin to creep in.

Jerry Potts strode across the parade ground, the elaborate fringe on his buckskin pants slapping and snapping against his legs. Colin looked up from his desk by the window in time to see him pass. A slight man with stooped shoulders, Potts was tough as they came, a native of land they now sought to conquer.

Son of a fur trapper and a Peigan Indian woman, he had proved invaluable to the Mounted Police, leading them first to Fort Whoop-Up and then here, to choose this site on the Old Man's River for Fort McLeod.

McLeod had hired him in Benton as an interpreter and guide and had relied on his expert advice in matters of the Indians ever since then. A special bond had developed between the assistant commissioner and Potts, one based on unquestioning loyalty and integrity.

Potts hurried toward McLeod's residence, and Colin closed his book. Rumors had flown that McLeod was about to request a meeting with chiefs of the Blackfoot Confederacy—the Blackfoot, Blood, and Peigan tribes. He wanted to reassure the Indians that the Mounted Police were here for the good of their people and that the police would always be fair in any decisions made under the absolute power McLeod had been given in dispensing justice. And now Jerry Potts's haste seemed to confirm that the meeting was soon to be.

Colin gazed up at the sky. The day had been kind so far. Sun flirted with low gray clouds, taunting these poor souls housed in log houses with sod roofs that poured liquid mud when it rained or snow melted. Most men had suspended oilcloth over their beds to shield them from the downpour of mud when they slept.

Conditions were poor. Ottawa seemed to have forgotten them. They hadn't been paid in months, and every man was indebted to the traders in town. Mail had been nonexistent after that first delivery brought to them from Benton by one of I. G. Baker's wagons.

As always, he wondered about Maggie.

Two weeks had passed without a trace of her. He'd quietly asked patrols to watch for her, cloaking his request with concerns for her health and possible connections to her father, who was still unaccounted for. But no word had come back. It was as if she had dropped off the earth.

Colin rose when he saw Braden hurrying across the parade ground, headed straight for his door. He opened it before Braden could knock.

"McLeod wants to see ye in his office," he said breathlessly, his eyes bright with excitement.

Colin reached around the corner for his coat. "What about?"

" 'E's sent for the chiefs of the Confederacy, asked 'em to come here for a meetin'."

Colin closed the door behind him and started across the common ground. "Does he think they'll come?"

"Potts says they're anxious to meet the police. Wouldn't that be a sight, now, the chiefs here with us?"

"Yes, it would." Part of Colin thrilled to the chance to see members of the Blackfoot tribe, the powerful, intelligent people who'd carved rich lives from this land and governed themselves with the compassion and cunning that Parliament should envy. But another part couldn't help but think that if not for people like Maggie and her father, this meeting might never have taken place.

Colin glanced up to see Steven Gravel intercepting them on an angled course.

"Colin, could I see you a moment?" He caught up with them just as they were about to step up onto the porch of McLeod's living quarters.

Colin paused and turned.

"Constable, would you come in, please?" McLeod asked as Braden opened the door.

"Can it wait?" he said to Steven.

Steven glanced around quickly. "I've found Maggie," he said in a whisper.

Chapter Nine

Maggie batted at a fat snowflake, then watched its cousins whiten the thicket. She'd waited two weeks, and there'd been no sign of her father. She'd even ridden back to the camp a time or two despite her vows never to go there again. But the camp was just as she'd left it, with no telltale footprints except from the scurrying of small wildlife in the fresh snowfall.

She couldn't spend the winter here. December and beyond would bring hard snow and ice and plunging temperatures. Her tent wouldn't be adequate shelter. Where should she go?

Temptation drew her back to Fort McLeod and Colin, but concern over her father and pride kept her away. If she returned to the fort, it was as good as admitting she was unable to look after herself.

And besides, she'd never rest until she knew what happened to her father.

Painted Ax. The thought struck her. Maybe he'd know where her father was. He and his village had been some of their best customers. And she did have those six bottles of liquor to loosen their tongues.

She jumped up and began collapsing the tent and packing supplies onto the back of the bay mare. As the snow thickened, she was riding toward the north, swathed in a buffalo robe.

Night had fallen as the first flickers of Painted Ax's fires showed through the driving white blindness that surrounded her. Her feet had gone numb hours ago, and she struggled to stay astride her horse. Four men sat around a leaping fire, buffalo robes thrown across their slumped shoulders and drawn tightly under their chins. They jumped and reached for their knives at their belts as Maggie rode into the yellow circle of firelight.

She opened her mouth to ask for Painted Ax but succeeded only in mumbling something incoherent through numb lips.

They looked from one to the other; then one man reached up and pulled her to him. Her legs refused to work, and she fell heavily against his chest. He scooped her into his arms and strode toward a tepee that glowed a warm yellow through the snow. He rapped once on a lodge pole, and the flap slammed back against the side.

He asked for Painted Ax, then stepped through the doorway and into welcome warmth. Voices talked all at once, and Maggie lost track of who said what. She was growing warm against his chest, and her eyes grew heavy.

He laid her in a soft bed of furs. Someone bent over her and said her name. Vaguely, through the fog of sleep and cold, she mumbled something in response, then closed her eyes.

She awoke, kicked aside the buffalo robe, and reveled at the sensation of cool air against her hot skin. Daylight lit the inside of the tepee and snowflakes drifted down from the smoke hole and hung suspended in a sunbeam before plunging to the dirt floor. A group of people watched her from their seats around the firepit, fingers crammed in their mouths as they ate from carved wooden bowls. One of them was Painted Ax.

"Mag-gie Hayes," he said with a grin.

Maggie propped up on her elbows, her gaze scanning across the crowd now watching her. "Have you seen my father?"

He shook his head and glanced at a broad-chested warrior on his right. Dark hair swept over one ear, and the other side was held away from his face by a single braid.

"George Hayes has not been here," he said, his words spoken carefully and correctly. "He lost his firewater to the police."

Maggie rolled out of the furs, then stood and adjusted her clothes. "I have to find him."

"We heard you were taken as slave." He swiped at the air to emphasis his point.

"I ain't nobody's slave, and ain't gonna be, neither."

Their hands moved slowly from their bowls to their mouths, their eyes never leaving her face. She reckoned they'd never had so interesting a breakfast as this one.

"Do you know where my pa mighta gone?" Maggie moved toward her pack that someone had brought inside. Guilt gripped her as she wondered if anyone had cared for her poor horse. "Did anyone see about my horse?"

"Horse fine." Painted Ax waved at the air again as if the question were trivial.

"I got something I'll give you ifen you'll tell me where he is." She reached inside the bundled blanket, gripped the narrow neck of a bottle, and pulled it free. "Some of my father's whiskey." She waggled the bottle, expecting to see anticipation in their faces, but they watched her with expressionless stares, and Maggie began to chafe under their regard.

"We do not drink the firewater any longer," the young man said with measured words and tone. "It makes our young men angry. They get into many fights, get shot. The traders robbed us, took our women, our furs, our food. It is good that the redcoats come and chase away George Hayes."

Maggie suddenly wished she had her back against a solid wall. She lowered her hand until the bottle dangled at her side. Whiskey had always represented power over the Indians, and Maggie admitted to feeling a certain superiority to them when they'd stagger into camp, ragged and drunk, eager to trade anything they had for one more drink of the firewater. But standing here under their gaze, she felt very alone and small, and as she considered what to do next, threads of overheard conversations about the Mounted Police's mission to rid western Canada of illegal whiskey drifted through her thoughts.

She stuffed the bottle back into her pack, then straightened. No one had moved. She rubbed both hands down the back side of her breeches. "Well, I reckon I'll be gettin' along now. Much obliged fer the night's sleep." She bent to retrieve the bundled blanket.

"Where will you find your father, Maggie Hayes?"

She turned and found that Painted Ax had placed his bowl by the firepit and gotten to his feet.

"Well, I dunno. I got a few more places I can look fer him."

Painted Ax stepped carefully around the circle of stones and came to stand beside her. "Your father always make fair trade with me. He never steal from us. We ask him for whiskey." He clapped a large brown hand over his heart. "But days of whiskey drinking are past. All of the Blackfeet, Bloods, and Peigans decide that the redcoats are good thing. We act like children, and they come and take away what will hurt us. We are ashamed and grateful to the redcoats." He stepped closer and picked up a strand of hair that had slipped out from beneath her hat.

"I have daughter, young like you. She marry a good man, but he like the firewater. One time he beat her until she die. Then I kill him." He dropped the strand of hair and looked up into her face. "The whiskey is bad. You go back to police, live in new town at fort. Maybe someday your father find you."

Shaken by the detachment with which Painted Ax could speak of such sorrow, Maggie picked up her pack and backed out the lodge's door. She turned, the bundle clasped in her arms, and ran nose to nose with her bay mare, who whickered softly as she picked through a pile of dried grass at her feet.

Maggie tied the bundle behind the saddle and swung up, suddenly feeling alien and alone in the camp where once she'd danced around a leaping fire with a wolverine pelt pulled over her head. Painted Ax stepped outside as she pulled the mare around and set off at a trot. She glanced back over her shoulder once. He stood where she'd left him, his hands fisted on his hips, watching her ride away.

Maggie followed the river south, Painted Ax's words rolling around in her head like river rocks. What if she never found her father? And if she did, would he be back in the whiskey business?

The mare stepped on a rock and shifted her weight suddenly, causing Maggie to scramble to regain her seat. Why hadn't he come looking for her? He knew she was at Fort McLeod. But in all the time she was there, he'd made no effort to find her.

Maggie frowned. Somehow she hadn't considered that before now. She'd been so absorbed with her plan of escape, she hadn't stopped to wonder why she hadn't been rescued first.

* * *

Colin squatted down to study a smudged track. The pony was shod, the horseshoe biting deep into the snow, marring its pristine surface with dark soil turned from the ground below. The brambles around him were thick with snow, their canes fat and frosted. Even beneath the soft layer that had drifted down silent and thick, signs that someone had camped here were plain. The damp riverbank allowed snow to stick only on tufts of grass, and the dirt between them was worn slick and packed with use. Bark on a river birch was gnawed, as if a horse had chewed on it in boredom. Maggie had camped here. He was sure of it.

The camping spot had not been cleared of brush. Instead, the inhabitant had merely snuggled a tent in between the brambles, disguising the camp from three directions.

"Smart girl," Colin said with a smile.

" 'Tis cunnin' she is, I say," Braden said, shaking his head. "She'll be handin' ye yer head, if ye don't mind, lad."

Colin tossed down the stick he'd used to trace the track and stood. "I don't see another trail. I wonder how the Blackfeet knew she was here?"

Braden shrugged. "A woman selling whiskey— word would travel fast."

They'd returned to the traders' abandoned camp and found it deserted. Upon searching the buildings, they'd found small tracks in the layer of leaves and dust that had accumulated in the weeks since the raid. And then they'd found the hidden cubbyhole in the still house and round marks in the damp soil within.

"I don't think she's selling the whiskey. I think she's looking for her father. The bottles of whiskey were her bargaining chips."

"Would ye be thinkin' of lettin' her lead us to 'im?"

Colin swung around, a denial on his tongue, but in truth, the thought had crossed his mind.

But only briefly.

He was out here in a snowstorm searching for Maggie because he missed her.

And because he was in love with her.

Even letting that thought run free in his brain jarred him to the worn bottom of his boots. How had she crept inside him, embracing his heart like a fat cat curling up by a fireplace, thwarting every barrier he put up? But she had. While he had raged against love and mulled over the whys and hows of his sorrow, she had sliced him open and slipped inside.

"Would ye be steppin' over here, please?" Braden had dismounted and now squatted by a depression in the snow. "There's a trail so plain a blind man could see it. Following the river north." He pointed to the same sharp, digging tracks as before.

They led to level ground that followed the winding river. Word had circulated that whiskey traders were operating farther north, hoping to get far enough away from Fort McLeod that McLeod wouldn't come after them.

They sorely underestimated James McLeod.

Following the dim tracks, now rapidly filling with snow, they rode until dusk overtook them. They stopped on the outskirts of a village, the same village where Maggie had haggled endlessly with Painted Ax. *Was* Maggie going into business for herself? Or was she out drumming up business for her father?

Quietly, they sat in a copse of trees and watched the quiet village as the sun died. Wisps of smoke coiled up from the apex of tepees. An occasional bundled figure hurried from a lodge to the edge of the river, dipped a bladder of water, then hurried home. The sun set a miraculous pink that turned the snow into a confectioner's dream.

Near the center of the village, in front of a lodge, hay was scattered out across the surface of the newly fallen snow, as if someone had fed a horse. Odd, thought Colin. Most of the Indian ponies grazed peacefully on the outskirts of the camp.

He mentally sorted through the information Steven had given him. Blackfoot scouts had brought word that a woman was camped along the river—alone. They speculated that she was George Hayes's daughter, either looking for her father or picking up where he left off.

McLeod had sent word to all three tribes of the Blackfoot Confederacy that he wanted to meet with the chiefs, to discuss the police's role in the west. An answer had come back that the police were welcome and that the Indians had already decided that the policemen were their friends and the whiskey traders their enemies. Many were refusing to trade for the firewater any longer, and whiskey traders were quickly becoming a thing of the past.

So where did that leave Maggie? he wondered as he shifted in the saddle. Had she grown desperate for food and come here? Fear's icy fingers tiptoed across his skin. In a flash he could imagine her hungry, cold, desperate. Perhaps she had not fully recovered from her illness. Perhaps she had suffered a relapse and stumbled here seeking help.

"Colin."

Colin jumped and turned to look at Braden, who stared back with a frown knitting his brows together. "Ye looked as if ye'd seen a banshee. Is somethin' the matter?"

"No." He shook his head, embarrassed his thoughts had shown on his face.

"She could be down there in any of those lodges," Braden said with a nod in the direction of the village.

"Indeed she could. But maybe not." Colin turned his horse and rode around the village in the disappearing light. Equal distance around on the other side was a fresh trail. Same tiny hoofprints, same sharp angle.

"We'll make a tracker out of ye yet, lad," Braden said, a twinkle in his eye. "She's ridin' back toward the fort. I wonder now if she's comin' back to beg yer forgiveness?"

Colin stared down at the small, even tracks that led off into the encroaching night straight toward Fort

McLeod. "I don't know much about women in general, but I can guarantee you with complete faith that Maggie Hayes never begged for anything in her life. And she's not about to start now."

Maggie made camp in a group of paper birches that clung to the riverbank with gnarled roots. She cut tamarack branches, laid them on the ground to shield her from the cold, then spread a buffalo hide over their width. After the mare was tied, Maggie climbed into her bed and wrapped up in another robe, cocooned like a caterpillar waiting for spring.

Outside, the lonely plop, plop of snowflakes broke the silence, accompanied only by the sound of the river, now reduced to a whisper.

She had no idea where to start looking for her father. Had he gone back to Benton, thinking her dead? Was he waiting somewhere close, planning to steal her back from the police? He'd sent no word, no message.

Apparently the whiskey trade was dead, at least here in Canada. Would he have gone farther north, to the land of the Cree and out of range of the police? Which direction should she go?

Pulling the buffalo robe from over her face, she blinked against the snowflakes that fell out of the darkness to sacrifice themselves against her warm cheeks. Welcoming the cool air, she endured the attack for a few moments, then pulled the fur over her face again.

Perhaps she could go down into the Sweet Grass Hills and look up some of Pa's friends. Maybe he was there—if he was still making whiskey.

Angrily, she fought back quick tears.

She'd been a burden to him. That was it. Only a burden to be endured. Since her mother's death, she'd been a stone around his ankle, dragging him back.

Self-pity swallowed her, and hot tears streamed down her face, making the temperature inside the hide unbearable. She yanked back the fur again to endure the snow.

The mare snorted and rumbled deep in her chest, as if sensing Maggie's grief, and Maggie wished she were closer and could reach out and touch a warm hock and feel a soft nose nuzzling against her neck. She'd affectionately named the mare Belle. She'd named all the mules, too, and Pa had laughed and said not to waste good names on dumb animals. But he didn't know how many nights she'd fallen asleep in the wagon, waiting to meet another trader, comforted only by the closeness of the team and their soft horse noises.

Her path suddenly became vividly clear.

So much so that she sat up in bed and let the buffalo robes fall to her waist. She'd go back to Fort McLeod and wait for her father. Surely, soon he'd come to claim her. But she'd not go back empty-handed. She had nothing to trade, but she knew Painted Ax did. The police needed horses. The mounts they'd ridden across Canada had not recovered from their hard trip and were being sent south to spend the winter in protected coulees where forage was plentiful.

Trading was something she was good at. That and tending horses. She'd march right back through the same gates she'd slunk out of and announce that she could help them solve their horse problems. In return, they'd allow her to stay in the fort and help the veterinarian surgeon—just until her father came for her, of course.

Smiling to herself, Maggie lay back down and yanked the rough fur over her head and face. Closing her eyes, she summoned again the sensation of Colin's lips moving over hers, his hands trembling as they gripped her shoulders, the urgency in his kiss. She sighed and wondered if she'd ever feel those things again.

"Crowfoot's comin'."

Snow swept in through the mess-hall door flung open by young Constable Jackson.

"I beg your pardon?" James McLeod said from the head of the long plank table.

"Crowfoot's comin'. He's at the gate now." The young man's chest heaved beneath his uniform coat.

Slowly, McLeod dabbed at his mustache with a napkin and stood. "Open the gates," he said matter-of-factly, then stepped over the bench seat.

The young man disappeared in the patter of running footsteps. "I'd like everyone assembled on the parade grounds as soon as possible. Treat this as an inspection.'' Then he strode out the door. Stunned, the men stared at the door for a moment before benches scraped backward and men scurried out the door.

Crowfoot was the powerful head of the Blackfoot Confederacy, an organization that comprised three major tribes: the Blackfoot, the Blood, and the Peigan. Minor chiefs had answered McLeod's summons several days ago, expressing their pleasure over the presence of the police and their relief that firewater would be sold no more to their people. But no one had expected the great Ogemah of the Blackfoot tribe to visit. His word was law among the three tribes, his power indisputable. An alliance with him would secure peace in most of western Canada, and the Northwest Mounted Police would have struck the killing blow to lawlessness and illegal liquor.

Colin followed the crowd out the door, pulling at his jacket and gloves as he hurried to fall into formation. A cold wind whipped around his shoulders and teased the too-long hair over his ears.

The cottonwood log gates groaned, then opened slowly. A lone man stepped through. He wore a plain buckskin shirt and leggings. A blanket hung in folds around his shoulders and dangled to touch beaded moccasins. In one hand he carried an eagle's wing— a symbol of his position as ruler of his people.

With confident steps, he strode into the midst of the white men, his eyes darting quickly from side to side, not in fear but scanning intelligently, taking in all displayed for his benefit. And for an instant all held their breath. Hastily erected banners fluttered in the cold breeze. No one made a sound. Not even a cough broke the silence. Then McLeod stepped forward, resplendent in his red jacket and glengarry cap. This moment would change the course of life in his beloved Canada. The peace and well-being of all hung on what would occur in the next few seconds.

Chapter Ten

The two men stopped face-to-face. Crowfoot, long, dark hair hanging below his shoulders, looked McLeod in the eye, then turned to glance at the assembled men, as if assessing the commander by the look of his men. A shiver ran up Colin's spine as he stood on the front row, just feet from the most feared Indian in the Northwest Territories.

McLeod motioned in the direction of his quarters, and Crowfoot followed, still glancing around the fort. McLeod opened the door, and Crowfoot leaned forward to peer inside and looked up at the bull buffalo head hung over the door.

"Stamis Otokan," Crowfoot said, pointing at the head and then to McLeod's hat, which bore the crest of the McLeod clan. Then the two went inside and closed the door.

The fort heaved a unified sigh. Except for a small detail that lingered not far from McLeod's door, the men scattered back to unfinished tasks. Colin had turned to go when he caught a movement near the fort gates. Nerves still on edge, he whirled. Maggie sauntered through the gate, leading a bay mare.

Fighting the urge to sweep her into his arms, kiss her senseless, then strangle her, Colin walked toward her, careful to keep his gait unhurried and nonchalant.

She stopped in front of him, arrogance rolling off her in waves. "I come back to offer you a deal," she said without preamble or explanation.

Demands for explanations sprang to the tip of his tongue, but he fought down the urge and decided to let her lead the game. "A deal?" he said, and laughed, hoping she didn't see him glancing over her, assessing her fitness. Her eyes were rimmed with faint circles, and her face was a little gaunt. He quickly sorted through his images of her, comparing her now with the Maggie that had emerged from the grasp of typhoid. Yes, she looked well. Tired but well.

"You need horses. I know where to get 'em."

Only his Maggie, daughter of the most notorious whiskey trader in all of western Canada, would range the Canadian wilderness alone, then return and offer to make the Northwest Mounted Police a deal.

A deal for horses she did not have and probably intended to steal.

But they did need horses, and badly. McLeod had sent thirteen men and fourteen horses to spend the winter at Fort Kipp. Another seventy-seven had been sent south with Subinspector Walsh. They needed native horses, strong animals accustomed to the harsh winters and adept at pawing through snow for dried grass.

But the number of horses was the last thing on his mind as he gazed down at her. She had some kind of gumption, this bit of a woman with blue eyes and a forked tongue. Nothing seemed to daunt her.

Not typhoid.

Not the wilderness.

Not the Mounted Police.

And that was the Maggie Hayes he was in love with.

Cold realization settled on him, and he realized that all the arguments he'd staged with himself were for naught. She'd slowly worked her way past his grief and into his heart with the same persistence she used in everything else.

Her lips were rough and cracked from the cold, but he imagined them pressed against his cheek, his temple, his mouth. They were from different lives, separate worlds, the two of them. He had learned to shape life to his own needs; she had learned to take what life tossed her and make the best of it. How would they ever find common ground?

"You interested?"

"What?"

She cocked her head to the side and squinted one eye. "I said are you interested?"

"Yes, I'm interested."

"Well, let's get down to the hagglin' then."

She sashayed away in front of him and headed for his quarters, completely oblivious to the looks and guffaws drifting their way. Feeling like a complete fool, Colin strode behind her, mustering as much dignity as the situation allowed him.

She looped the mare's reins around a post and stepped up on the porch. Without waiting for him, she pushed open the door and stepped inside.

"Where did you go, Maggie?" Colin stepped in behind her and closed the door, abandoning his moments-old promise to let her explain in her own good time. All right, so she'd won this round.

She turned, the bravado gone from her eyes and a tiny slip of the woman beneath showing through. "I went lookin' fer my Pa."

"Did you find him?"

She glanced down at the floor. "No. I don't know where he is."

With a thousand voices screaming no, Colin stepped forward and tilted her chin until she looked into his eyes. "I was worried about you."

She blinked but made no move to pull away. "I didn't think—" She cut off the words and glanced to the side. "I thought he mighta gone back to the camp."

"But he hadn't."

She shook her head.

Colin trailed his finger to the hollow at the base of her neck where her pulse jumped softly. She raised her head and met his eyes squarely. The effect was jarring.

He traced the high points of her collarbone until his finger slipped beneath the fabric of the ragged white shirt she wore crammed into the waistband of his only pair of spare pants.

"You're wearing my clothes."

"They were all I could find, and I couldn't run away naked."

"No, you couldn't do that." Unwaveringly drawn to her, he stepped closer and lowered his head.

"I had to try and find Pa."

"Yes, you did."

"He coulda been hurt someplace."

"Yes, he coulda."

"Colin?" She looked up, her eyes large and moist, her lips only a breath away.

"Huh?"

"Are you gonna kiss me again?"

"Uh-huh." His lips touched hers, and her response was immediate. Warmth was all his addled mind could think as her mouth responded to his. She molded her body against him, her arms encircling him, pinning his arms to his sides. Vaguely aware he had lost control of the situation, Colin ignored the cautious voices and heeded instead the aged ones that stirred him.

No polite pecks for Maggie Hayes, he realized as she kissed passionately and without restraint, as wild and free as the prairie that had reared her, hinting at the untapped depth of passion within her.

Colin fought to keep his own emotions in check, to remind himself that she was an innocent with no idea what reaction her touch and kiss could produce. And yet somehow he felt she did know, that she heard the same gentle, wise voices as he instructing the body in the ways of procreation.

Her hands, gentle and strong, kneaded his back through the rough fabric of his jacket, bunching muscle and skin, lulling and exciting. He caught her to him, pressed her against him, the urge to have her even closer overriding every other thought.

He'd already thrown caution to the wind, abandoned every last shred of his grief and reticence in exchange for this wonderful liquid happiness flowing through his veins. The woman in his arms represented life and light and love—a multitude of pleasures—and he wanted them all.

His hands roamed over her back, returning again and again to trace the narrowness of her waist, the flare of her hips, the breadth of her shoulders. Some ancient voice urged him darkly to examine more intimate parts of her, to pull aside the serge and cotton between them and explore the softness of skin.

Colin caught her forearms and gently moved her back, breaking the embrace.

"What's wrong?" she asked, her eyes huge globes of sky quivering with tears.

"We can't do this."

"Do what?"

"What we were both thinking."

She tilted her head at an angle that said a closer examination of this issue was at hand. "What were *you* thinking?"

Colin felt embarrassment begin to roast the tips of his ears. Why had he not learned that if he dropped Maggie a crumb of information, she then wanted the whole loaf of bread? No medical-school exam had been as hard as the next few minutes were likely to be. He sorted through a dozen explanations, each one more absurd than the last, then abandoned them all in favor of the truth.

"I was thinking that I'd like to make love to you."

Her mouth formed a perfect *O*, fitting accompaniment for the shape of her eyes. "But we're not married."

"I know. That's why I pushed you away."

She twisted her mouth in a way that pursed her lips and made his knees go weak. "But you said that ifen two people ain't married, then they can't make love."

"I said they shouldn't, not that they can't."

"Shouldn't sure does get in the way of a lot of things, don't it?"

Colin nodded, already knowing that he was a condemned man, consigned to forever need Maggie Hayes in his arms. Turning away from her, he took off his jacket and draped it over a chair. After raking a hand through his hair, he propped his palm against the wall and wondered what he was going to do from this point forward.

She ducked under his arm and turned to face him. "Colin, what do you reckon it feels like?" she asked in a half-whisper.

"What what feels like?"

"Makin' love," she whispered, as if it were a secret between them.

Colin threw his head back and stared at the ceiling. "I would imagine that it's wonderful."

He could imagine her frown even before he looked down into her face. Nope, she wasn't through with this.

"No, I mean what it *really* feels like."

"We shouldn't be talking about this, Maggie."

"Why not? You're the one who said you were thinkin' 'bout doin' it."

Her face was so open, so expectant. She was trusting him to explain the mystery of life to her.

They knew so little about each other. Their entire acquaintance was based on a kiss, a bout with typhoid, and another kiss. He knew nothing about what she thought or wanted or dreamed. And she knew nothing about the deep, dark side of a man's soul or how she had lifted him free of that abyss.

How little any of that really matters, he thought as he watched her face. "Well, I could give you a medical explanation."

She shook her head. "I know *how* it's done, leastways with dogs and horses. I ain't stupid. I got eyes. I want to know how it feels to be that close to somebody." She fisted her hands and held them drawn up in front of her.

Her hunger reached across the space between them and intensified his own. *Indeed, how would it feel to give yourself over to someone with no barriers, no pretensions?* "I would imagine that making love is like taking another person into yourself, your thoughts being their thoughts, their pains yours, their happiness making you happy. I think that person becomes a part of you, and you them.''

The expected frown never materialized. Nor did the next question.

"And you wanted to feel that way about me?" Her voice was a soft, incredulous whisper that coiled tightly around his heart.

His next answer would change the direction of his life as surely as Crowfoot's sudden appearance this afternoon had changed the course of history. And as absurd as their situation might be, Colin knew beyond doubt that Maggie Hayes was the only woman he ever wanted to feel that way about again.

"Yes."

She stared at him a moment, and part of him braced for the next surprise. "Me, too," she said quietly.

His first impulse was to take her to the narrow cot and teach her everything she was burning to know. Instead, he put the width of the room between them by moving to the window, where a stream of cold air leaked in around the sadly warped frame.

Maggie watched the muscles of his back flex as he stood gazing out through the glass, arms crossed over his chest. He was angry. She could tell by the stiffness of his stance and the silence that was growing by the second. Sensing his anger was directed at her, she wondered what she'd done. She'd asked him a simple question. He'd answered it truthfully, and she'd replied just as honestly. The words had seemed so right, so true. But now she wondered if this was another part of loving she didn't understand.

And she did love him. That fact she knew absolutely to be true. From the first moment she'd seen him, she'd known deep within her that he was the only man she'd ever want. And the weeks she'd spent away from him had only reinforced that belief.

But his world was a mystery to her. He knew about medicine and healing, and he'd been to school, something she both admired and feared. He'd traveled across the ocean. And he'd been in love before. Yet she felt this intimate connection between them, as if each needed something only the other could provide.

She moved toward him, stopped facing his back, then put her hands on his shoulders, marveling at how comfortable she felt touching him. But his body tensed beneath her fingers.

"Did I do somethin' wrong?" she asked.

"No," he replied, and turned around to face her. One corner of his mouth tipped up in an attempt to smile, but the emotion never reached his eyes. "It's just that things are not always as simple as they seem."

She thought over the last few words of their conversation. Things seemed pretty simple to her. "What do you mean?"

"I mean that we're worlds apart, you and I."

So, he felt the differences between them, too. He thought she wouldn't fit into his world, that she was too simple, too ignorant. He hadn't described the woman he'd been in love with, but Maggie imagined her a sophisticated woman, with cultured ways and beautiful clothes. Like the women down in Benton who wore the lovely straw hats with sky-blue ribbons and walked down the street in their elegant dresses.

And the feeling of intimacy between them evaporated.

Maggie moved back a step. "There's more to the deal than just the horses."

He stared at her a moment. "Go on."

"In return for the horses, I want to work with the horse doctor. Stay here at the fort and help him doctor the horses you keep. Looks to me like he needs all the help he can get." She kept her voice and her gaze level. "And I ain't got no place else to go. Leastways right now."

The courage that admission must have taken. "Maggie." Colin stepped forward, a surge of protectiveness sweeping over him, but she backed away, making it clear she wanted no comforting.

"I'll have to speak to Assistant McLeod about this."

"Go ahead and talk to him." She yanked a chair out from underneath his desk. "I got all the time in the world." She straddled the seat and plopped down.

The hard-nosed Maggie Hayes was back, and Colin regretted seeing the other Maggie slip back into hiding. He'd hurt her. He could see it in her eyes. She didn't understand his withdrawal, and neither did he. Here they were, two fools awash in doubt.

She couldn't know the heights to which she tempted him, the thoughts that rioted through his mind when he was within her touch. This wonderful creature that survived by wit and instinct was offering him unconditional love, and he didn't have the good sense to reach out and take it.

"I'll talk to McLeod tonight, but I'm sure he'll agree to all you ask. In the meantime, I'll take you to Dr. Poett's office. He'll welcome the help."

Without meeting his eyes, she stood and proceeded him out the door. She unwrapped her mare's reins and followed Colin to the stables.

"John?" Colin called in the darkness of the stable, only the open door for light.

"Yes?" a voice answered from the other end of the structure. A circle of yellow light grew until it silhouetted a slight man holding a lantern aloft.

"John, this is Maggie Hayes. She lives in the area and knows a great deal about horses. She's offered to help with the sick animals. And she'd like to stay in the tack room."

Poett walked closer, stopped, and looked from Colin to Maggie as if they'd both lost their minds. "Is this the young lady that was brought in with typhoid a few weeks ago?"

"Yes. This is Maggie Hayes."

Maggie smiled a tight-lipped smile and nodded.

"I see," Poett said. "Well, the tack room is crowded, but with a little rearranging—"

"I ain't particular. I've done with worse." She pivoted and walked to the room where rows of pegs held saddles, bridles, and blankets.

"What does McLeod have to say about this?" Poett whispered as Maggie stepped into the room and out of sight.

"Actually, this was his suggestion."

"Oh?"

"When will you know about the rest of our deal?" Maggie asked, reappearing from the tiny room.

"Tonight. Maybe tomorrow."

"Good." Brushing past him, she lead the little mare into an empty stall and unsaddled her. Then she gathered her own saddle and bridle and dumped it unceremoniously onto the floor.

"Maggie. There's other places you could stay. More comfortable."

"No." She said, turning. "I don't want no special treatment. I'm here to do a job, not be in the way."

"I wasn't going to offer you special treatment, just better lodgings."

"Where? Your bed?"

Stunned, Colin stared at her and heard John discreetly walk away to the depths of the barn.

"I was going to offer to move over to the hospital and let you have my bed, yes."

Maggie shook her head. "I said I don't want no special treatment. I ain't like other girls. I don't need a soft bed and fine sheets before I can close my eyes. I just want a roof over my head and a warm blanket, and I got all that here."

"You deserve better."

She moved a step closer and narrowed her eyes. "Why? Just 'cause I'm a woman?"

"Well, no . . . I . . ." He stopped and collected his thoughts. "You can stay wherever you wish."

"That's what's scarin' you, ain't it, Colin Fraser?

The fact that I'm a woman and that I can drive a team and ride as good as any man here. You're afraid I just might be tougher than you.''

He turned to go, angry and heartsick at the insecurity that echoed behind her bold words. How could she not know how wonderful she was, how strong and inspiring? What kind of doubt had robbed that knowledge from her? And what kind of man was he to feel such passion for a woman, then doubt whether or not she would fit into the life he envisioned for himself?

He had reached the door when his temper boiled over—both at himself and at Maggie. "No, Maggie," he said, turning. "What scares me is that you think you have to be.''

Chapter Eleven

The pungent odor of horse permeated Maggie's clothes, her hair, and everything she owned. She breathed deeply of the beloved odor and marveled at how happy she was in the leaky, drafty stable.

The big black swung his head around and nudged her with his wide nose.

"Stop it," she said with a playful swat to his shoulder, and repositioned her feet so that his foreleg was firmly across her thigh. Bending his hoof up, she poked at the tender pink frog of his foot and rubbed her thumb across a purple bruise. He grunted and pulled against her.

"I know it hurts, boy," she cooed, smoothing a hand down his matted, rough coat.

Winter and the cross-continent march had been hard on the horses, and many of their injuries from the summer and fall had not healed. Inadequate hay had added to their problems.

Again adjusting the injured foot, Maggie dipped a hand into a bowl of slick, foul-smelling ointment and lathered it onto the bruise. Flaring his nostrils, the black hooked his neck around and gave the concoction a reluctant sniff.

"I know it stinks, but Pa always used this on our horses, and they healed just fine. You'll feel better soon."

The horse answered with a soft whoosh of breath and a grunt. Maggie lowered the hoof to the ground and straightened, working a kink out of the small of her back. The soft plop of snow was audible even on the sod roof. Snow had fallen for days, an abrupt change from the warm weather the Chinook had blown in a few days before. At least it was snow and not rain. Rain brought sluicing mud that oozed out of the sod roofs, pouring down like gray curtains of misery on all unlucky enough to stand beneath it.

Lifting the lantern off its wooden peg, Maggie closed the door of the stall behind her and set off toward her tiny corner in the tack room. The barn had no windows, and an oil-burning lantern provided the only light available even during the day. But the coziness of the barn suited her, and the horses were gentle listeners that neither judged nor commented. Trips outside were reserved for washing up in freezing water poured into a tin pan or dinner in the mess hall with the men of the fort.

She hung the lantern on a nail driven into a sturdy

cottonwood timber, and light flooded her small compartment, made from a converted stall. The tack room had proved too crowded, and the constant smell of leather and sweat had become cloying deep in the night. Yellow prairie grass littered the floor and lay in a heaped pile for a bed with a blanket spread over it.

Colin was a constant visitor, trying to convince her to move into his quarters while he moved to the hospital. Or to the storeroom. Or to some of the lodging offered by the merchants now firmly entrenched outside the fort gates. Every time their eyes met, she saw guilt in his blue gaze, guilt over his part in her present predicament. She couldn't make him understand she assigned him no blame. He was doing his job, just as the U.S. Cavalrymen that had chased her over hills and through coulees had been doing theirs. She held nothing against him. Except the fact that he would not let her love him or hold him or caress away that persistent frown that rumpled his brow. He was a man used to setting everything to rights, a man who left no loose ends dangling. Ever. And she was a loose end.

Maggie closed the door and savored the dim light and quiet for a moment. She was at home here among the beasts she loved, more so than she would be with strangers. The smell of horses and hay was familiar and comforting. In all other places she felt inadequate and stupid. Even eating meals among the men of the post. There was so much about so simple a task she did not know. Which side of the plate the fork was placed. How to juggle a plate and still lift a slice of beef from it without sliding its entire contents into someone's lap.

She peeled off her shirt and replaced it with one she'd hung carefully on a nail. This was her dining shirt, her only other one that didn't smell like the stables. She gave a cursory sniff to the leg of her pants, wrinkled her nose, and decided it would have to do. After all, this was her only pair of pants, a gift from Colin so that he might have his spare pair back.

She left the barn and waded through ankle-deep snow, the sharp wind cutting through her clothes. The lights of the dining hall glared brightly, reflected against the snow in yellow squares. Over the roof of the long building, the evening sky was a deep purple laced with ribbons of magenta, and for a moment she longed for the open prairie and the caress of the wind against her skin. She stopped and closed her eyes, concentrating on the soft kiss of a snowflake on her cheek.

Lilting laughter cut into her thoughts, and she opened her eyes. A woman stood on the porch of the dining hall, her dark hair swept up in soft swirls, a bright yellow dress belling out around her, accenting a tiny waist. Colin leaned against a post of the porch, his arms crossed over his chest, his scarlet jacket pulled smoothly over his hips. His velvet-rough voice tumbled across the space between them and held the attention of the beautiful woman on the porch. She laughed, her voice like the tinkle of a bell. Colin leaned forward and laughed, too, his deep chuckle creating perfect harmony.

Maggie stopped and stared. What a beautiful couple they made. She wondered if his lost love had looked this way. Beautiful. Fragile. Feminine.

Everything Maggie was not.

Suddenly seized with insecurity, she turned to head back to the barn. She'd sneak back to the kitchen later. Alton, the cook, would have saved leftovers for late diners and midnight wanderers.

"Maggie!"

She recognized Colin's voice but was tempted to keep walking and pretend she didn't hear.

"Maggie!"

With a sigh, she turned.

"Come and meet Abigail."

Abigail. Maggie snuffed her indignation to no one but herself and reluctantly plodded toward the porch.

"Maggie Hayes, this is Abigail Baker, recently arrived from Ottawa."

The beautiful Abigail smiled at her and held out a slim white hand. "I'm so pleased to meet you." A note of excitement quivered in her voice. "I'm told you are a true frontier woman. Those of us confined in the east can only dream of the sights and sounds you must experience here in the wilderness. That's why I came when my uncle invited me."

"Winter ain't no time to travel." The words came out gruff, almost growled, and Maggie felt her cheeks redden.

"Indeed, it was a cold, hard trip from Benton to

here," Abigail continued, undaunted. "The train ride was most satisfactory, however."

"You rode on a train?" Curiosity overcame Maggie's jealousy. She'd heard of the great iron horse, taller by far than any man and more powerful than a team of horses. Talk said it could traverse the prairies even in a blizzard and soon the entire country would be crossed by the iron rails it rode upon.

"Oh, yes. It was wonderful. All that power just plunging ahead. We saw buffalo, huge, shaggy beasts. I wonder if their fur is as soft as it looks."

"It ain't soft, but it's warm. If you can get used to the smell. They piss on their back legs, you know."

Maggie wished with everything she was that she could bite back those words the moment they left her lips. Abigail's face blanched, and Maggie heard laughter from inside the dining hall.

Colin's lips tightened into a line. Fueled by jealousy, Maggie enjoyed the slight surprise that registered in Abigail's eyes.

"Your father was a whiskey trader, I understand? Oh, how exciting." Abigail clapped her hands together, undaunted, and Maggie wondered how she maintained such levels of enthusiasm.

Maggie glanced at Colin. He was watching her, his dark blue eyes shooting sparks of reprimand. Something inside her was pleased that she was able to ruffle him this way.

"The newspapers at home were absolutely filled with stories of whiskey traders. What a dangerous life you must have led. Were you ever afraid?"

"A body'd be a fool not to be afraid. Especially when the U.S. Cavalry's on yer heels."

She could feel Colin's look of disapproval raking over her, but she was guiltily enjoying these few moments of notoriety.

"What do you think of the new name for our mounted police?"

"What new name?"

Abigail put her hands together beneath her chin. "Mounties. The eastern papers have become quite taken with the name."

"Sounds like a sissy name to me," Maggie said with a shrug.

"It's time to go inside," Colin said, taking Abigail's elbow and throwing Maggie a searing look that said, *Stop it.*

Oil lanterns hung over the long tables that spanned the length of the mess hall, their wicks softly glowing balls of fire encased in sparkling glass houses. The dim light softened the edges of rough logs and weary men. Plain dinnerware sparkled like fine china, and the sheets that covered the tables could pass as linen tablecloths.

Abigail smiled and graciously accepted words of welcome from the men of the post. She flirted outrageously, casting coy glances and feigning shyness. Maggie shoved her hands into her pockets and slipped to the other end of the room, moving in the shadows. She sat in her usual place, a chair near the second door. Two young constables, hardly more than boys, were her customary dinner companions, each one gratefully too shy to speak. But tonight their eyes, too, were trained on the other end of the room and the woman in the yellow dress.

Dinner was served and finished without so much as a glance from Colin. He seemed completely absorbed in Abigail Baker. Maggie ate little, unable to keep her eyes off the couple—Colin's hand touching Abigail's wrist, the attentive look on his face when she spoke.

When her stomach would tolerate no more tasteless food, Maggie quietly pushed back her chair and slipped out the door. A full moon peeped out from behind a cloud, bathing the deserted parade ground in silvery light. The snowfall had stopped, and now a new mantle of white covered wagons and fence posts without prejudice or favor. The night was quiet. Maggie closed her eyes and imagined she could hear the music of the stars, as she'd often done as a child. Then she opened her eyes, stared into a star-encrusted heaven, and wondered if there was anyone beneath this velvety night canopy that loved her.

Laughter came from the mess hall, and Maggie hurried away, kicking tufts of snow before her, eager to retreat to the dark recesses of her room, where she neither answered to nor envied anyone.

Soft horse noises greeted her as she opened the door and slid into the darkness. Somewhere at the back of the barn hay rustled, and the sound of chewing echoed loudly. The scurry of tiny rodent feet told her that the midnight grain patrol was on duty. She opened the door to the small stove and tossed in another stick of wood, then rubbed her hands before the flames, eager for the feeble warmth. When she'd insisted on moving out of the tack room, Colin had built an enclosure around the stall, and soon the room was toasty warm from the tiny stove.

She crawled into her hay bed and drew up her knees. Sleep came quickly on the wings of warmth and a full stomach. Her eyelids drooped, and wandering thoughts became soft and fuzzy.

Then, suddenly, she was wide awake. Senses alert, she listened for what had disturbed her. Horses still ate their hay. Mice still scavenged for food with faint squeaks and the scrape of tiny nails. All seemed right, yet the hair on the back of her neck stood at attention. With a faint rustle, Maggie reached down for her rifle, safely tucked beneath the hay. The cold metal slipped easily into her hand, and she felt better when her fingers closed around the stock.

"Maggie?" a slightly familiar male voice whispered through her door.

"Who is it?" she asked, swinging her legs over the side of the bed and tightening her grip on her rifle.

"Maggie, girl?"

"Able?"

"Yep, it's me."

Maggie lowered her rifle and opened the door to her room. Able Lent stood before her, one of her father's favorite partners in crime. He was hunched against the cold, an old ragged coat pulled around him, fastened over an expanding belly with the one remaining button.

"What are you doing here?" Maggie asked, suddenly seized with the disgusting urge to hug him.

"I come to find you. I promised yer pa."

Maggie's heart soared, and she clutched his coat sleeve. "You've seen Pa? Where is he? Is he well?"

"Easy, girl. Best we step inside." He stepped into her room and closed the door behind them both. "Yer pa's fine. Him and me and a few others got us an operation way north of here, out of reach of these damned red-coated devils. They got the Blackfeet so's they won't even drink no firewater no more. But the Cree, now they ain't so righteous, not yet at least, and it's like old times." Able grinned a toothless grin.

"Is he comin' fer me?" Half of her quivered in anticipation of the answer, and half of her quaked in fear.

A strange expression crossed Able's face; then his eyes returned to their customary shifty expression. "Not yet. Soon." He glanced around the small room and the piled hay bed. "Ye ain't advanced much, have ye, girl?"

"I got me a job. I work with the veterinary surgeon."

"With the what?"

"Horse doctor."

"Oh."

"He needed help and I . . . well . . . I didn't have noplace else to go."

Able looked uncomfortable for a moment, then looked at her from underneath bushy eyebrows. "We're fixin' to remedy that. Yer pa and me, we made arrangements for a shipment of prime whiskey from

Montana. Them boys got themselves a big operation just across the border. They can turn out more liquor in a month than your pa and me could even think about. And the Cree up north, well, they ain't got nothin' else to do in the winter." Able leaned closer. "We need you to drive one of the wagons."

Excitement sprang to life inside Maggie. Memories of breathless pursuits and near misses made her heart race, and the lure of freedom became almost irresistible.

"When?"

"Right after Christmas."

She glanced around the small room she called home. If she returned to her old life, fed the demon that hungered for risks and thrills, she could never come back here, never see Colin again.

"Yore one of the best, Maggie girl, and me and your pa need ya."

"Can I think about it?"

Able frowned. "What's there to think about? It'll be like old times. Don't you miss them times?"

Maggie sat down, the burden of responsibility suddenly too heavy to carry. "I don't know, Able. Some days I do. And other days, I don't miss 'em so much. Seems like we was always runnin' and movin'."

Able inched closer and took her hands in his. "Course we was. Weren't nobody a-tellin' us what to do. We was free to go anyplace we wanted."

" 'Cept where the law was."

"Yeah," he conceded, " 'cept fer there. But we had all the Territories to gallivant around in."

As she listened and remembered, suddenly the old life didn't seem so wonderful, after all. "Let me think about it. I got my job here and all."

Able studied her for a moment; then his face softened. "Well, you give it some thought, girlie. Me and yore pa'll be in touch. You've done better fer yerself than ye think. This here's a decent place, Maggie, with decent folks, even if they is the law. Yore a woman now. Maybe you oughta be thinkin' about catchin' yoreself a husband, not followin' a bunch of old whiskey traders around. These here folks can teach you stuff yore pa and me ain't never even heared of."

Maggie crossed her arms over her chest. "I don't want no husband. I just don't know ifen I want to go back to haulin' whiskey."

"I best be gittin' along. Somebody'll come a-lookin' fer you sooner or later.

"Ain't nobody gonna come," she said.

"How 'bout that Mountie feller?"

"Who?"

"The one what healed you up."

Maggie shook her head. "He doctored me. That's all."

"You sure?" Able pinned her with a steady look.

"I'm sure."

"Well, yore pa said to wish you a merry Christmas."

"Does he miss me, Able?"

Able took her hand in his callused one. "Every day and every night, Tumblebug."

Maggie's eyes misted at the long-ago nickname, and

she felt her resolve to stay wavering back and forth across an invisible line.

"I gotta go, girlie. These here Mounties are still lookin' fer yore pa and me. Wouldn't do fer them to catch me here."

Able rose with a soft groan and shuffled to the door. He opened it a crack, and Maggie was seized with the impulse to grab him and pull him back, to have a tiny piece of her father with her. But she kept her hands by her sides and watched Able start to step through the door.

"Wait." Maggie grabbed his arm, the incongruity of the situation finally dawning on her. "How did you know where to find me?"

Able smiled softly and nodded toward the dark depths of the barn. Maggie stepped outside her room and looked down the corridor that separated the rows of stalls. Faint light helped distinguish stall bars from darkness, and there in the corridor, a figure leaned with shoulder against the wall. Maggie squinted and thought she could make out the outline of a uniform and see the faint glint of brass against dark red.

"Hurry, Able. Go out the front door," she whispered frantically, shoving Able toward the door. "I'll distract him."

Able caught her hands. "There ain't no distracting to be done. He brought me here." Able nodded toward the shadowy figure who now walked toward them. Clinging to Able's sleeve, Maggie drew herself up, mentally preparing responses in Able's defense.

Then Colin walked into the lamplight, a smile tilting the corners of his mouth. Anger borne of jealousy and fear seared at Maggie's thoughts and sharpened her tongue.

"You bastard." Her hand itched to slap his face, to make him hurt the way his betrayal was making her hurt. But he caught her wrist before her palm connected to his cheek. "You set a trap fer 'im."

"I brought him here for you," he said, his voice a deep, soft growl. "He wanted to know that you were all right."

"And then?"

"And then I was going to sneak him out of the fort."

"That's so, the way he says, Maggie," Able said.

"Sneak him out? And break your precious oath? Liar."

Colin's face hardened above her, and his blue eyes turned as cold as ice. His fingers around her wrist tightened, and she could feel the tension mounting in his body, now pressed against her. "Why are you so damned suspicious of everyone and everything?"

"Ain't I got a right to be? Ain't nobody but Pa ever told me the truth."

"When have I ever lied to you? When?" He shook her captured wrist.

"You lied 'bout bein' a whiskey trader."

"That was my job. I explained that. When else?"

She stared up into his face, searching frantically for an answer. But there was none. Bitter words waited on her tongue, but the truth was, he'd never been anything but honest with her. He'd never lied or led her down false paths. The realization only made her angrier.

"Now, Maggie girl. I don't hold nothin' agin him. He was doin' his job, all right, just like we wuz doin' ours. Me and yore Pa knowed the law'd catch up with us sooner or later. And maybe things is for the best, after all," Able said.

Maggie look at Able, puzzled at his words, but she didn't dare ask him their meaning now.

"Let me go." She swung her attention back to Colin.

"Not until you tell me, Maggie. When have I ever lied to you?"

She stared up into his angry face for a moment longer, part of her quelling at the depth of emotion mirrored there. "You ain't." She jerked her wrist free and rubbed at the skin where his fingers had touched. "Is that what you want to hear?"

His face softened, and his shoulders relaxed. "I wanted you to see Able because I thought it would make you happy. It's as simple as that. No hidden purposes. No planned ambush, as I'm sure you thought. Even I have a heart, Maggie."

Faced with his brutal honesty, Maggie's anger faded into guilt, leaving her with a dissatisfied lump in her stomach. She wanted to rail at him, to beat out her frustration and confusion against his broad chest. Her whole world had been jerked out from beneath her, and he thought she should just go on as if nothing had happened. Did no one understand?

"You can take that heart of yours and give it to *Miss* Abigail Baker for all I care." Embarrassment, deep and hot, filled her as the bitter words rolled off her tongue. She sounded like the whores that gamboled about and argued in the saloons in Benton, sniping at each other with poisoned words.

Amazement filled Colin's face for a moment; then the dark anger returned. "What?"

"There on the porch. You and *Miss* Baker. Her all . . . prettified and you drooling over her like a . . . like a . . . dog in heat!"

Colin's face froze, and she could see him tremble as he fought for control. Maggie swallowed and glanced at Able. To her surprise, he was grinning, apparently enjoying the show. Chafed by this last desertion of support, Maggie plunged ahead. "Is she the kind of woman you want? Soft and silly? Ain't worth a pound of salt in a snowstorm? Hell, all she can do is smile and serve tea and . . . faint." Maggie crossed her arms over her chest and waited.

Without a word, Colin turned on his heel and motioned to Able with a nod of his head. Together they walked into the darkness of the barn. She heard the back door open with a squeak, then close. Crunching footsteps soon died away, and she strained to hear an altercation at the front gate. But only the silence of the night filled her ears.

Drained by her anger, Maggie returned to her bed, snuggled into the depression she'd made before, and tried to sleep, but the expression on Colin's face haunted her. He'd been just as angry as she, deeply angry. And only now, as her fury faded into reason, did she wonder why.

Chapter Twelve

"Come with me."

A swoosh of cold air swept into the barn and the horses turned their heads toward the light. Colin stood in the doorway, his mouth set in a stubborn line, looking more angry than he'd been last night.

"I said come with me." He took one step forward and grapped her forearm.

A shiver of apprehension and excitement ran through her as his warm fingers closed around her arm. "I ain't. What the hell's the matter with you, anyway?"

Colin took the currying brush out of her hand, placed it on a nail keg, then yanked her toward the door. Then he threw his overcoat across her shoulders. "School's in session."

"What do you mean, school?" Maggie asked as he pulled her out into the dying light. She struggled to keep her feet under her as they waded through the snow toward his quarters.

"What are you doing? Have you gone plumb crazy, Colin? Let me go!"

He paid her no mind and ignored the curious stares and outright laughter that came from the men assembling for the evening meal.

"Permission to be absent from dinner?" Colin asked, stopping suddenly. Maggie ran into his back and stumbled backward a step until his grip stopped her. Peeping around him she saw the amused face of Assistant Commissioner McLeod.

"Granted, Constable Fraser," McLeod answered with a cocked eyebrow.

"He's gone crazy. Make him turn me a-loose," Maggie shouted, looking back over her shoulder, but McLeod smiled that small, controlled smile of his, clasped his hands behind his back, and watched Colin drag her away.

Maggie grasped Colin's arm with her other hand and hauled back against him, succeeding only in stumbling and plunging to her knees in the snow.

"Colin, stop."

He halted and pulled her to her feet.

"Let me go."

"No."

Maggie searched his face for some semblance of sanity. "Where are you takin' me?"

"To my quarters."

Maggie's eyes widened, and Colin's narrowed. "Don't flatter yourself, Maggie. My intent is not nearly so pleasurable as that would be."

Maggie caught her breath. Who had stolen away gentle, calm Colin Fraser during the night and replaced him with this oaf of a man?

"Why are you taking me there, then?"

Colin resumed walking, and Maggie hurried to keep up, chafing at the cold that seeped in through the wet knees of her pants. "I've had as much as a man can stand, Maggie, and I'll have no more of it."

"Of what?"

They'd reached the front porch of his quarters. He shoved open the door and pulled her in behind him. A warm fire crackled on the hearth, and the scent of biscuits drifted up from a cast-iron pot nestled in the ashes, contrasting with the ever-present scent of chloroform.

In the room beyond, his blanket and sheet lay on the floor, piled in a tousled heap, evidence of a restless night. The door shut with a bang, and he released her hand. Maggie moved away from him, stopping when her back touched the shelf that held stoppered bottles of medicines and instruments.

He ran both hands through his hair, teasing it to stand on end in soft waves. Hands on hips, he paced to the fireplace, stared at the flames, then wrenched his coat off and tossed it over a chair back. He braced both hands on the mantel, leaned forward, and stared at the hearth. All the while, Maggie waited.

"You're not living in that damn barn another hour."

"But—"

"No buts."

Maggie raised her chin. No one told her what to do. Least of all Constable Fraser. She opened her mouth to retort.

"And you're not going to say a word until I'm finished. Is that clear?" Firelight caught faint strands of red in his hair, and one curl drifted down to kiss his temple.

Maggie snapped her jaw shut and nodded. Something about Colin Fraser angry rippled through her in a way she liked.

He took a deep breath and held it a moment before exhaling and pushing away the errant curl. "You're going to catch your death of cold in that barn. So, as of right now, you live here. Understood?"

"Where are you going to sleep?" Maggie glanced at the cot, fighting down the images that floated across her vision.

"Dr. Kittson has agreed to let me stay at the hospital."

"But—"

"I said no buts."

Maggie thought to argue further but nodded instead. There was always time later to wiggle out of anything she agreed to now.

"Take off your clothes."

She clutched the neck of his coat and wondered if he'd truly taken leave of his senses.

"In there, of course," he finished with a scowl, and pointed to his bedroom; the curtain still hung on the rope above. "There's a tub of water waiting for you."

She glanced toward the room again and found that, indeed, a large tin tub sat in a corner by the window, thin tendrils of steam rising from the surface of the water.

"You want me to take an all-over bath? In the winter? I'll die of pnewmonie."

"It's pronounced pneumonia, and you won't get it from taking a bath."

"Yes, I will."

"No, you won't."

Maggie glanced again at the tub. She'd never had an all-over *warm* bath. Just a little washing occasionally with water she heated in the kettle. Summer baths were taken in rivers and ponds. The thought of immersing herself in warm water was inviting, she'd have to admit. But should she let him win this round, sell her soul for a warm bath?

The set of his mouth told her he'd stand for no argument this time, and she chewed on her lip trying to decide just how far she could push him.

"If you don't get in, I'll strip you and put you in myself."

Well, that settled the issue. She knew he'd do that.

"All right."

"Then put on the dress there on the bed."

The blue calico dress he'd bought for her lay folded

in a neat square at the foot of his bed. She shuffled toward the room, pulled the curtain behind her, and sat down on the cot. The scent of him surrounded her, part medicinal, part male. Memories stirred to life, memories of sensations and thoughts she'd tried to put aside. Here she'd lain at his mercy. Here he'd leaned over her, cleaned her, fed her. Here, even before she was conscious, she'd learned to love the man that saved her life in so many ways.

Her wrath died, and curiosity took its place. What was he up to? Some elaborate seduction? She lifted the dress out of its protective paper and remembered the day he'd given it to her, hope and expectation in his eyes.

She shucked her dirty clothes and shivered when the cool air struck her bare skin. Dipping in a toe, she tested the temperature of the water. Then she stepped into the tub and crouched down, sucking in her breath as the water slipped up around her, warming her, encasing her in pure bliss. Hands around her ankles, she was content to crouch there and enjoy the sensation until his voice broke into her enjoyment.

"There's soap there on a dish," he called through the curtain.

She lifted the square of soap from a cracked saucer and held it to her nose. It smelled faintly of sun-baked roses, like the ones she remembered from her mother's garden. As she rubbed the bar between her hands, the scent grew stronger. She smoothed the lather down her arm, expecting the stinging that usually accompanied lye soap. But this soap went on as smooth as her mother's best salve, sinfully soft.

She ducked her head underneath the water, then lathered her hair with the soap. Outside the curtain, Colin rattled pots and pans, whistling an off-key tune. She stifled a giggle, slid down until the water covered her shoulders, and wondered what he had in mind next. She closed her eyes and remembered their last kiss with a flush that could not be blamed on the cooling water.

She found a length of toweling by the side of the tub, then stepped out and dried herself off. The dress slid over her head as easily as she remembered, but the new garment lying beside the dress baffled her. Of soft white fabric edged in a tiny lace, the garment resembled men's drawers except for the gaping hole between the legs. She supposed she should put it on, but where?

"What's this thing?" Maggie shoved aside the curtain and held up the garment.

Colin stared at her, dropped a plate, then caught it before it hit the floor. Obviously ruffled, he placed the plate on the table, then turned toward her slowly. "It's a lady's undergarment called drawers."

"Drawers? Like men's drawers?"

"Sort of."

She examined the garment again, shoving her hand through the gaping hole between what was now clearly the legs. "Well, somebody cain't sew. They left a whole seam loose."

Colin's eyes darted from her face to her hand as

color climbed up his cheeks. "It's supposed to be that way."

"Why?" Maggie examined the garment again and, for the life of her, could see no reason for the open seam.

"It's so you can—" Colin's hands waved in the air, and his eyebrows wiggled up and down. Obviously, he was trying to tell her something, but she'd be damned if she could figure it out.

"So I can what?"

He stopped gesturing and sighed. "Relieve yourself."

"Do what?"

"Pee."

She stared at her hand, thrust between the white fabric legs. "Oh." She glanced back at him, now red from his neck to his ears—an endearing shade of pink that made her want to follow that path with a trail of kisses. "That's pretty smart, huh."

"Yes," he nodded, "smart." Then he turned away, walked out the door, and closed it behind him.

Outside, a full moon dusted the snow with diamonds, winter's gift to those weary of her. Colin breathed deeply, inhaling the cold air as deeply within him as he could. Why did dealing with Maggie always leave him embarrassed and her with a new arsenal of ammunition to use against him? She treated delicate subjects with the same thirst for knowledge as she did everyday conversation. She knew no bounds of propriety, no taboos, no subjects to be discussed only behind closed doors and never in public. Maggie Hayes only knew that she wanted to know more.

Colin turned to put his back against the porch railing and watched her through the window. She turned the garment front to back, inside to out, examining every seam and stitch. Then she held the garment up at her waist and shook her head as if in amazement.

Raised in a household with no sisters, women's undergarments and other such subjects were never, ever discussed. The only knowledge he had, he'd learned in medical school, along with other information he quickly stored underneath the heading of "medical purposes only." How would he explain to her the things she would need to know to live in polite society? Especially when her store of knowledge of such things was so empty. Yesterday afternoon, when he'd been introduced to Abigail Baker, he'd seen her as an ally, someone he could enlist to help him explain to Maggie the things a young woman should know. Instead, his efforts at fostering a friendship between the two women had resulted in instant jealousy on Maggie's part.

He supposed he should be flattered, but instead, it hindered what he wanted most—to bring Maggie into his life. To help her learn to live among civilized people and feel at ease there.

To be happy living as a Mountie's wife.

He now knew this was the truth of his heart. She was the woman he wanted to bear his children and the woman he hoped would agree to follow him from posting to posting—the only woman he knew tough enough to do both fearlessly.

He was in love with Maggie Hayes, but if he asked her to marry him now, he knew she'd bolt, afraid of life away from her precious prairie, reluctant to give up her freedom. First, he had to prove to her she was the same Maggie Hayes inside *or* outside stockade walls.

Maggie eyed him distrustfully from across the table, then she looked down at the silverware, plate, and glass before her. Hands in her lap, she seemed uncertain where to start.

Colin ladled buffalo stew onto her plate, then returned the pot to the hook over the fire. He offered her a pan of biscuits warm from the oven, and she selected one with uncertain fingers. Placing the warm bread on her plate, she put her hands back in her lap and looked up at him with eyes so large and lost that his heart turned over.

Having already decided that instructing her on how to eat at a properly set table would only result in a yelling match, Colin elected instead to teach by example. He picked up a spoon and dipped up a portion of the stew. Maggie watched, then imitated what he did.

Colin began a one-sided conversation that represented six weeks' worth of gossip gleaned from fort discussions, anything to keep the awful silence from engulfing them again. While Colin talked, Maggie watched, ate, and occasionally nodded. When she tucked her napkin into the neck of her dress, he let the slip pass—for now. After all, she was wearing her new dress, and her new drawers, too, he supposed. She'd taken the undergarment, gone back into the bedroom, closed the curtain, then emerged later with a slight frown on her face. He supposed that after a lifetime spent in men's pants, open crotch drawers must take some adjustment.

After supper, Colin cleaned up while Maggie perched on a chair, hands in her lap, back straight, uncharacteristically quiet. Hardly the Maggie he knew and loved. He glanced around at her from the dishpan and found that she was nodding, weaving precariously with her eyes closed.

Colin smiled and wondered how long it had been since she'd eaten a hot meal and gone to a warm, soft bed.

"Stubborn brat," he muttered, drying his hands on a towel.

He scooped her into his arms, and she lolled her head onto his shoulder without waking. He carried her to his bed and laid her in it, dress and all. She turned over onto her side and sighed deeply. Fighting the urge to kiss her cheek, Colin settled for pulling the blanket up to her neck and closing the curtain between the two rooms.

He finished the dishes, turned down the lamps, and picked up a pillow and extra blanket from where he'd placed them in the examination room. Dr. Kittson had been happy to provide Colin with a bed in the hospital until it was needed by a patient. With a last look back, Colin closed the door and made the cold and lonely walk to the hospital.

Maggie woke up warm. She stretched and snuggled deeper under the blankets. Then she remembered where she was and why. What an odd evening they'd spent, chatting about inconsequential things over dinner while they both ignored the fact that neither one of them was acting like themselves. And while it had been on Maggie's tongue more than once to ask him just what nonsense he was about, she'd kept quiet, reluctant to spoil the mood.

And despite the oddness of it, she'd liked the feeling of home and hearth, of staring at him across a dinner table, sharing events of the day. Mulling over the mystery, Maggie smoothed a hand over the pillow and imagined his head there beside hers. The morning would be cold, and they would both be reluctant to let the cool air into their warm nest. He would reach for her and she—Maggie buried her face in the pillow and breathed in the essence of him. Maybe some things were better left unquestioned.

Then she sat up and looked around. Someone had been in and built a fire. A plate covered with a cloth sat on the hearth, and the curtain had been pushed aside. Maggie flopped back in the bed and let her mind rove over last night. In contradiction to his usual methods, Colin hadn't scolded her about a single thing since he'd explained about the drawers. In fact, he'd behaved very oddly, expecting her to know how to eat with all those things he put beside her plate. So she'd watched him and mimicked his motions. And for some reason he seemed very pleased she did.

Swinging her legs off the bed, Maggie quickly changed her dress for her old clothes. She had three horses due to have their hooves cleaned that morning. After lunch, Dr. Poett planned to do surgery on a leg, and he'd promised she could watch. She folded the dress and new drawers and laid them carefully on the bed. Perhaps she'd wear them again one day. Perhaps he'd invite her over again for a bath and a meal. Apparently, that's what young men did. But until then, she had work to do.

She ate the food on the covered plate, left it on the table, and hurried across the parade ground toward the stables. Midway across she met Colin, obviously headed for morning drills. He stopped in front of her, an odd expression on his face.

"Would you come for supper again tonight?" he asked as if they'd not spent an explosive evening together.

Maggie tilted her head. Maybe he had a stomachache. He was pale and acting very odd. "Sure. Have I gotta take another bath?"

He laughed a small, nervous laugh. "No."

"Do I gotta wear the dress?"

"Only if you want to."

Genuine concern began to form in Maggie's mind. This wasn't the Colin Fraser she knew. "I want to."

"Until supper, then." He nodded to her and strode away.

Maggie crossed her arms over her chest and watched him take his place in line and come to attention. Out of the corner of her eye she saw Abigail Baker, also watching Colin. Or at least that's the way it seemed. She was leaning on the porch railing of the mess hall, laughing and looking at the drilling. Jealousy reared its head again, and Maggie spun around and stalked to the stables.

By nightfall, Maggie was dirty, bloody, and in a rage. Who was he to tell her where she could and couldn't live? And him with that Abigail leering after him. Did he think she was an idiot? What did he think she was going to do? Live in his house while he slept in the hospital? She could damn well look after herself. She'd been doing it for years. So, she'd have Dr. Poett put a larger barrel heater in her room if that would shut him up.

Stalking across the snow, Maggie cursed Colin with every step, composing the tongue-lashing she'd give him the moment she saw him. But when she rapped on the door and he opened it, all arguments left her mind. He wore his dress jacket, brass buttons gleaming in the firelight. His pants were pressed and brushed. Beyond him the table was set with lanterns turned low and dishes carefully placed on a white cloth.

"Guess I better take a bath, huh?" she said, peeking hopefully around him.

Colin smiled and opened the door to let her in.

Later, after a bath, a change of clothes, and dinner, Maggie watched Colin take off his jacket and start for the dishpan.

"No," she said, catching his arm. "You did 'em last night. I'll do 'em tonight."

"Are you sure?"

Maggie nodded, then poured water from the kettle into the dishpan. Colin sat down at the table and watched her as she put their dishes into the warm water and lathered soft soap between her hands. His gaze followed her every movement, and she wished he'd get mad again, yell at her or something. This new behavior was both intriguing and unsettling. He carried on a pleasant conversation consisting of the day's activities around the fort. His words were a steady drone until she heard Abigail's name mentioned.

"She came to visit her uncle," he was saying.

"You think she's purty?" Maggie asked as she dried a plate.

"Who?"

"You know who." She threw him a glance over her shoulder, and he grinned.

"Abigail? Yes, she's very pretty."

"You're a sucker fer them pretty, soft women, ain't you?"

When he didn't throw back a comment, Maggie turned around.

"No, actually, I'm a sucker for tough, dirty-mouthed prairie brats." His words were light, but his eyes darkened as he rose from the chair. Maggie watched him close the distance between them, and her heart began to pound.

When he was beside her, he took her hand, still damp from the dishwater, and pressed it to his chest. "There's a dance on Christmas Eve. Would you do me the honor of accompanying me?"

"I cain't dance."

"I'll teach you." He took the dishtowel out of her hand and draped it across a chair back. Her other hand he took in his own and pulled her out into the center of the room.

"Put your hand here on my shoulder." He placed her palm flat against the rough fabric. "Now, put your other hand in mine." His fingers laced through hers, and his arm went around her waist, pulling her close to him.

"But we ain't got no music," she mumbled against his jacket front.

"We'll make our own." He commenced humming softly, and his body began to sway. "Relax and do what I do," he said into her hair. Maggie looked down and watched his booted feet, stumbling along after him, threatening to send them both crashing to the floor.

"Here. Put your feet on mine."

She looked down at his polished boots. "Ain't I gonna mess 'em up?"

He shook his head, and she stepped up onto the tops of his feet. He pulled her tighter against him until her cheek rested against his chest and his hand settled into the small of her back. When he moved, she struggled to keep her feet on his, stifling a laugh and remembering doing the same with Pa when she was a child.

"This is called a waltz," he said, interrupting his humming. "A very romantic dance," he said, his words a soft rumble beneath her cheek.

"Uh-huh," Maggie replied, moving closer to him until their bodies touched full length. She closed her eyes and concentrated on feeling rather than seeing. His chest muscles flexed and knotted beneath his clothes. His hips swayed gently, keeping time to his humming. His long, lithe fingers caressed hers, his thumb rubbing a tantalizing path on her palm.

"People don't dance this close together in public, though," he said.

Maggie started to pull away, but his hand on her back pulled her closer. "But it's all right here." He rested his chin on the top of her head and sighed.

"Why are you a-doin' all this?"

"All what," he murmured into his hair.

"Dressin' me in this dress, makin' me take a bath."

"I didn't make you do anything."

Maggie looked up. "You said if I didn't get into that tub, you'd strip me yoreself."

"Well, maybe I was a little forceful the first time, but you're a stubborn woman."

Maggie harrumphed and put her head back on his chest.

"But you like it, don't you?" he asked.

Maggie opened her eyes and stared at the fireplace.

"Yeah, I like it, but I don't understand why yore a-doin' it."

He stopped and lifted her chin with his fingers. "To prove to you that you could live anyplace you want to."

Maggie frowned. "Even where I gotta wear a dress every day. Is that what yore a-tryin' to tell me?"

"Yes."

"Why?"

His head lowered until his breath brushed across her face. "Oh, Maggie. How can you not know?"

Then his lips covered hers, claiming her thoughts, warming her more than the fire. Maggie cupped his face in her palms, feeling the prickle of beard stubble beneath her fingers.

"I love you, Colin." she whispered against his lips. "Make love to me."

The request weakened his knees and made him summon every ounce of decency within him to deny her. Words of commitment perched on the end of his tongue, promises that would bind their hearts together. But did she understand what she asked? Could she give up her carefree existence, her life on the edge of adventure, and adopt the regimented, scheduled life of the Mounted Police? No, it was too soon. If he confessed his love now, before he was sure she knew what she asked, the consequences could break her heart. For he was as sure of her love as he was of his own. Once her promise was given, he had no doubt she would follow him to the ends of the earth, if necessary. But could he ask a wildflower to become a hothouse orchid?

"We can't," he whispered against her lips.

She pulled away, hurt brimming in her eyes. Seconds ticked by, and he knew she was waiting for his declaration.

"I better take you home," he said finally.

She dropped her gaze from his face and stepped out of his embrace.

"I'll change my clothes."

"No." He caught her arm as she moved away. "They're yours. Take them with you."

She offered no argument and moved to the door. He draped his winter coat over her shoulders and opened the door.

"I'd rather go alone," she said with a hand on his chest to stop him. "I'll bring your coat back in the morning."

He nodded, and she moved toward the edge of the porch.

"Maggie?"

She stopped and turned. "Yeah?" she said, her voice hopeful.

He waited a moment, teetering again on the edge of uncertainty. "I'm sorry."

She nodded and stepped into the snow. He watched her wade toward the stables, dragging his heart along behind her.

Chapter Thirteen

A sharp rap on the door surprised Abigail Baker.
She laid aside her crochet, rose, and answered the
door. A bundle of rags and boots stormed into her
uncle's parlor and shoved back a furry hood to reveal
the strange, sharp-tongued woman the whole settlement was talking about.

"Do come in," Abigail said, and closed the door
against the cold wind.

"I come to ask your help."

Abigail watched her pace back and forth across the
brown and red hooked rug, leaving little puddles of
water wherever she stepped. Ever since their bizarre
meeting at supper that night, Abigail had been
entranced by Maggie's story, one that was oft repeated
in fort gossip and enhanced whenever possible. Most
people thought she was as guilty as her father and

should have been fined or jailed along with the rest of the men. Others thought her an unfortunate victim of circumstance. Whatever the verdict, the overwhelming opinion was that Constable Colin Fraser was in love with her, and the whole settlement was watching their every move.

"Of course. What can I do for you, Maggie?"

Maggie stopped pacing and looked up. Abigail was struck by the clear blue of her eyes and the obvious intelligence reflected there. Score one point for Maggie.

"I was rude that night at supper, and I'm sorry." There was no groveling in her tone, just simple facts. Abigail found herself liking Maggie more every moment.

"Apology accepted. You said you needed my help? May I take your coat first?"

Maggie took off the cumbersome garment lined with buffalo fur and held it out. Abigail took it and hung it on a coat tree with as much dignity as she could muster, expecting to see some creature crawl out at any moment.

"I gotta know one thing first, and it's gotta be the truth."

"Of course."

Maggie planted her hands on slim hips that were buried in too-big pants and shirt, apparently one of her father's castoffs. "Are you in love with Colin Fraser?"

Abigail gasped, then quickly covered her surprise. Constable Fraser was quite handsome and obviously a gentleman, but anyone within fifteen feet of him could see his heart was already stolen.

"I consider Constable Fraser an acquaintance, but no more than that."

Maggie's troubled face brightened. She was very pretty when she smiled.

"Well, I am."

Abigail stifled a giggle. Oh, this was just wonderful. A real-life Cinderella story right here in Fort McLeod.

"Indeed? And does Constable Fraser know this?"

Maggie looked down at her oversized, muddy boots. "He does now."

"Oh, dear. Are your affections not returned?"

Maggie looked up with a frown. "Say again?"

"Doesn't he love you?"

"Well"—Maggie poked at a ridge of the rug with her boot—"he didn't say. I just sort of blurted it out, and I guess I surprised him. I thought he might. Especially after he kissed me like he did and all."

"How can I help?" This was better than any fairy-tale book in any library.

"I want you to help me make him love me." Her plea was so plaintive, so brutally honest, that hot tears sprang to Abigail's eyes, and she wrapped her arms around Maggie.

"What did you have in mind?" Abigail lead Maggie over to the settee and pulled her down beside her, ignoring the dirt and mud encrusted on her clothes.

"He seems to set great store on eatin' and dressin' properlike, and he tried to teach me some, but I just couldn't make heads nor tails out of what he was a-tellin' me. I just did what he did, and that seemed to make him happy. I was a-hopin' that you'd know how I could do it right."

Abigail wiped a splatter of dirt off Maggie's cheek. "We'll start right away. Now, you'll need a dress."

"Oh, I got one of those." Maggie jumped up and ran to her coat. She wrestled a package from inside the great bulk that Abigail hadn't noticed, then hurried back to the settee.

"He bought this'un for me." Carefully, Maggie untied string and opened the paper wrapping to reveal a blue calico.

"It's lovely, and perfect for you, I think." Constable Fraser had excellent taste. The pattern was fresh and innocent. No heavy laces and silks for Maggie Hayes, Abigail thought.

Maggie looked up at Abigail's hair. "Could you teach me to do up my hair like yorn? I've tried, but I just cain't do nothin' with it but stuff it under my hat."

Abigail pulled the floppy hat off Maggie's head, and a fall of beautiful, blond hair tumbled out. It would look perfect pulled up in combs.

"And the eatin'. Can you teach me how to do that without embarrassin' him?" Maggie looked down at her lap. "Seems like I embarrass him every time I see him."

Abigail stood and took both Maggie's hands in hers, then pulled Maggie to her feet. "When you and I are through with Constable Fraser, he won't know what hit him."

* * *

A brutal wind tore at Colin's buffalo coat, threatening to rip it away, while bits of ice stung his face. The prairie was an ocean of white, sky and land blending as if an artist had melded the two with a deft brush. Winter had a firm grip on the Northwest Territories.

Colin had had some trouble convincing McLeod to let him ride this one-man patrol. McLeod preferred to have his medical officers close in case they were needed and had at first resisted Colin's request. In the end, however, he'd relented and allowed Colin to track down the source of rumors brought in by Blackfoot scouts. There was a whiskey operation, they said, to the north, almost in Cree country. Rumors stated that the leader of the operation was George Hayes and he had moved his whiskey camp north, hopefully out of the reach of the Mounted Police.

But Colin wanted more with George Hayes than to arrest him for making and selling illegal whiskey. As long as Maggie wondered about her father and fantasized about the carefree life she remembered, she'd never be happy with him. She'd always wonder about the life she'd left behind. He had to find Hayes and convince him that if he truly wanted the best for his daughter, he needed to put to rest her illusions.

Blackfoot scouts had given him a detailed map, which he followed north, riding deeper and deeper into forests of lodgepole pines and tamaracks. Now he sat overlooking a copse of trees where thin tendrils of smoke drifted up to blend with the monotonous sky.

No lodges were scattered out across the wide plain. No ponies pawed for grass beneath the cover of snow. Only white men would camp so. Prodding his cold horse, he rode closer.

The camp had the same layout as the one along the Bow River, only smaller, less organized. There was a central house to protect the distilling equipment. Tents were scattered out around it instead of cabins. The market for illegal whiskey had dwindled. Word had spread among the Indian tribes that the white man's firewater was a bad thing and the whiskey trade was dying.

Taking a spyglass from his saddlebag, Colin focused on the camp and saw figures bundled in brown moving around in trodden, dirty snow. He studied one figure in particular, a stout man with a floppy hat.

George Hayes.

Colin lowered the glass. So the stories were true. Maggie's father had resurfaced. He thought back to the letter and Hayes's words begging him to watch and keep Maggie. But had he fulfilled that promise? He thought back to Maggie's profession of love for the thousandth time and wondered again why he'd been unable to answer her. The words were there in his heart, but what if he'd confessed he loved her? What if he married Maggie and gave her a child? Would she be happy living such a life? Married to a man gone perhaps for months on patrol? Left home alone to raise children and fill empty hours? Would she one day curse the first moment she kissed him?

She was so naive, so innocent. Her world consisted of the wind and rain, sun and shadow. She knew the seasons and the earth but nothing of the way bodies collide and human emotions entwine.

If he opened his heart, she would give all of herself. He was certain of that. She would make the commitment to him with the same infuriating honesty with which she approached everything else. And such complete devotion placed a high debt upon the receiver.

Colin replaced the glass to his eye and saw a wagon now positioned near the large log dwelling. Men were loading crates of bottles into the wagon, obviously bound for a Cree village. George Hayes himself climbed up on the wagon seat. Colin lowered his glass and rode down the incline where he could not be seen. Soon the rattle of the wagon drifted across the empty prairie, and the wagon and team topped a rise. Lumbering along like a brown bug on a white carpet, the wagon left deep tracks in the snow as it wound its lonely way north.

Colin followed, and near nightfall the wagon stopped in a thin stand of trees near the river. Hayes climbed down from the seat and soon had a campfire blazing in a cleared area. Colin waited until the scent of cooking bacon filled the air before he rode into the camp.

"Constable Fraser," George Hayes said as he calmly turned a slice of bacon with a long skinning knife.

Colin swung down from his saddle and walked toward the fire.

"How's Maggie?" Hayes looked up from his task, expectation on his face.

Colin squatted by the flames. "She's fine. She misses you."

Hayes stirred the meat around in the pan for several silent seconds. "She's better off without me," he said finally.

"No, I don't think so. She thinks you've deserted her. And she's right."

Hayes flipped the bacon out onto two tin plates. "Saw you following me about midafternoon. Figured you'd make your move come nightfall."

Chafing from the flush of embarrassment, Colin accepted the plate, pulled his own knife from a leather scabbard at his belt, and speared the meat.

"You come to run me in?" Hayes asked.

"No. Just to talk."

Hayes glanced sidelong at him. "Rode an awful long piece just to talk, didn't you, Mountie?"

"I want to marry Maggie." Colin bit off a piece of the bacon and reeled from the coating of pepper.

Hayes stopped in midbite. "What's she say?"

Why was he doing this? Colin wondered briefly, then dismissed his doubts and followed his instincts and Maggie's tenet of honesty. "I think she wants to marry me, too, but her answer depends on you."

"Why's that?"

Colin coughed, then stood and got his canteen of water from his saddle. "She thinks you need her here.

She thinks this is where she's supposed to be. How can I compete with the life you offer her? Unending adventure. Life-and-death scrapes every day. Freedom to do anything she pleases anytime she pleases."

Hayes smiled. "I'll admit she got the upper hand on me after her Ma passed. Never could tell her no. She just took right to this life. She could drive a team better than any man I ever hired. And she's smart." Hayes pointed at Colin with the end of his knife. "She outfoxed the U.S. Cavalry many a time. But," he said, lowering the knife, "she don't remember the bad times. Blizzards. Not enough to eat. We all protected her from that as much as we could."

"This way of life is dying, Mr. Hayes. I think you know that. The west is being settled quickly. Now that we've built Fort McLeod, towns and people will follow, and she *and* you will have to learn another way of life."

"I'm too old to change. But my little girl, I only want what's best for her."

"Come to see her, then. Settle her mind on this. I'll see that you have immunity while you're there."

Hayes shook his head. "It's better if she keeps on thinkin' I've just disappeared."

"She knows better."

Hayes frowned. "How's that?"

"She had a visitor a few nights ago."

"Who?"

"Able Lent."

Hayes sighed and stared down at his plate. "What'd he tell her?"

"I don't know. I didn't stay to listen."

Maggie's father shoved his food around in the tin plate until a thin layer of bacon grease began to congeal on the cooling metal. "Able and me, we been together a long time. Afore Maggie was born. He's all the family I got 'ceptin' for Maggie."

"I believe that he was trying to get her to come back here."

Surprisingly, Hayes nodded. "Probably. He knows I miss her somethin' fierce."

"Come back to Fort McLeod with me," Colin said in a sudden flash of inspiration. "There's jobs around. You'd be close to Maggie. I'd speak to McLeod on your behalf."

Hayes raised his head and smiled sadly. "Like I said, I'm too old to change. This here might not look like much of a life to somebody like you who's seen better, but at least here ain't nobody a-tellin' me what to do. I ain't a-watchin' no clock and beggin' fer my money."

"And you're not with your daughter."

"I always meant fer Maggie to leave me when she was a woman proper. I promised her ma." He wiped his knife across his knee and shoved it into the leather sheath at his side. "Just didn't know it'd be so hard to let her go off on her own."

Colin stood. "Until you tell her that, give her permission to live her own life, she'll hang on to the notion that one day you'll come riding in and sweep her off to her old life. I can't compete with that, Mr. Hayes."

He started for his horse, expecting Hayes to call him back, but when he turned, Hayes sat staring into the fire.

"Thanks for supper." Colin swung up into the saddle and gathered his reins.

Hayes turned his head. "You gonna tell her you saw me?"

"No. That's your job."

Colin wheeled his horse around and headed toward Fort McLeod, a three-day ride away. He'd make it back just in time for the Christmas Eve dance if he made camp late and rose early every day. But he'd found nothing he'd sought when he left. He knew no better either Maggie's heart or his own. He only knew that his future was in George Hayes's hands.

"No, no. Always keep one hand in your lap."

Abigail shook her head, and Maggie sighed. "How'm I gonna eat when I gotta think all the time?"

Abigail laughed. "It'll become second nature soon, and you won't have to think."

"I ain't never gonna learn all this stuff." Maggie threw down the linen napkin, left her chair, and walked to the broad window that looked at the front gate of Fort McLeod. Abigail's uncle ran one of the dry-goods stores built outside the nearly finished fort, and the living quarters were upstairs. Their home was beautifully decorated, from the cut-glass lamps on the walls to the linen cloths that covered every table, and Maggie felt even more out of place.

"Of course you will." Abigail came to stand behind her. "It just takes some time."

"I'm just stupid." Maggie pressed her forehead against the cool glass. Colin had ridden out of the fort three days ago without a good-bye or an explanation. She had asked around discreetly, but no one knew or else they wouldn't tell where he'd gone. Perhaps he had gone back home to Ottawa. Perhaps he had asked for a transfer to one of the forts farther east.

"The dance is tomorrow night. We have a lot of work to do before then."

"I don't care anymore." Maggie turned from the window. "Thank you for what-all you've done."

"He'll be back, Maggie. He's not the kind of man to leave without saying good-bye."

"He's already done that."

"Maybe he's on a secret mission he couldn't tell you."

"And maybe I'm a duchess."

Abigail grabbed her hand and pulled her into the center of the room. "We have to practice our waltz." Abigail assumed the position of the man and began to count. "One, two, three. One, two, three. Remember to walk in a box."

Maggie stumbled after her, trying to remember the steps and to count at the same time.

"This was a lot more fun with Colin," Maggie grumped, casting another wishful glance at the fort.

"I'll bet he's a wonderful dancer. One, two, three. One, two, three."

"He's a better kisser."

Abigail stopped in her tracks. "Oh, tell me all about it," she whispered, and pulled Maggie toward the settee, then forced her to sit down by her side.

"You ain't never been kissed?"

"Oh, no. Not yet. Uncle would never permit it. But"—she lowered her voice to a whisper—"I'm just dying to know what it's like."

Drawn into her enthusiasm, Maggie outlined, in detail, her first kiss with Colin. Abigail's eyes widened; then she covered her mouth to stifle a round of giggles. "It all sounds so sinful," she said.

Maggie watched the delight in Abigail's eyes and smiled. Abigail had turned out to be a true friend. Hour after hour she had patiently doled out instructions on table manners, party behavior, dressing, and on and on. While such details seemed to come so easy to Abigail, Maggie's head spun with the number of things she wasn't supposed to do.

Don't stuff your napkin in your collar, no matter that it makes more sense than placing it on your lap.

Don't talk with your mouth full—even if someone speaks to you first.

Don't say "ain't"—even if it ain't.

Don't talk about bathrooms matters or births or underclothes or barn smells or surgeries or barn chores at the table or in polite company. Actually, the list was much longer, but Maggie could only concentrate on a few "don'ts" at a time, so she picked the ones most likely to come to mind.

And don't, don't, don't, kiss him in public.

"Why?" Maggie had insisted.

"Kissing in public is considered lewd," Abigail had whispered with a gleam in her eye.

"What's lewd?"

"Bad, like a . . . saloon."

"Saloons aren't bad. I used to eat in the saloon every time Pa went to Benton."

"Don't discuss that, either."

Maggie sighed. Just what was she supposed to say? "So it's all right to kiss him later, just not in public."

"Well, Uncle says not until a young lady is engaged, but I'm going to if I ever get the chance."

"Ifen you don't kiss somebody, how are you gonna get engaged?"

Abigail had shrugged her shoulders.

"Maggie? Are you ill?"

Maggie shook herself out of her musings. "No, I'm fine. Just thinkin'."

"Oh. Tell me more about kissin'."

"That's all I can think of—exceptin' it made me feel funny in my stomach."

"Like you're going to throw up?"

Maggie thought a moment. "Sort of, but better. It musta made him feel in his stomach, too, cause his face looked funny."

Abigail leaned forward, her face suddenly serious. "Mama always said men couldn't control themselves in some situations and a girl had to be awfully careful."

Maggie frowned. "What'd she mean by that?"

Abigail raised her eyebrows. "You know. Making love." Her voice was a forced whisper.

Maggie remembered Colin's face, his eyes dark and dangerous, his body tense, and how he had stepped away from her, trembling. "Colin said he wanted to make love to me."

Abigail gasped so loudly that Maggie was sure her uncle heard it downstairs at the bolt-goods counter. "He didn't!"

"But he wouldn't hurt me. I know he wouldn't."

Her hand half over her mouth, Abigail leaned forward again. "Men are all the same. They really like making love. Mama says ladies just put up with it, after marriage, of course, cause that's how we get babies."

"I don't know about just puttin' up with it, Abigail. Kissin' Colin and holdin' him felt awful good. All I could think about was how his skin would feel next to mine."

Abigail clapped her hand over Maggie's mouth. "Don't you even think such a thing, Maggie Hayes, or you'll end up a disgraced woman."

"I'm a disgraced woman now."

"It's not the same. Quick, promise me you won't ever do anything like that, at least not until you're married." Abigail grabbed Maggie's hand and held it tightly. "Please, Maggie."

Her face was so distraught, Maggie wondered what about this she didn't know. "All right, all right. I promise."

"Good, now let's get back to the waltz."

They moved across the floor in tempo to Abigail's off-tune humming, interspersed with "one-two-threes." To her amazement, Maggie discovered that soon the steps came easily, and she began to enjoy the motion of the dance.

"See," Abigail said with genuine delight, "I told you you'd love it. Nothing is as exhilarating as a waltz in the arms of a handsome man with the skirt of your dress billowing out around you." Abigail let Maggie go and spun around the room on her own. Maggie laughed and wondered what it must have been like to grow up so carefree.

A movement outside the window caught her attention. A lone rider trotted through the fort gates leading a packhorse. He raised a gloved hand to the sentry and headed for the stables.

"Abigail, I gotta go."

Abigail stopped spinning and staggered a step or two. "But we haven't gotten to your hair yet."

"I'll be back later." Maggie grabbed her coat and opened the door.

"Remember what I said, Maggie Hayes."

Maggie looked over her shoulder at Abigail's' worried face. "I'll remember." Then she shut the door and sprinted toward Fort McLeod.

Chapter Fourteen

Colin stood in the center corridor of the stables, wearily unsaddling a wearier horse. He dragged the saddle off his bay mare's back and let it drop to the ground. Tan mud spattered the horse's belly and Colin's pants. Head hung in exhaustion, the mare stood patiently while Colin rubbed the dark square on her back with a cloth and spoke to her in soft tones discernible only to the two of them.

Maggie leaned a shoulder against the wall, content to watch him work. As much as she wanted to rail at him for disappearing, she also knew that he owed her no explanations. He was a constable in the Northwest Mounted Police and therefore subject to orders and patrols. She was his patient, bound to him only by compassion and a few unforgettable kisses.

Maggie pushed away from the log wall and walked

forward. Colin didn't notice her until she passed by him and bent down to examine the mare's trembling forelegs.

"I'll put some salve on her. You musta rode her hard."

Colin paused, his movements reflecting his exhaustion. "I did."

Maggie fiddled over the mare a few moments longer, hoping for more of an explanation, but when he didn't offer one, she took the reins from him and led the horse away.

When the mare was fed and her forelegs rubbed with a herbal balm, Maggie latched the stall gate and headed for the door, battling the disappointment that threatened to consume her. Tonight was Christmas Eve, and the dance was only hours away. Colin was obviously exhausted, and with the terms on which they'd parted, she'd be relegated to sneaking peeps at the whirling dancers from outside the window.

But as she reached the door, she was surprised to find Colin sitting on a bale of hay, elbows on his knees, head drooped and nearly asleep.

He roused himself as she neared and looked up at her with bloodshot eyes. "Shall I call for you at eight?"

Maggie looked down at the sweat-encrusted bridle in her hand. "You ain't gotta, since you're tired."

He stood, arching his back and bending his hips slowly. "I wouldn't miss it."

A tingle of excitement ran through her even as her conscience pricked her. "I'll be at Abigail's."

He frowned and wiped his palms down his mud-flecked blue pants. "Abigail's?"

"It's a surprise."

He nodded absently, obviously missing the excitement in her voice, and Maggie wondered if he could waltz while asleep on his feet.

"I'll see you at eight, then." He strode to the door with a stiff gait and stopped with his hand on the latch. He looked back as if he were about to say something, then stepped out into the darkening afternoon.

A guilty lethargy drugged Colin's limbs, making him reluctant to stir from the tub of hot water that eased the ache in his legs and back. Only the chilling of the water reminded him that an evening of dance and merriment awaited him outside this paradise. Reluctantly, he stepped out of the tub, dried, and donned his spare uniform. Peering into a cracked mirror, he fastened the last brass button and stepped back to make sure that all accoutrements were in place. McLeod took dress occasions very seriously, no matter they were hundreds of miles from civilization. A carefully groomed demeanor had to be maintained was McLeod's edict. The scarlet jacket was a symbol of justice and fairness in the west and should be well-groomed when at all possible.

Lifting his white gloves from the chair, Colin stepped out into the icy night, strains of Christmas carols already wafting on the still air. Quivering brilliance filled the inky night sky that stretched wide and wonderful above. No clouds dulled the brilliance of a full moon that dominated the east. Hearing only the crunching of his boots as he walked through the gates toward Baker's General Merchandise, Colin let memories of Christmas at home edge into his thoughts for only a moment.

He stepped up onto the covered porch and knocked. The wooden floor reverberated with footsteps, and Abigail's face appeared between two hanging lace-curtain panels. She smiled and opened the door.

"Come in, Constable. Maggie will be ready in a few minutes. Won't you come upstairs for some eggnog?"

The store was dark, its familiar items now mysterious shapes, but the scent of leather and molasses was unmistakable.

"Eggnog?"

Abigail climbed the stairs ahead of him, carefully lifting the hem of a shimmering golden gown edged with elegantly draped lace. "One of Uncle's customers gifted him with some fresh eggs, and another brought fresh milk."

"I haven't had eggnog . . . in a very long time," Colin said, half to himself. More memories of home elbowed their way into a brain too tired to resist. A sliver of vulnerability worked its way into his good mood. Last Christmas he'd been safe and warm beside a fire, his future certain, his path charted. And now . . .

Abigail opened the door to their living quarters, and the scents of home and Christmas poured out.

The sharp twang of tamarack permeated the air. Something warm and cinnamon baked in an oven. He stepped into a room filled with elegant creature comforts. The sofa was a medallion-back, all the rage back east. Colorful, soft rugs covered the wooden floors. Yards of opulent lace draped the windows. A cheery fire burned in a fireplace, brass firedogs grinning beneath fragrant logs.

"Please, sit down and I'll bring you your eggnog." Abigail flashed him a quick smile and disappeared behind a door. Colin sat down on the sofa and sank into its softness. Candles reflected against the glass, throwing back cheery yellow circles that chased away the cold starlight beyond. Colin's eyes grew heavy as the heat from the fire seeped through his clothes. Thoughts spun and wavered, and he was back home, the year before he left for Scotland. Father was there in his chair, pipe firmly clamped in his mouth. Mother brought in a tray of drinks and Christmas pastries.

"Colin?" A familiar voice worked its way through his dream. A nice voice, soft. Something about it was comforting, calming.

"Colin?"

He opened his eyes and stared. Was this Maggie Hayes?

She straightened and smoothed her dress—his dress, the one he'd picked especially for her. Blue calico. A small frown marred the happiness in her eyes, and he shook himself fully awake.

She was beautiful. Golden tendrils of hair swept up over her ears, anchored in place by plain golden combs. She backed away, looking uncomfortable, worrying the fabric of her skirt with nervous fingers.

Simple and beautiful. His Maggie, this wonderful gift that came hidden in plainness, begging to be unwrapped and discovered.

He moved toward her and saw first joy, then uncertainty, flash through her eyes. Her hands were cold as he took them in his own and kissed her fingertips.

"You're beautiful," he murmured against her skin.

She blushed the color of a snowy sunrise and glanced away. "Thank you. Abigail did all this." She whirled around and spread the skirt to reveal tiny golden slippers.

Colin smiled. "While Abigail's work is admirable, we can't give her all the credit."

Maggie met his gaze with bold, undisguised desire, shaking him to his core. Despite the coy trappings, she was still his prairie brat.

"We should be going," he said, pulling himself out of the spell she'd cast and fetching her cloak. He allowed himself the pleasure of sweeping his fingers across the skin of her neck as he settled the soft white wrap across her shoulders. She shivered beneath his touch, and he thought he would burst from needing her.

They stepped into the night and breathed out wispy clouds of moisture. Yellow patches of light filled the windows of the mess hall, silhouetting shadowy figures. For all he was worth, Colin wished they didn't have to join the crowd that awaited them, to smile and pretend interest in the twenty conversations swirling around them. He'd much prefer to spend Christmas Eve in a remote copse of trees with a campfire for warmth, the stars overhead for ornaments and Maggie in his arms.

Maggie threw her head back to stare at the night sky. "You reckon we'll see the Christmas star tonight?"

Colin followed her gaze upward, where pinpoints of light winked and flirted with their cousins below on the mantle of snow. "I don't suppose that sort of thing happens very often."

Maggie slipped her hand into his. "I suppose not."

They reached the porch of the mess hall, and the door burst open.

"Welcome, all who enter," bubbled Braden Flynn, already obviously imbibing Christmas cheer. Despite the Mounties' stern position on illegal whiskey, a certain amount of whiskey making went on within the walls of Fort McLeod, all done very discreetly but nonetheless general post knowledge. McLeod tolerated the practice with a blind eye, and Colin suspected he figured it was a small allowance for the misery his men had endured thus far.

"Enjoying yourself, Flynn?" Colin asked, smiling at Braden's ruddy cheeks and dancing eyes.

" 'Tis nothin' like Irish whiskey, but 'twill do on a cold night, Colin Fraser." Braden brandished a coffee cup and slammed the door shut behind them.

Colin removed Maggie's wrap and hung it on a pegboard that usually housed scarlet jackets during meals. Braden looked Maggie up and down, then glanced at Colin. "Is this lovely creature Maggie Hayes?"

"You know it's me, Braden," Maggie hissed, coloring a delicate shade of pink.

Braden looked delighted with himself and chuckled. " 'Tis Maggie Hayes, to be sure."

A quartet of musicians began to saw out a waltz on fiddle and harmonica, and Maggie looked up at Colin. "Ain't no time like now," she whispered.

She moved into his arms and laced her fingers with his. The other hand rested lightly on his shoulder, barely discernible through the thick serge.

He stepped into the crowd, and she followed him easily. Relaxing, he moved with more surety, and she matched him step for step. Abigail, it seemed, had been busy.

Whirling around the floor, Maggie watched her feet for the first few minutes, then looked up at him, childlike delight on her face. How he would have liked to reach down and kiss her, to draw her breath deep within him and keep it there forever. The music ended. Maggie stepped out of his arms, and he felt adrift, alone, without her body pressed to his.

"Would you like something to eat?" he asked, and she nodded.

Leading her by the hand, he moved through the crowd, fielding comments and questions. Maggie smiled and nodded and made conversation as if she'd been born to it.

Abigail made her arrival accompanied by a flock of young constables, each eager to take her coat and fetch her a plate. She caught Maggie's eye briefly, smiled warmly, then turned her attention back to her admirers.

The rough plank table nearly groaned beneath the weight of food spread upon it, most prepared and brought by the women of the community of Fort McLeod. Roast meats, breads, cakes, and pies loaded the table that had been pushed to one end of the building. A punch bowl squatted on the end of the table, a cluster of men gathered around it. Despite the best efforts of the hosting ladies, it was bound to already be laced with the post's best bootleg.

Colin filled a plate with holiday treats for Maggie, then one for himself, and accepted two cups of punch. He led them to a small table at the other end of the long room and pulled out a chair for her. Seated, Maggie examined every item on the plate before she bit into a bell-shaped cookie. Closing her eyes, she hummed her approval.

"This is better'n sorghum biscuits," she said, leaning forward, her eyes dancing with delight.

"Are you sure?" Colin snatched the cookie out of her hand and popped it into his mouth.

She looked so crestfallen for a moment that he laughed. "Don't worry, there's plenty more cookies."

She shot him a sidelong glance, then turned her attention to the dancers now whirling by to a fast jig. Chin propped on her hand, she watched, her shoulders jiggling in time to the music, reminding him of a young horse eager for a gallop.

"Do you want to try that?" Colin asked with a nod toward the dancers.

She shook her head. "I can't do them fast steps."

"Sure you can." Colin pushed back his chair and held out his hand to her. She looked up at him, her eyes bright with uncertainty.

He stretched his hand out further. "Trust me," he whispered, meaning far more than teaching her the steps to a dance.

She put her fingers in his palm, and he pulled her against him, put an arm around her waist, then whirled them both into the flow of the music.

She learned quickly, allowing him to lead her into the rhythm. She tossed back her hair and laughed, a tiny tinkling sound that reminded him of Christmas bells teased by the wind.

The room became a swirl of color and light, and all he could focus on was the woman in his arms. She was soft and pliable against him, moving in perfect sync with him, as if she were reading his mind, anticipating his next step.

Would they move through the joys and sorrows of life with as much ease and grace, anticipating each other's needs as they now did each other's moves? He was sinking fast in his self-made ocean of righteousness. For all his words and lofty ideals, he wanted her at this moment with a wantonness he had only before imagined. He wanted her love, her trust, and her body promised to only him.

"It shore is hot in here. Can we go outside?" The music had ended, and Maggie looked up at him, a damp curl teasing her eyebrows. The party swirled around them, but Colin barely noticed.

He took her hand and lead her to the door, thankful for the cheerful fire in the cavernous fireplace. Another moment and he'd have kissed her deeply and intimately in front of the entire post.

The sharp bite of the night air was welcome and invigorating but did little to cool the ardor brewing in Colin as they stepped onto the deserted porch. The merriment from inside was muted, and shadowy corners tempted Colin's already weak resolve.

Maggie walked to the edge of the porch, looked up, and planted both hands on the top railing. "You reckon there's folks livin' on the moon?"

Colin glanced up at the silvery orb greedily guarding her portion of the night sky, then stepped to Maggie's side. He touched her wrist and felt her pulse leap against his fingers.

She turned toward him, an escaped curl bouncing against her cheek. "What?"

"I—" The rest of the sentence deserted him. Were there adequate words to ask for her heart? Were there enough adjectives in the world to make her see he was completely and happily lost in her eyes.

Her expression turned to concern. "What's wrong? You want to go?" she asked, moving a step closer.

Colin backed away a step. "No, I'm fine."

She tilted her head a fraction. "You sure?"

Colin swallowed. "I'm sure."

She shot him a look filled with doubt, and he had the sudden feeling that his most intimate thoughts were etched across his forehead for all the world to read.

They went back inside and danced more dances, ate more Christmas fare, and listened to Assistant Commissioner McLeod toast the new fort and this new era in Canadian history.

"Are you ready to go?" Colin asked when he couldn't stand sharing Maggie with the post another second.

"Sure," she said, and moved to get her coat.

Colin draped the wrap across her shoulders and ushered her outside. The quietness of the night echoed for a few seconds as the noise of the party faded behind them. They walked across the now-quiet parade ground and stopped when they reached the center of the open space.

"Thanks fer takin' me," Maggie said, staring down at her feet.

"You're welcome," he babbled, his response barely registering.

"Stay in my quarters tonight," he said, the idea of sending her back to the stables in her finery unacceptable.

"All right," she answered, uncharacteristically agreeable.

"You wanna come inside and git warm afore you go?" she offered when they'd reached the porch.

He should refuse, he knew, for once alone with

Maggie, he could no longer guarantee his actions, a prospect that both aroused and terrified. "Yes, I'd like that," his traitorous tongue responded.

Maggie opened the door, and they stepped into the examining room. Beyond, the bed was turned down, and a fire burned merrily.

"I lit the fire before I left," he said. "I'm surprised it hasn't burned down to ashes," he said as he retrieved a log and threw it onto the orange flames.

Colin pulled her coat off her shoulders, shutting his eyes against the image of more of her clothing falling away from milk-pale skin, marred only by faint freckles that begged to be traced and connected with a single finger. A cool, soft hand pressed against his forehead.

"Are you gettin' sick?" Maggie asked. "You sure are actin' strange."

He opened his eyes and stared at her concerned face. When he'd asked Elena to marry him, it had been for complex reasons. He'd loved her, of course, but she'd also been an excellent choice as a doctor's wife. Smart, educated, socially adept, she would have moved through any social engagement with ease and aplomb. They'd been good together, and the passion between them was an extra.

But Maggie came to him with only her wits and her love. Colin would have once considered those qualities sought only by fools and romantics. Now he could think of no greater prize.

"I got somethin' for you," she said with a coy smile,

and pulled a package from her coat. A lopsided bow adorned the crookedly folded paper.

Colin untied the ribbon. The paper fell away exposing a pair of socks, one two inches longer than the other. He held them up, their obvious difference in length swaying Maggie's enthusiasm not at all. Eyes bright, she gazed up at him. "Do you like 'em? I used to knit fer Pa, but I ain't done it in a while."

"They're perfect," he said, and meant every word. They were perfect because they'd come from her hands, crafted with love, a gift of her time. His gift paled in comparison.

He moved to the cabinet and returned with a package wrapped in plain brown paper. Eagerly, she unwrapped it and lifted free two lengths of scarlet ribbon.

"For your hair," he said, guilt gripping his insides. When he'd seen them in the store, they'd seemed the perfect gift, but now he wanted to give her more, something that said how rare and perfect she was to him.

Tears glistening in her eyes, she held up the ribbons. "They're the color of your uniform."

He glanced down at his sleeve. "Yes, they are." He took the ribbons from her trembling fingers and turned her around. Lifting her blond mane of hair, he breathed in the sweet, soapy smell that teased his nose, then tied her hair up with the ribbons, leaving long streamers of scarlet cascading across her shoulder.

She turned around, her heart in her eyes. How

ittle it took to please her. And how ready she was to
please.

"Guess this means you're my girl," he said, the
playful tone of his voice falling far short of the seri-
ousness of the words.

"Am I?"

He stepped closer, knowing he was nearing the
edge of the precipice upon which he'd danced a
dangerous jig for weeks now. She was soft and willing,
molding intimately to his body as he gathered her
against his chest. The top of her head nestled beneath
his chin, and she fit against him as if they'd been
carved to fit together, like the pieces of a carefully
planned puzzle. Eternity would never be long enough
to hold her this way.

"I saw your father." The words bubbled out unbid-
den, a guilty conscience purging itself. He'd debated
whether to tell her, more for a selfish reason than
for protection of information. He was afraid she'd
leave if she knew her father was close, seduced away
by the lure of adventure and fetterless freedom.

She pulled back and looked up, excitement replacing passion, and he could almost see her riding away.
"Where? Was he well? Is he coming here?"

"He has another whiskey operation about three
days' ride north of here. He was well, and no, he's
not coming."

A frown knitted her eyebrows together. "He's not
coming?"

"He wants you to stay here in Fort McLeod, Maggie,
to make a new life for yourself. The whiskey trade is

dying. Soon there'll be no more market for the stuf
even without the Mounted Police.''

She stepped out of his embrace and wrapped her
arms around herself as if shielding herself against his
words. "How come he couldn't tell me that hisself?'

"He asked me to tell you."

She spun around and paced to the fireplace. "He's
just gonna disappear without so much as a good
bye?''

Colin followed her and cupped her shoulders in
his hands. "He was afraid it would be too hard to say
good-bye in person." Putting words in George Hayes':
mouth, Colin plunged on, desperation beginning to
nibble at him.

She turned in his embrace, tears slipping down her
cheeks. "He's all I got, Colin. I ain't got nobody else
in this world. How can he just go off and leave me
here?''

Colin tightened his grip on her arms. "You've got
me.''

Her eyes flickered back and forth across his face,
searching for sincerity, he knew.

"What are you a-sayin'?''

Colin swallowed. "I'm asking you to be my wife.''

His life was already eternally linked to Maggie Hayes.
She was there inside him every moment of the day and
night, and life without her physically at his side had
become unimaginable. Their union was inevitable, as
unstoppable as the spring thaw that would make the
ice-covered rivers groan. He'd rehearsed the words over
and over, envisioning her expression as everything from

joy to downright rejection. And now the world seemed to stop and hold its breath as he waited for her response.

Her face paled, and she reached for the back of a chair. Slowly, she shook her head. "I can't marry you."

Chapter Fifteen

While the world shattered into a thousand pieces, Colin stepped toward Maggie and noticed that her knuckles were white where she gripped the back of the chair.

"Why? Maggie, look at me." He touched her cheek, and she raised her face, her eyes dark and sorrowful.

"Don't you believe that I'm in love with you?"

"You ain't never told me."

Her words produced an ache deep in the center of his chest. She was right. He'd never said the words to her. He felt this love so strongly, so deeply, he'd assumed she did, too.

"I love you." He moved toward her again, but she took a small step back that moved her out of his reach, and the inches between them now yawned like miles. "What's the matter?"

"I reckon no girl in her right mind would say no, but I just cain't believe you really want to get married."

A tiny barb of truth buried itself beneath his skin. So, all those months he'd wrestled with his conscience and doubted his heart, she'd sensed his reluctance. He should have known Maggie would see right through him.

"Why do you think I don't want to marry you?"

Maggie looked down at the floor and scuffed a toe at an uneven board. "I reckon I loved you the first time I laid eyes on you. But I knew you was a man with a demon clawing at his insides. You weren't no whiskey trader, that was as plain as anythin', but you had Pa fooled. Then, when I woke up and you was bendin' over me, well, I thought you was one of them angels Ma used to tell me about."

A tear rolled down her cheek. "A man's gotta know what he wants afore he takes himself a wife, and you don't know what you want." She raised tear-brimmed eyes, and Colin's heart wrenched. "You cain't make up yore mind ifen you want to stay here in the Territories or go back east. I seen it in yore eyes every time you look at the prairie. Yore a-judgin' it against what you left behind. I might not be so smart 'bout some things, but I know ifen a man ain't happy in his work, he won't be happy at home, neither."

Colin felt like an insect specimen pinned to a collection board. Her insight and logic were infallible. He'd often wondered if he should return east and pick up life where he'd left off before medical school in

Scotland. But now the images he remembered of Ottawa, of gray buildings and dirty snow, paled against the beautiful starkness of the prairie, the wide winter sky and Maggie.

"I'm needed here, Maggie. More and more settlers will follow, and doctors will be needed. We could make a good life here."

Her lips began to quiver. "There's another reason."

"What?"

"Pa needs me. Ifen the whiskey trade is a-dyin', like you said, he ain't gonna have nothin' left."

Colin took a step toward her, but she stood her ground in front of the fireplace. "He's a smart man. He'll find something else to do. Many of the whiskey traders have gone into legitimate businesses and are doing quite well." Another step brought her within arms' reach.

"Pa ain't no young man. What ifen I don't never see him again?"

"I'll make sure you do." Colin drew her into his arms, and she came without protest. Thumbs on her cheeks, he drew her head back and kissed her, open-mouthed. No more prudishness between them. No more wasted time.

She tasted of cinnamon and punch and responded with a need as desperate as his own. Knees trembling, Colin endured the first rush of passion that poured over him and trailed kisses down her neck to the hollow of her shoulder. Her skin tasted both salty and sweet as he nipped at the ridge of bone and clasped her to him.

"Dear God, Maggie, I love you. How could you ever doubt that?" he choked out against her skin. "How could you think I wouldn't want you here in my arms for the rest of our lives?"

She clung to him with shaking fingers that kneaded into his back. He lifted her into his arms and held her against his chest, in awe of this perfect moment in time. She stared into his eyes, confident and unafraid, as if she knew and accepted what was to come next.

He hesitated, remembering his lofty words and admonitions about right and wrong, spoken by a man never before this desperately in love. He would take from her a precious gift, albeit one given willingly. And even though tender, simple words now bound their hearts together, did he have the right to seek this intimacy now, without the benefit of marriage? What if she conceived a child?

He laid her on the prairie-grass mattress that crackled its protest, then surrounded them with the aroma of sun-dried grass and memories of warm, sun-lit days. Fingers fumbling, she worked loose the brass buttons of his jacket and shoved the heavy scarlet serge off his shoulders, letting her fingers slide slowly across the bare skin of his collarbone.

He yanked first one arm out, then the other, and let the jacket drop to the floor. Then he sat up on the side of the bed and stared down at her—hair fanned across his pillow, the tiny hollow at the base of her throat pulsing slowly, her eyes heavy with desire—and suddenly he felt enormously undeserving.

"Maggie," he began, but she covered his mouth with her fingers.

"Fer a smart man, you sure think way too much, Colin Fraser." Her voice had the effect of pouring warm honey down the center of his chest. Before he could pull her to him, she replaced her fingers with her lips.

He slid the combs from her hair and watched it fall in golden waves across her shoulders. "Are you sure you understand what we're about to do?" he asked, pulling his fingers through the silky strands.

She nodded and sat up to meet him.

He began to unbutton the tiny pearl buttons on the front of her dress, but his hands shook so badly, Maggie covered them with her own.

"Here, let me," she said. Enjoying the look of urgency on his face, she purposely undid each button slowly and deliberately until the thin fabric fell away, baring her borrowed shift.

He glanced down, and she knew that the thin white fabric hid nothing from him.

He closed his eyes, his lashes dark semicircles on his cheeks.

"Colin?"

"I have no right," he said, head bowed.

"Please don't talk right and wrong." She grabbed his forearm. "I want this. I want you. I'm givin' you the right."

"But after what I said . . . what I believed about marriage."

She eased her grip and slid her fingers up and

down his arm. "I ain't educated like you, but I believe the Lord is more concerned over whether two folks love each other before they make love than he is over what preacher spoke over 'em."

She slid forward until her lips brushed his. Taking his hand, she pressed his palm against her upper chest, over the spot where her heartbeat raced. "I studied on this since you and me talked that day. I been a-carryin' you in here all this time. I reckon that's what you meant that day 'bout bein' a part of somebody else, and that's what you and me is, parts of each other. Folks don't get no more married than that."

With one finger, she traced his eyebrows, down his temple, and circled his lips. "I know you ain't gonna do nothin' to hurt me."

He studied her face for a moment, and she could see him weighing, deciding, measuring all the consequences of what they were about to do. Perhaps that's what educated people did. Weigh the outcome of every situation before it happened.

But Maggie had always lived by her wits, hanging her future on instinct and intuition. And every intuition and instinct she possessed was telling her that tonight she belonged in Colin's heart and in his bed.

She put a hand behind his head and dragged his mouth to hers, tumbling them both back onto the mattress. She worked loose the buttons on his undershirt and slid his suspenders off his shoulders. He left her arms only long enough to remove the rest of his clothes, then returned and slowly peeled away the layers of her clothing until she lay bare to his gaze.

"You're beautiful," he whispered, his eyes suddenly bright with moisture.

She reached for him again, intent on dragging him back into her arms.

"Wait," he said breathlessly holding out a hand and running the other through his hair. "There's things about a man—"

Drunk on the newfound power she held over him, Maggie ran her hand across the muscles of his chest, marveling at how the chafe of his hair against the sensitive skin of her palm could be so arousing. His gaze never left her face as her fingers feathered out across the washboard surface of his ribs and back up the sinewy surface of his arms.

Suddenly, Colin captured her hand and pinned her wrist to the pillow beside her head. Raised up on one elbow, he returned the examination, trailing one finger across her collarbone, around the delicate hollow at the base of her neck, and sweeping in tiny, circular patterns across her chest and down to her belly.

Then his weight was on top of her, his fingers laced with her fingers, his warmth becoming her warmth. The contrast of their bodies was perfect—his rough where hers was smooth, his hard where hers was soft.

"If you don't want this, say so now." He lowered his head and nipped at her collarbone, her shoulder, her bottom lip. His voice was rough and unsteady, an intimate voice she knew he would share with no one else.

"I want you," Maggie said, begging for the unknown something she knew only he could provide.

"Say you'll marry me," he said, a glint of mischief in his eye as his bare toes rubbed up and down her leg.

"Colin—"

He kissed her again, crushing her lips beneath his. The core of her turned to liquid, fogging her good sense and eroding away her reluctance. "Say it," he whispered against her lips.

"Yes. I'll marry you."

His expression softened, and he released her hands to cup her face and kiss her tenderly. "You'll never regret it, I promise."

Maggie laid her hands on his forearms, amazed that they trembled with such intensity. "Will it hurt?"

"Only for a minute or two and then never again," he replied in a whisper that brushed her ear. Maggie closed her eyes as he began a more intimate examination of her body, touching her, caressing her until she thought she would burst for want of him. And as their bodies merged, she wondered if anyone else had ever been so loved.

An ember popped, its explosion loud in the predawn hours. Maggie stirred, aware of a strange warmth lying next to her. She opened her eyes and looked into Colin's sleeping face. One arm was curled beneath his head, and the other rested on her hip with careless possessiveness.

Maggie smiled, remembering, and moved to lay her cheek on his bare forearm. Today's beard was a dark shadow on his cheeks. Sprigs of hair lay mussed on his temples. They'd joined not only their bodies but their souls as well in one joyous moment. Deep within her she carried his seed. He'd explained the intimate details in a lover's whisper that had ruffled the curly fringes of her hair and made her want him again.

There was a chance, he'd cautioned, that she might conceive a child. His cheeks had turned a delicious pink as he'd fumbled with a half-apology for his actions. She'd dismissed his concerns with a kiss that said she was as guilty as he, and that reassurance had lead to more very unremorseful actions.

She rolled onto her back and stared at the bare beams overhead. Then she glanced toward the window. A few stars peeped above the plain cotton fabric that covered half the glass. Christmas morning was young, and in the course of a few hours, her life had forever changed, leaving the path she knew and embarking on one that she desired. She was a woman now, loved by a man, offered a life at his side and in his heart. And she'd pledged her life and her heart as well. Pa always said a man was only as good as his word. Did she have the courage to back up what she'd promised in a fog of desire?

Wife. A powerful word grown more so in years of girlish fantasies. Companion. Lover. Confidante.

Nurse. The weight of the responsibility was already growing alarmingly heavy. She turned her head to look at Colin, and the alarm dissipated like mist in the morning sun. He was now hers, and she, his. The seductive mysteries that had swirled around him were now intimate secrets between them. No words or papers could ever make them more so.

In her joy, however, one thing was missing. Where was Pa? The question haunted her like an unfinished song or a missing sock. Colin had said he was fine, that he was happy and wished her the same. But if she could only know that for herself, hear the words from his lips and see the truth in his eyes, she would be truly happy.

She glanced again at Colin. He would be her husband by this time next year. They'd live together, sleep together, make love. She'd have left Pa and her other world far behind.

The world was open to her, Colin had said. More people would be coming to the Territories. Soon Fort McLeod would be a regular town, and the carefree life she and Pa had lived would be gone forever. She had Colin to fill that gap. What did Pa have?

She turned onto her side, snuggling into the curve of Colin's body. Could she embark on this new path without first knowing what had become of the only family she'd ever known? Would he continue to make and sell illegal whiskey, moving farther and farther north until the mysterious icy land swallowed him?

Sudden panic seized her, and she felt the cozy walls of the cabin close in around her.

She had to know.

Before she looked in Colin's eyes again.

Before he touched her and drew her into his seductive embrace.

She had to know.

Easing aside the blankets, she rose and winced as the cold floor met the warm bottoms of her bare feet. Quickly, she located her pants, shirt, and hat. Dressed, she placed a log on the fire, praying the greedy embers wouldn't pop and crack their eagerness and awake Colin.

She straightened from the hearth and moved toward the bed to stand over him. Sleep bathed his face in innocence. No one would guess that only hours before his eyes had darkened with passion and his body had trembled beneath her touch. One bare shoulder poked above the blanket, and she longed to cover it. But one movement and he'd be awake. She couldn't see him before she left. One touch and she'd abandon her intents and follow him wherever he led.

The cold air made her chest hurt as she drew in deeply and eased the door closed behind her. Stepping into the snow, she crunched her way to the stables, praying the noise wasn't as loud as it sounded. She'd be back in six days, seven at the most. Maybe Pa'd come back with her, take a job in the settlement like so many other whiskey traders divested of their liquor and trade goods.

In a few minutes, she had her horse saddled and packed with the equipment and spare provisions she'd kept hidden just in case she ever had to flee the fort. A body couldn't be too well prepared, she always said.

She led the mare in a roundabout path to the front gate, avoiding buildings as much as possible as the crunch of snow sounded deafening in the reverent quiet of Christmas morning. As she lead the horse through the gates, a lone sentry raised a hand in a sleepy salute. Head and neck swathed in hat and scarf, Maggie doubted he recognized her. And what did it matter if he did? She'd left Colin a note explaining as well as she could what was in her heart. She could only hope he'd understand and not come after her. She had to do this alone, make this last break with her old life on her own terms, under circumstances most likely to lure her back. How would she know her heart was true if she didn't test it?

The unmistakable chill of bare skin exposed to a cold room awoke Colin. He groped for the blanket and pulled it up to cover a cold, bare shoulder. He squinted at a rude sunbeam that crept in the window and turned to nuzzle Maggie awake, pleasant memories of last night flooding his now-functioning brain.

All he found was her pillow with a note attached. Swinging his legs over the side of the bed, he quickly recoiled from a cold floor and cursed under his breath. He reached back, picked up the note, and pushed his hair out of his eyes with one hand.

Maggie's large scrawl nearly filled the page. She'd

gone to find her father, the note said, to settle in her mind that their paths must part. There were no coy entreaties or morning-after doubts in her words. Only straightforward facts, given in Maggie's no-nonsense way. This was something she had to do alone, and she asked that he not follow her. The last line said simply, "I love you."

Colin let his hand fall to his bare thigh, still clutching the note. Even as his mind formulated a plan to stop her, he knew he wouldn't. She had given him her promise, opened her body and her heart to him and welcomed him inside. He could only trust that she would return to him and give him her hand.

A bright bit of ribbon caught his attention. He leaned down and picked up the package Maggie had given him, abandoned to the floor when passion overrode them both. He lifted out the socks and pulled them on, surprised that they fit well—except for the unequal lengths. He wiggled his toes and stared down at the slightly irregular stitches. So like Maggie. Unpredictable, undisciplined, unforgettable.

With a resigned sigh, Colin searched the floor for his clothes and pulled them on, wrinkles and all. As he stared in the cracked mirror, he marveled that he looked no different. He had proposed marriage, taken a virgin to bed, and lost his virginity in the same night, all with no evident change in his appearance. How could a man endure such a gambit of emotion without some lasting effect? Maggie would laugh to know that he entertained such romantic nonsense.

Worry elbowed its way into his thoughts. She knew the prairie, as well as her own limitations, and could find a needle in a snowstorm. She'd come back when she was ready; to have her before was to have the shell and not the woman within. And he wanted the woman within with every ounce of sinew and muscle inside him.

Three days.

He said he'd ridden three days.

Maggie shielded her eyes from the sun's glare glancing off the surface of a startling new snowfall. As far as she could see, the prairie was white with occasional rolling hills, distinguishable only by the shadows that haunted their depressions.

She eased herself back down into the saddle and sighed. Any turn of the river could be hiding a camp. Any coulee. Any hill. This was a foolish idea, coming out here to find a man that didn't want to be found. After all, George Hayes had hidden a large bootleg whiskey operation right under the nose of the U.S. Cavalry. He could certainly hide a small operation in thousands of acres of wilderness.

From her vantage point on a slight rise of land, she could see the lavender silhouettes of the Rockies thrusting themselves against the belly of heaven, snow frosting their summits. The river ran below her, its twists and turns now silent and frozen. She'd have bet money that Pa would have picked that turn right down there to camp. Willows grew thick, and the curve of the river afforded protection from the north wind and a screen from sight.

Slitting her eyes, Maggie studied the copse of trees one more time. A thin tendril of smoke puffed up, tentative at first, then stronger.

Maggie smiled. Dawn was still a memory in the east, and Pa never could resist coffee in the morning. Gathering her reins, she punched the mare in the sides and rode straight for the thicket of willows.

A neat log building sat surrounded by square white canvas tents whose sides were patched and dingy. Faint voices floated on the morning quiet, and the smell of frying bacon joined the scent of coffee.

She dismounted and tied off her horse to a willow branch. Then she walked straight into camp without being challenged. The floating aroma of coffee unleashed memories of similar mornings—shivering before a fire awaiting Pa's special flour bread, the delicate touch of frost on autumn leaves, the smell of sour mash and wood smoke. But now these memories seemed far away, as if they were from someone else's life.

A group of men sat hunched over the small fire, holding outstretched hands over the feeble flames. Holding a black iron frying pan was her father, hat pulled low over his forehead, explaining in detail to the group the intricacies of making flour bread.

"Merry Christmas, Pa."

He jerked his head up, sentence unfinished, and the pan teetered uncertainly for a moment. He sat the pan on a rock, then struggled to his feet.

Maggie flung herself at him, warm remembrances erasing the weeks apart.

"Maggie girl," he said, holding her tightly against him.

"Merry Christmas, Pa," she said, sobbing into the bulk of his ragged coat.

"Merry Christmas, girlie." He held her away from him and searched her face with a quivering smile. "You've got rosy cheeks—like yore Ma."

"I had to come."

"I know you did," he said softly, rubbing her back with his broad, warm hand.

"How are you? Have you been well?" He seemed paler, gaunter, but with the heavy winter clothes, she couldn't be sure.

"Well enough. Come over to the fire. The bread's almost ready."

He led her to a place at his side, then sat down and neatly flipped the bread over in the pan. Maggie met Able's gaze across the ring of stones, and he smiled as if he'd known she'd come. Other introductions were quick and mumbled.

"I ain't a young man no more. Can't stand the wind and the cold like I used to." He turned the cake of round bread onto a tin plate and drew a long hunting knife from a leather scabbard at his belt. First wiping the blade on the knee of his pants, he then sliced the cake into six equal portions.

The stares of the men made the skin on the back of her neck crawl. White women were scarce in the Territories and nearly unheard of this far north. She sensed from them danger, not camaraderie, as with the camps before. She glanced briefly around the circle of faces and saw only desperate, hard men.

"I was just tellin' the men how you used to love this bread," he said with a soft smile as he speared a still-steaming piece for her and placed it on a tin plate.

Maggie bit into the bread, and a thousand memories flooded back. "How's the whiskey business?" she asked as the platter of bread went from hand to hand around the circle.

Pa shook his head. "Ain't much whiskey business anymore, least ways not here. Now further north, there's the Cree, and they ain't so particular as the Blackfeet. They still know a good bottle of firewater when they see it, and they ain't shy 'bout askin' fer it, either." He took a bite of bread, seemed to have trouble swallowing it, and reached for a steaming cup of coffee. After several swallows, he cleared his throat and coughed.

"You boys go on now and run off that mash." The sullen, silent men obediently stacked their plates and shuffled off toward the log house, leaving Able, Maggie, and her father to huddle around the fire.

"That there's the last of the mash. We ain't got no more grain. Ain't nobody got any. Bad crop year up here." Pa threw another piece of wood onto the fire, and a shower of orange sparks danced into the air. "You remember old Tom Boggs? Seems he's done gone down to Benton and bought hisself a dry-goods store with whiskey money. He sent word that me and Able got a standing job there if we want it."

"I think that's what you oughta do, Pa. You wouldn't have to spend no more nights outside." Could she be about to get her Christmas wish?

"Don't be so fast to put yore pa out of the whiskey business. The Lord don't close a door but what he opens a window. I'm grateful to old Tom, and one day I might take him up on his offer, but me and Able got us a plan fer now." The men exchanged knowing glances, and Maggie's heart sank.

Chapter Sixteen

Huge monoliths of fur and horns, snow and ice hanging from their grizzled beards and fur, barely moved aside as Colin and Braden rode through the buffalo herd. As unconcerned with the driving snow as if the flakes had been flower petals, the herd moved in a slow, plodding gait, stopping only occasionally to paw at the snow and unearth dried grass.

Colin shoved at the rump of a cow with his boot as she refused to move and threatened to rake him off his mount as he passed. She shuffled forward a step or two and otherwise paid him no heed. Leading a packhorse apiece, Colin and Braden emerged from the herd and headed toward the towering backbone of lavender granite and pristine snow dominating the western horizon.

"I wonder if I'm wearin' one of their relatives,"

Braden said through the furry collar of his buffalo coat.

Colin smiled, but Braden's usually keen humor did nothing to improve his mood. Two days had passed since Maggie left, two long, miserable days. And in that time, he'd asked himself a dozen times if he should have gone after her.

"Denny's goin' for the mail at Fort Kipp, did ye hear?"

"Yes. It'll be nice to get letters from home," Colin answered without feeling.

"I'm expectin' a letter from the prime minister complimentin' me on my fine Irish humor."

Colin nodded silently, then Braden's words sank in. "What?"

" 'Tis sure to be a woman," Braden said with a shake of his head, "causin' ye to ignore such a fine day and fine company."

Colin smiled at Braden's laughing eyes, the only part of him visible between his helmet and his snow-dusted coat.

" 'Tis Maggie, isn't it? I haven't seen her about in a day or two. Did ye step on her feet at the dance?"

They drew their horses to a stop beneath a group of wind-striped aspens. Limbs bleached white by the elements stretched toward the leaden sky like desperate arms, giving a pallor of hopelessness to the day.

"No. I asked her to marry me."

Colin swung down from his saddle and walked back to check the load of blankets and buffalo robes on his packhorse.

"Did ya, now? And did the lass, possessin' good sense, refuse to be associated with the likes of ya?" Braden swung down out of the saddle and *oofed* when his feet touched the ground.

Colin smiled and yanked on the packhorse's cinch. The little mare stumbled to the side and swung her head around to give Colin a disgusted stare. "Sorry, girl," he said with a pat to her neck. "No, she said yes."

"Congratulations, old man. And ye lookin' like ye've lost yer best friend." Braden walked stiffly around his mount and shook Colin's hand with genuine affection. " 'Tis an excuse fer another party, if I'm any judge."

Colin glanced around the grove of trees, then up to the threatening sky. "Maybe we should camp here for the night. Buffalo Calf's village is a half day's ride."

Braden nodded. "Looks like a good spot."

As darkness closed in around them, they unsaddled the horses, gave them a ration of grain, then made camp within some boulders that promised shelter from the north wind. Within the protective circle of rocks, they lit a small fire and heated tea and ate pemmican, traded for at the last Blackfoot camp they'd visited. Routine patrols through surrounding villages ensured that no more whiskey traders plied their goods among the people huddled together for the winter; in return, the police traded blankets for needed buffalo robes.

After supper, all that remained was to roll up in the thick buffalo hides and sleep until morning. But sleep would not come, and Colin sat by the fire in companionable silence with Braden, feeding precious firewood to the flames.

"Does McLeod know ye intend to marry?" Braden asked, poking at the fire with a burned stick.

"No. I haven't asked permission yet."

"Ye know Ottawa frowns on the men marryin'. They think it's too hard on the women."

"I know."

"What do ye intend to do if Ottawa refuses to give ye permission?"

Colin shrugged. "Leave the Force. Open a practice . . . someplace."

"Ye'd leave the Mounted Police?"

Colin stretched out his legs to warm his feet. "The Mounted Police saved my life, but I'd give it all up to have her."

Braden's face sobered, and he returned to staring into the dancing orange-and-blue flames. "She must be a special lass, indeed."

Despite his constant joking, Braden Flynn was a compassionate and intelligent man, one who'd shown a particular talent for dealing with the Blackfeet, easily winning their trust and confidence with his warm wit and gentle ways. Colin longed to unburden his conscience to someone who had once deeply loved, to find out if other men felt so confused and out of control when they gave themselves completely, heart and body, for the first time. And Braden had once had a love affair, albeit a tragic one.

"Ye don't seem a man about to be wed. Is there

somethin' wrong?'' Braden asked, pulling the fur away from his face as the fire warmed them both.

"Maggie's gone to find her father."

"Is the old man still brewing firewater?"

"About three days' ride north of Fort McLeod."

"Stubborn old goat. So, ye've been to see him?"

Colin turned toward Braden and saw the unasked question in his eyes. "Yes, I've been to see him."

Braden nodded and poked at the fire some more. "I'm supposin' yer purpose wasn't to arrest him."

"No, it was to ask for Maggie's hand."

Braden laughed. "Yer a gentleman to the core, Colin Fraser. What did the old man say?"

"He gave us his blessings."

"But?"

"Maggie won't marry me until she knows her father is safe."

"And she's gone off alone to see to that."

Colin nodded.

"And therein lies the problem. Yer feelin' guilty that ye didn't stop her."

"She insisted." Colin tipped his head toward the snowy prairie beyond the fire's comforting ring of light. "She was born out there, and she's as capable out there alone as I. If I had tried to stop her, I might have lost her forever."

"She's a headstrong one, that Maggie. Headstrong women can be the death of ye."

They sat in silence a few more minutes while Colin bolstered his courage. He felt like an awkward thirteen-year-old, aghast at the first signs of sexuality, cowering outside his father's door while he worked up the courage to ask questions.

"That's not all, is it, Colin?" Braden asked suddenly, staring down at the ground, his voice solemn.

"No . . . it isn't."

"Well, as me dear mother used to say, ' 'Tis a foolish man that carries the weight of a burden when there's willin' ears nearby.' "

Colin picked up a stick and traced patterns in the dirt. He'd never even envisioned broaching this subject with his father, let alone a man he'd known only a few months. But Braden had a way of cutting through such barriers.

"The woman you were in love with, in Ireland. Were you and she ever . . . intimate?"

Colin raised his head to look at Braden, expecting to see shock on his face. Instead, Braden wore a soft half-smile. "So that's how it is, is it?"

Colin nodded, waiting for the admonitions about decency and morals.

"Ah," Braden said. "Makes a different man of ye, doesn't it? Giving yerself to the woman ye love?"

"Yes, it does."

"Lads aren't supposed to talk of these things. We're coldhearted bastards, you know." Braden threw Colin a sidelong glance and a quirky smile. "Her parents thought she was too young to wed, and we couldn't wait. Now, in my prayers at night, I give thanks we didn't. I have that small bit of her to meself, at least."

"Did you want her even more . . . afterwards?"

"With every breath I drew. She was all I could think

of, and it was then I realized the benefits of marryin' first. 'Tis a foolish man that thinks makin' love once to the woman ye intend to marry will cure the appetite until the weddin'. It only opens the door to the heart, his and hers.''

"I always believed that intimacy was a thing meant only for marriage, that men and women didn't bare their hearts or their bodies until they were wed. I was shocked at how easily I succumbed when tempted and how that's all I seem to be able to think about now.''

"Nonsense. Yer a healthy man in love. In yer heart of hearts, she's already yer wife. She's in yer arms, alone, with a soft fire on Christmas Eve. Many's the man that's fell to such temptation.''

Colin stared at Braden and his sly smile. "How did you know?''

"The two of ye'd been drownin' in one another's eyes all night. I went lookin' fer ye after the dance. Constables Baxter and Wilson were in on leave. We thought to have a hand of poker. Two sets of footprints led to yer door, and none led away.''

Who else had noticed? Colin's heart began to pound. If word had gotten around, his request to marry might be denied, after all. Maggie's future at Fort McLeod would be compromised. Why hadn't they been more careful?

Braden reached over and touched his sleeve. 'Don't look so stricken, lad. No one else is the wiser. tromped around in the snow and wiped out the prints, then paraded myself back to the hospital, layin' down the loveliest set of footprints ye ever saw."

"We were fools. How can I thank you?"

Braden shook his head. "No thanks needed." Then his face saddened, and his eyes grew wistful. "Maybe someday ye can do the same for me."

Muffled shouts filtered through the canvas-tent wall. Maggie turned over and drew her knees tighter into her chest. She couldn't remember ever being so cold, and her dreams had been scattered and disturbing. Able's voice carried over the others with an edge of concern that set Maggie's hair on end. She swung her legs off the cot and drew the buffalo robe around her. Parting the tent flap, she looked out as men hurried past. Next to the firepit her father lay sprawled on his back, chunks of firewood scattered out beside him.

"Pa," she cried, and ran toward him, throwing off the robe.

"I'm all right," Pa said, struggling to sit up. "Just twisted my knee's all."

Able and another man hauled him to his feet. He wobbled for a moment and looked around, a blank expression on his face. Then he brushed their hands away and staggered off toward his tent. Not the gait of a man with a twisted knee, Maggie thought, a premonition creeping up her spine with tiny cold fingers.

"This has happened before, hasn't it?" she asked Able, somehow knowing the truth.

He glanced at Maggie and set his mouth in a hard line. "He didn't want you to know."

"Well, I know now. What happened?"

"Two or three times he's stumbled without no good reason. Afterwards, there was always somethin' wrong. He couldn't talk right, or one eye sort of drooped down. Last time he started talkin' out of his head, talkin' about your Ma like she was walkin' right beside him. That's why I come to you that night. He's got his head set on this last haul, and I was hopin' ifen we did it, he'd be satisfied to go on down to Benton and take old Tom up on his offer. But we ain't got nobody here who's half the driver you are."

Maggie took a deep breath of the cold air to still her heart and stop her head from spinning. She felt as if she were riding a raft on a wild river, rushing toward an unknown end with no control over her fate. There was no time to think, only to react. She glanced at the faces of the men around her. In times past, her father's companions had been mostly other traders who threw their lots in together, some having left comfortable jobs below the border to answer the call to adventure for a few years before returning to become sheriffs, ranchers, and merchants. Even as a child, she'd felt no threat from them, but the men staring at her now with dark, hooded eyes and blank faces set alarm bells to ringing in her head. She wouldn't trust the whole lot of them out of her sight.

"When did you want to bring the whiskey in?"

Able slanted her a glance. "Things is already set up. We're supposed to be at the border in ten days from tomorrow. The load'll be waitin' there at midnight."

"If I do this, will you promise you'll help me convince him to give all this up and go down to Benton? No matter what happens?"

Able nodded eagerly. "I sure will. I'm gettin' too old fer all this sneakin' around, too. Me and yore Pa already talked about it. We're gonna get us a warm house together, one with soft beds and feather pillows. Always wanted me a feather pillow."

Maggie glanced toward the tents and saw her father standing with his back to them all, staring up at the snow-crested Rockies. He stood in his shirtsleeves despite the cold wind that made teeth chatter.

"Pa?" she said as she walked up behind him.

He turned watery, painful eyes to her. "Maggie girl. Do you know where we are?"

A bolt of alarm shot through her so strong that she struggled not to stagger backward. "We're at home, Pa."

He shook his head slowly, glanced at the tents, then returned to staring at the distant mountains. "I can't see your Ma's flowers. She's always got flowers in the windows."

Maggie laid her hand on her father's shoulder. "Ma's not here, Pa."

He shuddered beneath her touch and whirled around. "What are you talkin' about?" He grabbed her upper arms so tightly she winced. "Did something happen while I was gone?" His eyes were bloodshot and wild, his mind in another place and another time.

"No, Pa, no. She went . . . to get some more flowers. In the woods."

His face calmed, and he loosened his grip, ending with a soft pat to her shoulders. "You scared me there." His hands slid off her shoulders, and he turned back around to stare into the distance. "I don't know what I'd ever do ifen I came home and she weren't here." His voice was soft and weak, almost a whisper. "I sure don't know why she stays."

"Don't you want to lie down for a while?" Maggie tugged on his elbow.

"I think I just might do that. I'm feelin' sorta tuckered out." He turned and walked back toward the center of camp, then stopped abruptly. "Where's our house?"

"We moved down here near the river for the summer, Pa."

"Oh, that's right," he said with a wave of his hand. "Yore ma talked me into that. Said she wanted to hear the water as it went over the rocks. I never could tell her no." His gait was stiff and shuffling, and one leg dragged slightly behind the other. "Ain't it cold for summer?" he asked as a gust of wind tore through the grove of aspen, stirring dead leaves into tiny storms.

"Yes, it is," she said, throwing a glance at Able as she ushered her father into his tent.

With a groan he sat down on his cot, then stretched out. Maggie covered him with a buffalo fur and took off his hat. Sparse sprigs of hair sprang free, and he suddenly looked feeble and haggard. Fighting the lump in her throat, she smoothed back the errant wisps, and he smiled up at her. "You're a good girl, Tumblebug."

Tears brimmed her eyes, and she didn't trust her voice to answer him. She patted his arm and ducked outside. If she brought this whiskey across the border, she would be committing a crime that could see her locked up and fined. But worst of all, one that could separate her from Colin forever. She heard again his voice professing his love, asking her to spend the rest of her life at his side. But she also heard her father's voice, feeble and needy, asking her to do this for him. And it might well be the last thing he'd ever ask her to do. There simply was no choice.

"Able."

Able stood from his seat by the fire and looked at her expectantly.

"Have you got a map of the Montana border? I know all the limits of the Mounties' patrols. I can find us a route where we won't be seen."

Subconstable Cecil Denny dismounted his horse and stumbled into the waiting arms of his comrades. He'd ridden four long, cold days to bring to the lonely men a mail packet dropped off at Fort Whoop-Up by a supply team out of Benton. He withdrew the packet from his saddlebag and laid it in James McLeod's waiting hands.

"There's bad news," he said through cracked and cold-chapped lips.

Colin's heart skipped a beat at the words. Maggie was his first thought.

"Baxter and Wilson never made it to Kipp."

The crowd rumbled, and McLeod frowned as Denny related the news. The two men, on leave and at the Fort McLeod Christmas party, had left McLeod accompanied by pleasant weather for their return trip to Fort Kipp. Winter, however, had exercised her ability to change her mind, and a blizzard closed in around them, obliterating trail and landmark. Sometime during the night, they fell from their saddles, and their horses continued on through the storm, riderless, reaching the fort the next morning. The next day, the two men were found, one frozen to death, the other barely alive. He only lived a few hours longer.

Mail was distributed without excitement or joy.

"Fraser," McLeod called, and held up a package.

Colin stepped forward to receive it, then waited to open it until he was warm and seated before the barrel stove in the hospital's main ward. Wrapped in cheerful paper was a new pair of gloves, a scarf, and a letter in his mother's elegant hand.

Her large script read

I pray this finds you well and happy. Your father and I miss you and wish you could come home for a visit, but we know that is impossible for now. No exploit of the Mounted Police fails to make the newspaper, and we all find your lives out there adventurous and exciting, although your father and I know your life is probably not nearly as glorious or grand as the articles paint. We have heard rumors that you have not been paid in months and that your supplies are long in coming.

The letter went on to relate bits of family and community gossip, and a tug of homesickness began to nibble at Colin like the many mice that had moved inside the post buildings for the winter.

How easy it would be to long for civilization, he decided, reading descriptions of balls and teas. A sturdy house without a sod roof; floors covered with rugs and carpets; food warm and ready at a table set with crystal and china. He glanced up at the crude walls and lines of cots, then back down to his letter.

We received a letter from Elena's parents in Scotland, and they asked after you. They have come to accept that her death was God's will and no fault of yours. They ask in their prayers that you will find the same acceptance within yourself.

She closed with a plea that he come home when given the opportunity and wished him a Merry Christmas and a Happy New Year.

Carefully, he folded the note. Later, he would read it again when loneliness set in and the Territories seemed overwhelmingly large and empty. He slipped his hands into the gloves, reveling in the soft fur lining, and draped the scarf around his neck. Then he opened the door to the stove and stared into the flames, allowing Maggie to invade his thoughts. He'd held her memory at bay for the last four days by busying himself with whatever he could find to keep his hands and his mind occupied.

Inspector Walsh had arrived from the south bringing with him newly purchased horses, and Colin had helped John Poett examine the new stock and treat any minor injuries. The sudden holiday blizzard had produced cases of frostbite, various minor injuries, and colds among the men, and he'd thrown himself into their treatment. But despite his best efforts, concern for Maggie lingered there in the depths of his mind, haunting him like a persistent little ghost. Where was she? Was she warm? Fed? Happy? Had she found her father, or was she dead, frozen like Baxter and Wilson in the blizzard that had swept the area?

"McLeod wants to see you," Steven Gravel said from the doorway.

Colin removed the gloves and scarf and returned them to their carefully packed nest in the box, then placed the present on the cot he called his own. Since the night he'd lain with Maggie, he hadn't been able to sleep in his quarters. Every crack of the fireplace, every whistle of wind around the corners, evoked a memory of that night, and he needed no help remembering the pain she'd left.

McLeod's door brushed open with a familiar groan, worsened by the wet, cold weather. He was seated behind his desk in suspenders and undershirt, his scarlet jacket thrown over a nearby chair. A quill pen bobbed and scratched its way across a sheet of paper in the center of his desk. He acknowledged Colin with a distracted nod and continued his task until he laid aside his pen, raised his head, and steepled his fingers.

"Constable Fraser. Have you had any word from Miss Hayes since she left our midst?"

Taken aback, Colin hesitated for a moment. "No, sir. I have not."

"Do you know where she might have gone?"

None but the foolish tried to outfox James McLeod, and Colin felt just that—a cornered fox. "I believe that she went to find her father, sir."

McLeod watched him with dark eyes that could both impart compassion and pin a man to his chair. "And how do you suppose she knew where to look, Constable?"

Colin drew in a deep breath, possibly his last as part of the Northwest Mounted Police. So McLeod knew of his betrayal, his lie by omission. "I told her, sir."

"You knew of his location?"

"Yes, sir. I rode to his camp just before Christmas. He and a few of his men have a whiskey operation three days' ride north of here." The words tumbled out as if glad to be out of their prison of guilt.

"And you didn't share that information with the rest of us?"

"No, sir."

McLeod drummed his fingers on his desk. "What

purpose would you have to keep that information to yourself?"

"I did not go to him as a member of the Mounted Police, sir. I went as—"

"As what, Constable?"

"As a potential son-in-law, sir."

McLeod propped his elbow on his desk and cradled his cheek in his palm. "Come here and sit down," he said, waving at the chair that fronted his desk.

Colin sat and felt a wave of guilty sympathy for his commander. What an overwhelming task it must be to see to the well-being of one hundred and fifty men, police a huge territory, and deal with the native peoples with grace and compassion, much less with the individual problems of the men under his command. And Colin was about to add a huge one to the top of the pile.

"You're aware of the Force's opinion of their men taking wives?"

"Yes, sir, I am."

"Were you thinking of leaving us? If so, it would be our loss. You're a valued addition to our numbers, Constable."

"I was hoping to apply for permission to marry and present a good argument in my defense, Commissioner."

"Have you asked Miss Hayes for her hand?"

"Yes, and she has accepted my proposal."

"But she has gone to find her father?"

"She felt that she had to see that her father was well and cared for, sir. She had hoped to talk him into leaving the whiskey business and turning to more legitimate pursuits, as others have done."

"And do you think she will be successful?"

Colin stirred in the chair. "I think that George Hayes takes great pride in what he does, pride and enjoyment. He has managed to elude capture for many years. I think it will be difficult for him to turn to a life less exciting."

"Do you know where Miss Hayes is now?"

Colin felt again the stab of fear that constantly circled his heart. "No, sir. I hope she arrived at her father's camp safely."

McLeod sat up straight and ran a hand through his curly black hair. "I have a visitor who assures me that George Hayes is still very interested in trading whiskey." McLeod nodded toward the corner of the office, and a Blackfoot brave materialized out of the shadows. Dark, hollow eyes searched the room and settled a steely gaze on Colin.

"Calf Man works for Jerry Potts off and on as a scout. He recently came from Montana and brought information that a large shipment of whiskey is poised to be brought across the border for transport north and to be distributed there among the wintering Cree. He also says that George Hayes is the man coming for it." McLeod leaned back in his chair. "I'll give you two guesses who's driving the wagon."

Chapter Seventeen

Windswept and desolate, the prairie lay beneath an ocean of wind-carved waves, snowdrifts piled and sculpted like icing on a cake. Only winter on the prairie could both bedazzle and belittle. Like far-flung jewels, the fresh snow glistened and shimmered beneath a pale winter sun, making the prairie seem larger than it did when covered with grass.

Maggie shifted on the hard wagon seat. In front of her, Pa had stopped his wagon and sat staring at the distant gray horizon.

"Let's go, Pa," she called.

He turned around, his face blank. "Where was we a-goin'?"

"We're goin' to Montana, Pa, after that load of whiskey." She swallowed back the fear that threatened to choke the wind out of her. After three days

on the trail, she'd convinced herself that his spell
in camp was a passing thing, perhaps the result of
drinking his own brew. She'd almost put out of her
memory the cold dread that had poured into her
then, but now . . .

He frowned and looked around him, turning his
head slowly, like a doll she'd once seen in a Benton
store window. "Montana?"

"Don't you remember, Pa? There's a load of whiskey waitin'. You and Able did some tradin'."

He stared at her a moment, then his face brightened. "Oh, yeah. I remember." He turned back
toward his team and clucked softly to the horses. With
a jingle of harness, they started forward, puffing little
clouds of steam.

"Maybe I oughta go up there and ride with 'im,"
Able said, clutching the seat as the wagon lurched
into and out of a buffalo wallow.

Maggie nodded and pulled her team to a stop. Able
clamored off the seat and trotted to catch up with
her father. They exchanged a word or two, then her
father's wagon stopped, and Able climbed up onto
the seat.

Welcome solitude closed in around her, punctuated by the huff of the horses as they strained against
their harness and the muffled plod of their feet breaking through the thin crust of snow. Now she could
think and plan. As soon as they delivered the whiskey
to her father's camp, she'd convince him to come
back to Fort McLeod with her. Colin would know
what to do about her father's sickness. And after she

and Colin were married, perhaps Pa'd stay with them; she could care for him, keep him warm and fed, make his last days comfortable.

She shooed that thought out of her mind with a shake of her head. Pa wasn't going to die. She wouldn't let him. But even as she banished the thought back to the depths of her mind, a lingering doubt, a whisper of truth, remained behind.

He talked of her mother often, sometimes as a fond memory and sometimes as if she were standing by their sides. And as the days wore on, the distinction between the two blurred.

Maggie inhaled the biting air and shook all such thoughts from her mind a second time. They'd seen no other people so far, only the occasional buffalo herd hunched against the cold and sometimes a wolf, a lone silver sentinel that appeared on a rise of land, then vanished, blending into the shades of white and gray that surrounded them.

They should reach the border tomorrow and the trader's camp the next. Six or seven days back to her father's camp, then three to Fort McLeod. If she was lucky, she'd be in Colin's arms in two weeks.

Two weeks.

An eternity.

Dark, little doubts crept into her thoughts, shadows of guilt already forming. Would he ever find out she'd returned to her old ways? James McLeod seemed to know everything. Would he find out about this? If so, what would Colin do? What would he say? No, he wouldn't find out, she reassured herself. He'd never know, and she'd never do this again. There'd only be one little secret between them.

A dark, dirty length of fabric wound around Calf Man's head and spilled over his shoulder to mix with his long black hair. He fixed an expressionless gaze on Colin and moved another step forward, the long buffalo coat sweeping behind him. Fashioned with sleeves and a collar, the garment had obviously come from Benton or an industrious trader outside the gates of Fort McLeod.

"Calf Man, tell Constable Fraser what you told me."

The scout stepped forward, and Colin saw that he clutched a rifle at his side. Colin's hand slid across his thigh, closer to his Adams pistol.

"Big load of whiskey at border waiting for George Hayes, men say. He come in two weeks," Calf Man held up two fingers.

"When did you learn this?" Colin asked.

Calf Man added three more fingers. "Five day ago."

"Who told you this?"

"Men who make whiskey. They have camp down in coulee. Say U.S. Cavalry not come out in winter, and they sell much whiskey to Indians in Canada."

"Did you see the whiskey?"

Calf Man nodded. "Yes, see whiskey. Firewater in bottles packed in crates."

"How much? One wagonload?"

Calf Man shook his head. "Two wagons, maybe three."

Colin glanced at McLeod. "Able could be driving the second wagon."

McLeod nodded slowly. "Could be."

But probably not, Colin thought, his heart sinking. Duty was duty. He'd sworn an oath. "I'd like to go along, sir," Colin asked.

McLeod leaned forward and toyed with the ends of his mustache. "Pick your men, Constable. I'd like you to command this patrol."

What was McLeod saying? Was he testing him to see what he was made of, or was he giving him the opportunity to save Maggie?

"Braden Flynn and Steven Gravel." Then he named two other constables he considered friends.

"Calf Man has agreed to act as your guide." The Blackfoot glanced at McLeod. "At the usual rate, of course," McLeod said quickly.

Calf Man nodded.

Colin stood, anger and disappointment warring within him. How could she do this? How could she risk all that they had, all they would have, to return to her old way of life? Calf Man swept out the door, promising to return in the morning, when they would set out.

"Constable."

Colin stopped with his hand on the door.

McLeod stepped in front of Colin. He raised a hesitant hand and placed it on Colin's shoulder. "The danger to Miss Hayes does not lie with us. If caught, she can be fined and released. But if the U.S. troops were to capture her on their side of the border . . .''

Colin nodded, his already sinking heart taking a deeper plunge. ''There would be nothing we could do.''

''At least nothing to be done at that moment. We could write Ottawa, who in turn would—''

''I'll find her before she crosses the border,'' Colin said, hoping he could make good on that promise. Then he walked out the door to speak with Braden and Steven, wishing he could jump on the nearest horse, race to her rescue, and strangle her with his own hands—after he kissed her senseless.

McLeod watched the door swing closed, then walked back to his desk. He picked up the letter he'd been writing and reread the even script.

''Constable Colin Fraser has requested permission to marry . . .''

McLeod lowered the sheet of paper and glanced out the window. Fraser strode away, his gait even and determined. James sat back down in his chair and ran both hands through his hair, teasing it into disobedience. Across the desk his Mary smiled at him from a delicate silver frame—a smile that hid a constitution of steel. He dipped his quill into the ink and scripted ''Miss Maggie Hayes.''

Frantic flames consumed the sticks of firewood desperate to survive against the howling wind. The bulk of the wagon bodies broke some of the fury o

he wind that whipped snow into tiny icy knives but
unneled more underneath to torment both fire and
hose huddled around it. Maggie hunched her shoul-
lers and pulled her buffalo pelt closer around her.

They'd eaten a meager supper of pemmican and
vater, then lingered by the fire, reluctant to leave its
varmth. They spoke little, conserving their energy
or shivering. Pa nodded, alternating between watch-
ng the fire with bright eyes, listening to silent voices
n his head, and staring blankly out into the bitter
iight.

"Reckon we better turn in," Able muttered from
ehind the layers of cloth that muffled the bottom
f his face and his neck. "We're across the border
iow. Gotta watch fer them boys in blue."

Maggie nodded, too cold to form words. She glanced
t her father, but he was staring and seemed to hear
iothing they'd said.

"Pa? You ready to go to sleep?"

His gaze seemed fixed on some point far out into
he dark night, and his face wore an expression of
xpectancy.

"Pa?" She shook his shoulder, and he looked up
t her.

"What?"

"You ready for bed?"

"Sure. Sure," he said, scrambling to his feet.

"Able's got a place fixed for you in the wagon."
he grasped his elbow, and he leaned into her slightly.

shiver of premonition passed over her. He was
iding, disappearing into that imaginary world that

went on in his head, a place where Maggie could neither follow nor rescue him from. Brushing aside the feeling of helplessness that threatened to engulf her, Maggie helped him up onto the wagon seat, and he scrambled into the back to where Able held up the canvas cover they would sleep under.

Maggie checked on the horses, which stood with heads bowed against the wind. Stout beasts, they'd weathered many winter storms. Bellies filled with grain and hay, they'd doze away the stormy night, the snow barely an irritation to their thick coats. Maggie patted their necks, then climbed into her wagon and snuggled beneath her own canvas cover.

Dreams came on tendrils of emotion, images and feelings rioting through her slumber, filling her with joy and sorrow. She was a little girl again, chasing a butterfly that was suspended for a moment in a dusty sunbeam. Then she was older, driving her wagon, rattling pell-mell across the prairie, blue-coated soldiers giving chase.

She stirred in her sleep, hearing something . . . her mother's voice—that was it.

Calling.

Come home!

Yes, ma'am. I'll be right there.

Her father's face floated into her dreams for an instant, a clear, vivid picture that jarred her and filled her mind with his image. He was laughing, his hat pushed to the back of his head. Now there was someone else in the picture.

Mama.

Pa was swinging her around. She had a bunch of flowers in her hand. Brilliant blue flowers with delicate heads that bobbed in the slightest breeze. Ma was laughing, her head thrown back, her rich brown hair fanning out behind her like a child's. The warmth of their love infused Maggie, and she felt safe and loved and secure. She smiled and snuggled farther down into her nest of warmth. Tomorrow she'd go flower picking with Ma and have some of those blue flowers of her own in a jar on the table.

"George!"

Maggie frowned in sleep, and the beautiful images faded.

"George!"

Who was calling? A seed of panic began to spread as Maggie fought her way out of sleep.

"George. Where are you?"

She sat up, fully awake, and flung back the canvas cover, spraying a curtain of snow. Able stood in the bed of his wagon, hands cupped around his mouth. "I can't find your Pa," he said, fear in his eyes.

Maggie dropped to the ground and sank into snow several inches deeper than last night. She waded to the wagon and searched the ground. There were no footprints leading away, so he must have left soon after they went to bed.

The panic grew and spread. Her heart began to thump, and her thoughts tumbled over each other.

"Pa!" she called, and strained to hear a response. But only the remains of last night's wind dragging itself across the snow-covered prairie answered her.

She circled the wagons, watching the ground, but the mantle of snow was undisturbed and pristine. Walking in ever-widening circles, she alternately searched the horizon and the ground, shielding her eyes from the glare of sun against snow. Then she saw a lump about forty feet from the wagons, and somehow she knew.

She ran, then fell to her knees, her hands tearing at the snow and icy crust, and uncovered the red wool of a scarf.

"Able! Here!"

She yanked off her gloves and raked the snow away with bare, reddened fingers until she'd uncovered a shoulder. She pulled and rolled the body onto its back. Hands frozen in grotesque claws, her father stared sightlessly at the sky, a slight smile on his face.

"Oh, dear God. Able, hurry!" She cupped his cheeks in her hands and rocked his head back and forth. "Pa? Pa, answer me."

His skin was cold, his flesh hard. He was frozen.

Able's hands closed around hers and drew her to her feet and against his chest. "Ain't no use, Tumble-bug. He's gone to yer Ma."

Maggie buried her face against Able's chest, her mind numb. He couldn't really be gone. Why just last night . . .

She turned to stare down into his face again. Had he and Ma really come to her one last time to reassure her they were finally together, if only in her dreams? Tears spilled over her cheeks and made icy paths down her face.

Able's hands came up to clumsily rub her back. "He's been a-leavin' fer some time now. He just couldn't make up his mind when to go."

They buried him underneath a pile of rocks, a lonely monument on a wide prairie. Maggie laid down the last rock, then straightened and stepped back. Come the spring thaw, she'd return, she promised herself, and see that he was buried proper. Closing her eyes, she waited for the world to stop spinning, then opened them again.

Able watched her across the grave. "You wanna go back?"

"You?"

Able nodded. "I lost my appetite fer this life a long time ago. I just been going along to keep an eye on yer pa."

"Where will you go?" Maggie asked.

Able sighed and looked down at his boots. "I was a-hopin' I could maybe come back to Fort McLeod. Work in a store there or somethin'. I sorta feel like I owe it to yer Pa to watch after his grand-young'uns."

Maggie hurried around the grave and into Able's arms. "You'll always be welcome in our house," she said, her face buried in his coat.

"Now ain't this a purty picture."

Maggie jerked her head up and swung around. A U.S. Cavalry patrol surrounded them, their dark blue overcoats stark contrast to the brilliant white snow. The commanding officer shifted in the saddle and smiled.

"Might I be addressin' Maggie Hayes?"

Maggie glanced at Able. "You might."

"Well, Miss Hayes, you've provided me with many an afternoon's exercise. I'm pleased to finally meet you face-to-face." He swept off his hat and nodded.

Maggie glanced around. They were outnumbered five to one. They didn't stand a chance of escape. "What can I do for you?"

"Lieutenant Tom Cross," he said with a smile. "Just what are the two of you doing out in a storm like this?"

"I could ask you the same thing," Maggie retorted.

"You could, but I suspect you know that we're here on the same business." He nodded toward the grave. "Who's that?"

"My pa."

The lieutenant look surprised. "George Hayes?"

Maggie nodded.

His eyes softened, and his face lost its arrogant expression. "I'm very sorry."

"We're on our way back across the border," Maggie lied, her numbed brain struggling to think.

Cross looked toward the wagons—both pointed south—and raised his eyebrows. "Are you, now? And what was your business on this side of the border?"

"I ain't gonna lie. We was on our way to pick up a load of whiskey, but Pa died and . . . well, me and Able have lost our taste for this business."

"Lost your taste." Cross nodded and chewed the side of his mouth. "Miss Hayes, do you have any idea how many men and hours I've expended in the last few years chasing you and your father?"

"No."

"Plenty of both. And I'm not about to let you back over that border. Your Mounted Police with their fancy uniforms might think they've got the problem licked in Canada, but all they've done is run their vermin across the border into Montana. Then they become my problem."

If he arrested her, she might never get back home to Colin—and Colin couldn't cross the border to get to her.

"Are you arresting us?"

Cross swung down out of the saddle and nodded to two men, who also dismounted. "You're a smart girl, Maggie. I always thought so." Cross pulled her arms around behind her back and secured them with a rope. "Now get up on the wagon box."

Maggie obeyed, seeing from the corner of her eye that Able was treated the same way. Two men quickly hitched the teams' harnesses as Cross climbed onto the wagon seat. "I'll ride with Miss Hayes. Have one of the other men accompany Mr. Lent."

Cross spoke to the team, and they leaned into their harnesses, struggling to pull in the snow. "We found your customer's camp about three days ago. Nice little coulee they had. Sheltered from the wind. Plenty of whiskey to keep warm. All they had to do was sit there, drink, and wait for you." He flipped the reins and clucked softly to encourage the horses. "By the time we arrived, their tongues were pretty loose. They were more than happy to tell us everything we wanted to know about your little operation."

"What are you gonna do with us?" Maggie asked, twisting around to get a last look at her father's grave as the increasing snow quickly disguised the rocks. She fought tears as she turned back around and was surprised to find Cross watching her with compassion.

"I'm truly sorry about your father," he said softly. "I understand the two of you were very close."

Maggie stared straight ahead, concentrating on not making a fool out of herself in front of him, and let his apology go without comment. She raised her chin a bit when she felt his gaze sweep across her face.

"We have a camp not too far from here. I'm taking the two of you there, for now. Eventually, you'll go to Benton, and we'll decide then what's to be done with you."

A tiny tear squeezed from the corner of Maggie's eye. With her hands tied behind her back, she could only endure its humiliating trip down her cheek.

Colin shook his head and sent a cloud of snow flying off his buffalo fur cap. At least last night's wind and stinging snow had given way to a soft, gentle snowfall. He glanced over at Calf Man, seemingly impervious to the wind and snow, his face a stone mask no matter the weather or situation.

They'd crossed into Montana a few hours back. Since that time, Calf Man had lead them in a straight line toward the rolling Montana hills.

"Wagons here," Calf Man said suddenly, and reined in his horse. Colin yanked back on his own reins and looked down at the churned ground, faint depressions only faintly visible. A little farther away, a pile of horse dung marred the smooth white surface. A few feet farther, a pile of stones wore a fresh dusting of snow.

A grave.

Colin's heart twisted. He swung down and walked to the stack of small rocks. "Are you sure we're following Hayes?" Colin asked.

"Follow George Hayes," Calf Man said, still astride his horse.

Braden came up behind Colin. "It's not Maggie," he said softly.

"It's not Maggie," Colin repeated. He drew in a breath. "But I don't know for sure."

Braden stepped away, and Colin heard steps in the snow.

"Let's have a look, lads," Braden said to the other three men, and they began to move the stones.

Frozen in his tracks, Colin could only stare at the grave—and pray.

Braden dropped to one knee, scraped away a bit of snow, and lifted away a stone. A man's face appeared, colorless lips curled into a smile. Colin released a held breath, and his head spun for a moment.

"It's her pa," he said, hating the waver in his voice.

"Looks like the poor buggar froze to death," Braden said, replacing the stone. Colin quickly turned, looking for more graves, but saw only the smooth surface of snow.

"Too many horses," Calf Man said, pointing to churned ground rapidly being covered with snow.

While Braden and the men reburied George Hayes, Colin knelt and examined the ground. The prints were smudged and rapidly disappearing, but the fact that the horses were shod was clear.

Colin rocked back on his heels and drew in a deep breath.

U.S. Cavalry.

Chapter Eighteen

A thin pallor of smoke hung over the coulee, held low to the ground by the approaching storm. Colin would never be so stupid, Maggie told herself, glancing at Lieutenant Cross on the seat beside her. He saw the smoke, too, and a frown darkened his face for a moment as they topped a rise. The American Sioux were still raging across the west, resisting the cavalry's efforts to herd them all onto reservations, as were other tribes equally threatened by the United States's policy of "shoot first; ask questions later." A body was foolish to advertise their location so blatantly.

The wagon hit a bump and groaned and yawed in protest. Maggie braced her feet but nearly bounced from the seat just the same, unable to hold on with her hands.

Lieutenant Cross leaned toward her and grasped her wrist. "Are you all right?" he asked with a quick glance at her, then back to the trail before him.

"I'm fine," Maggie retorted, and yanked her arm away.

He frowned again as he straightened and returned his hands to the reins. "If I thought for a second you wouldn't try and get away, I'd untie you. But you would, wouldn't you?"

"Why don't you untie me and find out?"

Cross shook his head. "Nope. Lady, I swore if I ever got my hands on you—" He stopped and clamped his teeth together.

Maggie studied him out of the corner of her eye. He was clean-shaven and young, probably about Colin's age, but the lines around his eyes said he'd spent more than a year underneath the western sun. From Pa's stories, she'd have expected him and his company to be whiskey-swizzling, foul-mouthed bastards, bent only on pleasuring themselves and tormenting anyone unfortunate enough to cross their path. The lieutenant, however, seemed quite the opposite. Perhaps he was a man she could reason with.

"Was that really you chasing me all those times?" she asked.

Tom nodded and looked straight ahead. "Yep, that was me. Unfortunately. You sure didn't do my reputation any good. I've skinned many a knuckle over you."

"What do you mean?"

The lieutenant slanted a glance at her. "I was a

shavetail sergeant back then, fresh from back east. My captain assigned me the task of stopping you and your father from crossing the border with your loads of whiskey. Needless to say, I failed in my assignment. And not without consequences.''

Maggie felt a stab of guilt. "I'm sorry."

Tom shifted on the seat and rethreaded the reins through his fingers. The distant smoke was drawing closer, and Maggie's heart began to pound.

"Don't be sorry. You taught me a valuable lesson, one that has served me well since then."

"What was it?"

"Never underestimate the enemy, no matter how attractive she is."

A flush of embarrassment warmed Maggie's cheeks. Was he toying with her? Hoping to seduce her? But when he turned, his face held no sign of disrespect. "Where did you learn to drive like that?"

"My pa taught me."

"Oh. I'm truly sorry about your pa."

The sting of tears was close behind her eyes. "He'd been sick. I guess I shoulda tried harder to talk him outta this trip."

Except for the crunch of wagon wheels and the occasional jingle of harness, quiet fell between them. "From what I know of him, your Pa strikes me as the sort of man who died doing what he loved best," he said after a long pause.

Maggie turned to stare, but the lieutenant kept his eyes on the last few feet of trail and the group of men walking to meet them.

* * *

"White men foolish," Calf Man said from his prone position on the snowy ground. "Can see smoke long way when it lay low like that." He pointed toward the long plume of gray that arched across the prairie, pointing to the cavalry camp like a long, crooked finger. "Sioux and Cheyenne come here, kill them all." his statement was punctuated by a shake of his head that said he'd never understand the white man.

Colin put the spyglass back to his eye and watched the wagons stop and the man driving Maggie's wagon throw the brake with a booted foot, then jump down and speak to the gathering of men that quickly surrounded them. Then he walked around the team and reached up to help Maggie down. She leaned down into his arms, and for an instant, Colin felt a foolish stab of jealousy.

She stumbled when her feet touched the ground, and Colin bit back a groan. She must be cold and tired and sore. With every fiber of his being, he wanted to charge into that camp, sweep her up behind him, and gallop for the border, consequences be hanged. But that would be no way to start their life together. She'd not only committed a crime in Canada, but she'd crossed the border on the same foolish foray and placed herself in jeopardy and out of the reach of his influence.

He wanted to wring her neck.

Damn her muleheadedness.

He sighed as he lowered the glass, and Braden

moved in to lie in the snow beside him. Colin's pants and boots were soaked through, the wet fabric turning his skin to ice, but he didn't dare build a fire for fear of making the same mistake as the cavalry camp.

"We could take her," Braden said in a low whisper, echoing Colin's thoughts. "Scatter the horses, then snatch her up and ride for the border."

"I'd already thought of that," Colin said, smiling at the grin on Braden's face. "But we have to think of something a little more . . . legal."

Returning the spyglass to his eye, he watched as the lieutenant held Maggie's elbow, slowing his steps to match her stumbling ones, shifting some of her weight against his hip. The subtleties of compassion in his motions struck a note of jealousy in Colin but at the same time presented him with a solution.

"I'm going in to talk to them," Colin said, sliding backward from the apex of the hill until he could stand unseen.

"I'm goin' with ye," Braden said, brushing the snow from his wet pants.

Colin shook his head. "We have no jurisdiction here, and what I'm about to do isn't exactly legal. I don't want to involve any of you in it." He cast a glance at the group of men surrounding him.

"No self-respectin' Irishman ever ran from a good fight," Braden said with a lopsided grin. Then his face sobered. "I came to Canada with nothin' but my life and a broken heart. Ye've been a good friend, Colin Fraser, and I don't forget me friends."

Steven Gravel stepped out of the group, produced

three small blue balls from his pocket, and began to juggle them with one hand. "I've been known to create a diversion or two in my time."

Leaving two men behind as watchmen, Colin, Steven, and Braden rode over the crest of the rolling hills, straight into the line of sight of the cavalry detachment.

Maggie balanced the tin plate on her knee, eagerly scooping the warm stew onto her spoon while watching the blue-suited cavalrymen clustered around the fire. They were a jumble of types. Some strictly military, their uniforms carefully brushed and groomed. Others wore a haphazard mishmash of cavalry uniform, trapper's garb, and buffalo robe. All looked tired and cold. As they ate, they sneaked glances in her direction, their expressions ranging from curiosity to outright lust.

Across the flames, Tom Cross squatted on his heels, intent on devouring Sergeant Ben Bradford's buffalo stew. Despite the months on the prairie, his clothes were unerringly military issue. He'd been kind enough, helping her to the fire, untying her hands, and giving her a plate of warm food and a cup of cool water. Beneath his unsmiling exterior she sensed a gentleman, a man like her Colin, one devoted to his country and his mission, yet able to temper both devotions with common sense.

Maggie laid down her spoon and rubbed her wrists, chafed red by the rough rope that had bound her.

The snowfall had increased, and the large, feathery flakes that had drifted down at leisure were now angry specks of ice that stung and chilled. The surrounding prairie disappeared behind a thin veil of snow, closing them all in together.

She felt Tom's eyes on her and glanced in his direction. He'd abandoned his plate and stood buttoning his blue cloak tighter around his neck. Nimble fingers worked the brass buttons into holes. He glanced at her, then quickly away, almost as if he were afraid to be caught watching her.

Able sat at her side, his attention completely absorbed by the meal at hand. He'd been supplied with a second buffalo robe and now sat hunched against the cold like a bull in a blizzard. If she could escape, what would she do with Able?

Dishes rattled, and tack squeaked. Maggie looked at the men. They were breaking camp, moving. Fear began to weave its sickening web. Where were they taking her?

"Where are we going?" she asked as Tom stepped to her side and took her wrists in his cold hands.

"We're taking you down to Helena to turn you over to the authorities there." Gently, he pulled her hands behind her and began to lace her wrists together again.

Maggie wrenched around until she looked directly in his face. "What will they do with me?"

He met her eyes, and she was surprised to find his a gentle deep blue. "You'll be held for trial," he said without preamble.

"What about Able?" She nodded in his direction.

Tom glanced at Able. "Him, too."

"They wouldn't put an old man in jail, would they?"

Tom tugged on the leather strap he now used to bind her and slid a finger underneath to see that it wasn't too tight. "I suspect they'll let him go with a warning."

"And me?"

Tom looked down, the brim of his hat hiding his face. "I don't know."

A commotion at the edge of camp brought his head up, and he turned swiftly at the sound of rifles cocking. Three snow-covered men rode out of the snowstorm, their glowing scarlet jackets unmistakable.

Tom stepped to the front of his patrol, who stood with guns ready, chagrined at having been surprised. "Ah. Three of Her Majesty's finest," he said.

Colin.

Maggie's heart soared as he swung one leg over the back of his horse and dismounted. Reins in his hands, he stepped forward. "Constable Colin Fraser." He held out a hand. Tom hesitated a moment, then shook it.

"What can we do for you, Constable?"

He glanced at her, then turned his attention to Lieutenant Cross. "Those two"—he nodded in her general direction—"are known whiskey traders running an operation north of the Belly River. I was on their trail when they crossed the border. Since their crimes were committed in Canada, I'd like to take them back to Fort McLeod for trial."

The lieutenant smiled tightly. "But I captured them in Montana Territory. Constable, I've spent most of my career chasing George Hayes and his daughter. Hayes is dead, and I'm taking his daughter to Helena to stand trial."

Colin exchanged glances with Braden, and again his oath weighed heavily on his shoulders. Were he to storm the camp and sweep Maggie away, there'd be no safe haven for them, no peace of mind. And their actions would surely ignite an international incident that would be heard all the way to Ottawa and Washington, D.C. He met Maggie's pain-filled gaze across the fire. She looked sad and cold, and he wished with all his being that he could enfold her inside his buffalo coat and take her home to his hearth and his bed. But two countries and a mountain of laws stood between them. And as he gazed into her eyes, seeking reassurance of the love he knew was there, he felt an edge of anger, a resentment that she'd allowed anything to come between them. Not when, only days before, there'd been only the soft mantle of night between them.

She glanced away first, and he thought he saw the glimmer of tears shining in her eyes.

"May we speak alone, Lieutenant?" Colin asked.

Cross nodded, and together they walked out into the storm, where the wind would sweep away their words.

"There's more at stake here than the punishment of a crime," Colin began.

"I thought so," Cross replied.

"Miss Hayes is my fiancée."

Cross looked down and scuffed his black boot against a frozen tuft of grass, its brown spikes poking through the snow. He smiled and shook his head. "How'd you get yourself into that predicament, Constable?"

"How does a man ever get himself into trouble with a woman?"

Cross laughed and looked out across the snow-tormented prairie. "Point well taken. Well, despite this dilemma, you're a lucky man, Fraser. I hope someday I find someone as smart and savvy as Maggie Hayes." He brought his gaze back to Colin's face. "But I can't release her. Not because I don't want to. Hell, the whiskey trade's nearly gone. The Indians have lost their taste for the stuff, and I'm due to be reassigned soon. Just knowing that I had her in my grasp, if only for a moment, is at least some solace to my ego for her outfoxing me more times than I'll ever admit to anybody." He smiled. "But my captain's another matter. He's bucking for reassignment to the Seventh Cavalry. They're making a name for themselves in the Dakotas, and he's an ex-Confederate with a permanent itch to scratch. Bringing in George Hayes's daughter will be one more notch in his gun. He'd have me shot if he knew I let her go."

The first tiny, cold feet of true hopelessness began to run up Colin's spine, and the true irony of the situation struck him like a blow to his stomach. His only hope was to place absolute trust in the words he'd pledged on that rainy day in Toronto, to believe that the blind maiden of justice would see the truth and return Maggie to his side.

"I'll stay with her." Cross's hand rested on his forearm. "I'll testify in her defense. My word's good with the courts in Helena. I'll do everything I can to get her released."

"I could come to Helena, try to convince the court, too."

Cross shook his head quickly. "No, that's not a good idea. You 'knights in scarlet' have made us boys in blue look bad, it seems. At least in the eyes of the eastern newspapers. You'd do more harm than good by being there."

Colin nodded. He was boxed in, cornered.

"I'll take care of her like she was my own," Cross said, his gaze even and sincere. "I give you my word as a gentleman."

Colin nodded, not trusting his voice, hopelessness settling like a weight in his heart.

They turned and walked back to the camp. Colin met Maggie's expectant eyes as he approached and read in them her trust that he would make this right, that he would save her from herself.

Not this time.

Cross untied her without a word of explanation and withdrew along with his men to saddle their horses and load their supplies.

Maggie threw her arms around Colin, her body

quivering with excitement. Colin closed his eyes, fighting away the images of her exquisite naked body lying inside the circle of his arms.

"I knew you'd come," she whispered, planting a kiss on his ear. Then she moved to his mouth, kissing him with all the passion she'd learned in their months together.

"Maggie," he began when he could catch his breath.

"Don't talk; just kiss me again."

"Maggie." He gently pulled her away, and she knitted her brows together in confusion.

"What is it?"

Of all the painful truths he'd ever had to confess, he knew that the next words would be the hardest he'd ever uttered. "I can't take you back with me."

She blinked and looked stunned. His heart twisted.

"You mean not now? Not until the storm breaks?"

Colin swallowed, and his insides clenched. "I mean you have to go to Helena with Lieutenant Cross."

Her eyes widened, and for the first time since he'd known her, he saw fear in their depths.

"For how long?"

"For as long as it takes to . . . try you."

Panic flickered through her eyes, followed quickly by bright tears. Seconds passed, and words deserted Colin. Traitorous schemes wrestled themselves out of the arms of common sense and rose into his thoughts. Then Maggie chased the emotion from her face and pulled herself together as only she could do in the face of adversity. "I'm sorry I gotcha into this," she said calmly. "I reckon I finally gotta pay the price, huh?"

"Lieutenant Cross is going to take you there, and he promised me he'd stay with you through the trial."

"You ain't comin'?"

"My presence there might complicate things."

She nodded her understanding of the situation. "Whadda you reckon they'll do to me?"

McLeod had been content to spill liquor and seize buffalo pelts to punish most traders brought before him, but the United States had taken a more serious view of the whiskey trade, using it as a ready excuse on which to blame the difficulties with the Plains Indians. Punishment, it was rumored, varied from seizing property to hanging.

"I don't know," he said on a breath. Maggie always wanted to hear honesty, she'd said, no matter how badly it hurt.

She watched him a moment, standing just out of his reach. "Ifen I get off, can I come back to you?" She made the statement without emotion, as if she were wrangling a business deal.

"You can come back to me anytime, anywhere," he whispered.

She stepped forward, slipped her arms inside his coat, and laid her cheek against the rough serge that covered his chest. "Whatever happens, you ain't got nothin' to be sorry for. You've done yore job just like you outta." She raised her face and looked up at him. "I knew what I was a-doin' was wrong. I ain't no fool.

I just gotta pay the piper, as Pa used to say. Might as well stand up and take it like a man."

Then she stepped out of his embrace before he could sweep her into his arms and ride into the blizzard.

"Lieutenant," she called. "We ready to go?"

Cross stood beside Able, whose face looked paler than the snow dusting his shoulders. He nodded slowly.

"Let's get on with it, then."

Maggie turned and walked toward the waiting cavalry patrol. With the lieutenant's help, she swung up into the saddle and gathered the reins in her hands. A puff of wind stirred the falling snow into spinning dervishes. When the snowfall slowed, she was gone, and the world was a great, empty white.

Chapter Nineteen

A herd of buffalo grazed peacefully on the newly sprouted grass that carpeted the rolling hills. Smaller in number than Colin remembered from last year, the herd still dotted the landscape before him. Young calves, wobbly from birth, stumbled after their mothers, tails switching and bawling for attention. A warm breeze buffed his cheek. He removed the hated white helmet and ran a hand through his hair. Above, the blue sky was deep and wide, and all seemed right and safe with the world.

But it was not.

McLeod had barraged the U.S. authorities with letters after Colin returned to Fort McLeod, hoping to sway their opinion in Maggie's case, but all correspondence had gone unanswered. February had passed, as had March and April, and still there had been no word.

In May, after passing the winter in misery, Colin had demanded to go to Helena and bring her back. Or at least find out her fate. McLeod reluctantly relented, and Colin rode hard for a week and arrived to find that no one knew of Maggie Hayes or her fate. Lieutenant Cross had been reassigned to a posting farther east. There were no records of a trial, no witnesses to her arrival. She had simply vanished.

Heartsick, Colin returned to Fort McLeod, clinging to the hope that one day she would return to him as she'd promised. He wrote letters to Lieutenant Cross, whose answers came in mid-May. Cross had turned Maggie over to the authorities in Helena, then immediately received word he'd been reassigned. Despite his own paper campaign, Cross, too, had been unable to find out her fate.

On lonely nights, when the stars shone brightly overhead and the fort was quiet and peaceful, Colin would lie awake and wrestle the voices that whispered he should have taken a different path that snowy afternoon—snatched her out of Cross's custody and disappeared into the Canadian wilderness. True, they'd live life looking over their shoulders, but at least he'd know where she was and how she was.

Had she conceived a child from their union? Was she somewhere alone, outcast, struggling to feed herself and an infant? Had she escaped in Helena, tried to make her way north, and fell victim to some misfortune? Was she buried someplace unmarked and wind-wept? And during those long, dark days, Colin had found solace where he least expected—his parents.

They arrived in April after receiving several long, heart-rending letters written by a desperate man on desperate nights. Quietly, they sat and listened to him pour out the pain and uncertainty that had shadowed him for the last year and a half. He was brutally honest, keeping nothing from them except the intimacy of his relationship with Maggie. That he kept to himself, locked tightly in his heart, where only he could take it out and remember.

On the day his parents left for Ottawa, his mother had pressed into his hand a small velvet bag. When he opened it, he found a small golden ring, its smooth surface entwined with finely carved vines. His grandmother's wedding ring. "When Maggie returns," his mother had whispered tearfully, "slide it onto her finger."

He had sewn the pouch into a secret pocket in his uniform jacket to keep it safe and close. And every day he watched the southern horizon, hoping to see her top a rise, silhouetted against the blue prairie sky.

He reset the hat onto his head and touched the small, round bulge beneath the serge of his jacket to assure himself the ring was still there. The band of delicate gold had become a symbol of faith and hope to him, a promise that hadn't left his grandmother's hand in forty-three years, until the day she died. As long as it was there, riding just beneath his jacket,

he could cling to the hope that one day Maggie woul⌐
come home.

A new Blackfoot encampment had sprouted int⌐
existence only a few miles from Fort McLeod. Th⌐
Indians were concerned about the dwindling num⌐
bers of buffalo, a direct result of the burgeonin⌐
settlement of Fort McLeod, and had met several time⌐
with McLeod on the subject. Colin was on his way t⌐
the camp to make arrangements for yet another o⌐
these talks.

He turned his horse back toward the Fort. Calf Ma⌐
would accompany him today as interpreter, but h⌐
rarely needed one anymore. He'd picked up the lan⌐
guage quickly, and what he hadn't learned, Brade⌐
tutored him on at night.

The rattle of a distant wagon didn't register at first⌐
so accustomed was he to the constant squeak an⌐
whine of wagons and carts in and around the for⌐
As it drew closer, he pulled his horse to a stop an⌐
sat listening without turning. The sound came fron⌐
the south, not from the settlement. It was a two-hors⌐
hitch pulling a heavy wagon. He closed his eyes an⌐
tortured himself for a few seconds. What if it wa⌐
Maggie? He let the rush of anticipation pour ove⌐
him just to see if he was still alive inside. Then h⌐
quickly damped it out and turned around.

But there was no loaded supply wagon lumberin⌐
along. Instead, the large wagon was almost empt⌐
except for a few boxes and crates neatly lashed towar⌐
the front of the wagon bed. Two matched horse⌐
pulled in equal yoke, fine animals obviously accu⌐

tomed to pulling together. The driver wore shirt-sleeves and a floppy hat pulled low over his face.

Despite the clothes and hat, there was something familiar about the driver. True anticipation burst to life, and Colin struggled to snatch it back. The man was slight, with small hands that confidently held the reins. Colin kicked his horse into a gallop. Tomorrow he'd be touted as three kinds of a fool, he knew, when word got around that he'd charged up to a wagon and snatched the hat off some old man returning home after a long ride to Benton.

Heart pounding and hating in advance the disappointment that would surge through him and haunt his sleep that night, Colin galloped toward the wagon. Did he have a morbid tendency toward self-destruction? An urge to further punish himself for not throwing his career to the wind and following Maggie to the ends of the earth? No, a small voice of self-preservation piped up. Maggie wouldn't have wanted it that way.

When Colin reached the wagon, the driver didn't look up or slow his pace. When he could stand it no longer, Colin took the nearest horse's bridle and hauled the team to a hoof-skidding stop. Maggie pushed back her hat and smiled, her eyes sparkling with mischief.

"Hey," she said.

Colin leaped down from his horse and dragged her off the wagon seat and into his arms, nearly sending them both tumbling to the ground.

"Maggie" seemed to be the only word circling in his head.

She slipped her arms around him, clutching him to her with a grip strong and sure, and for a fleeting moment he wondered if he was in his narrow cot in the hospital asleep and dreaming. Then she kissed him, and he knew she was real.

"Where have you been?" he asked, knowing the words sounded stupid and demanding.

Maggie ran her hands over his shoulders, across his chest, back up to his neck, and into his hair, making him want her with an intensity that left his hands trembling. "I just wanted to make sure you was real," she said, her voice dropping into that range that made the hair on his neck rise.

Colin glanced around and for a second actually entertained the idea of making love to her in the wagon bed. More than he wanted his next breath, he longed to remind her that they belonged to each other and make her think twice about going wandering ever again.

"Didn't you get my letters?" she asked, stepping a safe distance away as if she read his lecherous thoughts.

"No, I didn't get any letters."

Maggie frowned, then compassion flooded her face, and she cupped his face with her hands. "You didn't get no letters at all? You didn't know nothing about me all this time?"

Colin shook his head. "There was a flood this

spring. One of the mail packets washed downstream.''
Why hadn't he thought of that before now?

"Well, I wrote you. The judge turned me a-loose
with a good tongue-lashin'. Said ifen he ever saw me
across the border again, he'd turn me over his knee.''
She smiled, and her eyes sparkled. "I believe he'd
do it, too. He said the only reason he was a-turnin'
me a-loose was I'd give them boys in blue somethin'
to think about 'stead of sittin' around playin' poker
when they shoulda been on patrol.''

Colin would have given two months' pay to have
been in the courtroom.

"But Able got sick.'' Her eyes grew shiny. "He died
last month. I been nursin' him all this time.''

"You were there in Helena?''

She shook her head. "No, me and him went on to
Benton. He wanted to see that house and soft bed
that Tom Boggs promised him. That's where he died.
Right there in that bed with a feather pillow at his
head. I reckon he went on and told Pa what a pleasure
it was.''

Colin pulled her against him and pressed his cheek
against the top of her head. She'd lost so much so
quickly, and still she'd had the gumption to drive a
wagon two hundred and fifty miles to get to him.

"Marry me. Today. Now.''

She raised her head. "But I ain't got no weddin'
dress.''

"Yes, you do.'' He leaped into the saddle and
reached down to pull her up behind him. She planted
her hands on her hips and squinted up at him. "I

ain't leavin' my team here. I worked for months to buy 'em."

"Worked?"

"Sure. I worked in the livery stable. Percy, he cried when I left. Said I was the best horseman he'd ever had." She grinned and rocked back on her heels.

"I'll send Braden back for it. I don't want to let you out of my sight."

"I ain't leavin' my horses."

Colin straightened in the saddle. "All right. Drive them in, but I'm riding beside you every step of the way. You're not getting out of my sight again until you're my wife."

She slanted a mischievous glance at him as she braced a foot on the wagon wheel and climbed up onto the seat. "You might be biting off more than you're bargaining for," she said with a wink.

"Sir, I—" Colin rapped on McLeod's door and shoved it open but was stopped by the sight of paper waving in his direction from McLeod's left hand. With his right, he continued to write with his quill pen.

"What's that, sir?" he asked as he stepped forward.

"Permission from Ottawa for you to marry Miss Hayes."

"We'd like—"

"Yes, as soon as possible. Today. Two o'clock. Just beyond the gates."

"How did you—"

"Half of the morning patrol raced back here to tell me."

"Who's—?"

"Father Brannigan from the mission is standing by."

"Sir—"

McLeod put down his pen and folded his hands. "Constable Fraser. You're a fine officer, one I expect to have a long and distinguished future with the force. But I have come to the conclusion, as did my superiors in Ottawa, if you do not marry Miss Hayes as soon as possible, the future of westward expansion in Canada may be jeopardized. So, if you would be so kind, please be at the appointed place dressed and on time so that we may return to the business of settling these Territories."

There was a glint in McLeod's eye as he spoke, and Colin knew that although the words were in jest, the meaning was sincere.

"Yes, sir."

"And do ye, Maggie, fair lass, take Colin here as 'er husband?"

Braden leaned forward. " 'Tis a blessin' on yer union that yer vows are bein' spoken in the golden Irish," he whispered in Colin's ear.

Colin smiled but never took his eyes off Maggie. The day would come when this moment would be a fuzzy memory, the warmth of it more memorable than the details. But he knew when that time overtook them, he would always remember the light in her eyes, the weight of her hand in his, the slight quiver that ran through her as she said, "Yes."

Colin held out his hand, and Braden placed the ring in his palm. And as he slipped the narrow band of gold onto her finger, he remembered the love his grandparents had shared and said a small prayer to be blessed with the same.

"Then I pronounce ye man and wife." Father Brannigan snapped his Bible closed and clapped Colin on the back. "Then let's get to the celebratin'."

Night cast a sultry net across the earth, filling the sky with sparkling stars and the air with a balmy breeze perfect for teasing filmy curtains and caressing bare skin.

Maggie held her hand up to the shaft of moonlight that lit their bedroom and admired the tiny glowing band nestled on her finger. Colin lay on his side, content to prop his cheek in his palm and memorize the way her hair kissed her shoulders.

Abruptly, she flopped over onto her side and snuggled closer to him, her feet tangled in the sheets. The brush of her bare skin against his sent his blood racing again, and he shifted positions.

"Do you think I'm gonna have a baby?" she asked, her eyes bright with curiosity.

"Well, it's a little early to tell. It's only been . . maybe fifteen minutes."

She shoved at his shoulder, then laid her head on his bare arm. "No, do you think we did it?"

Colin touched the tip of her nose with his finger. "I hope so. I certainly tried."

She nipped at the tender inner muscle of his arm, and he yelped in mock pain. With an arm hooked around her waist, he pulled her closer, and she curled against him with complete ease. He was truly blessed. During their lovemaking he'd prayed, when his time for release had come, that God would see fit to let her conceive.

A baby.

Maggie's baby.

With bouncing blond hair, blue eyes, and an appetite for danger.

Dear God, he was in trouble.

Author's Note

For many years after the initial organization and deployment of the Force in 1874, the Northwest Mounted Police discouraged its members from marrying, claiming that life in the unsettled territories was far too harsh for women. But they severely underestimated the women of Canada. Love conquered doubt, and before the turn of the century, many men returned east to marry the sweethearts they'd left behind. Some of these brave women left conveniences like indoor plumbing and running water to follow their new husbands into desolate wilderness without a glimpse of another soul, save each other, for months at a time.

Mountie wives quickly found that when they married their men, they also married the Force. They became adept at guarding prisoners, nursing the injured, cooking for stranded trappers, breaking up fights, and fending off marauding predators on cold, dark winter nights.

And yet they adapted and thrived, taking to heart their vows of for better or for worse, and raised happy, healthy families under what we would now consider almost impossible circumstances.

My deepest respect and heartfelt thanks go to Inspector (retired) Harold and Greta Routledge, whose own love story inspired me to write this series. Mrs. Routledge, along with her coauthors Wilma Clevette, Freda Heacock, and Gwen Skelley, put together a wonderful book entitled *Red Serge Wives* for the centennial celebration of the Royal Canadian Mounted Police in 1974. Contained within the gold-and-scarlet covers of this book are stories of love, devotion, and sacrifice submitted by wives and daughters, the most unrecognized members of the Mounted Police.

The story of the westward trek of the Mounties is well documented by many firsthand, day-by-day accounts in journals and diaries, so I feel compelled to confess to playing a little fast and loose with some minor historical facts to enhance the storytelling.

The first Christmas celebration at Fort McLeod actually occurred on Christmas Day and consisted of a feast, shooting matches, firing the cannon, and other outside activities. However, I could not resist a starry Christmas Eve night to further a budding love affair, so I changed the facts a little. I hope my dear Canadian friends will forgive me.

I hope you have enjoyed this first of three books on the Northwest Mounted Police. The next two will also be set during those first few tumultuous years in western Canada and will continue Braden Flynn's and Steven Gravel's stories.

Look for Book II, SECOND CHANCE in June 2001.

In May 1877, with Fort McLeod well established and the whiskey trade almost eradicated, Braden Flynn transfers to newly established Fort Walsh, still striving to forget the pain of losing all dear to him in the Irish potato famine.

Sitting Bull's band of refugee Sioux are expected to cross into Canada near Fort Walsh after their victory over General George Custer at the Battle of the Little Big Horn. Pursued throughout the vicious winter following the battle, the Sioux are exhausted and ragged when they cross into the jurisdiction of the Mounties at Fort Walsh.

There Braden meets Dancing Bird, a nontraditional Sioux woman who has lost her family and her hope in the flight across the prairies. Together they can mend each other's broken hearts if Braden can keep her on his side of the border when dwindling food supplies and increasing tensions with the Canadian Indians threaten to send the Sioux back across the border, where the U.S. Cavalry waits to condemn them to reservations.

You can write to me care of Kensington Books or e-mail me at *Ribbons@aol.com*.

ABOUT THE AUTHOR

Kathryn Fox started writing when she found herself devising alternate plot lines for *Cinderella* and *Sleeping Beauty* videos while at home with three toddlers. She lives in eastern North Carolina with her husband of twenty-three years, three sons, one cat, three dogs, and one cockatiel. She holds a bachelor's degree in horticultural science and has worked as a research technician, secretary, and wedding-dress seamstress. When she's not writing, she is the Nematode Assay Laboratory supervisor for the North Carolina Department of Agriculture.